STUCK PAGES

Vol. 1: Exposing the Heart of a Heartbreaker

Akim Bryant

Chris Omar LLC
15 Lexington Avenue
Mount Vernon, NY 10552

Copyright ©2012 by Akim Bryant

All rights reserved.

Cataloging-In-Publication Data: Bryant, Akim

Stuck Pages, Vol. 1: Exposing the Heart of a Heartbreaker
a novel by Akim Bryant

ISBN NUMBER 978-0-9992009-0-2

Edited by Katherine Faw Morris

Cover Artwork by Ceptian Suryana

Book design by Doug Barron

Printed in the United States of America, 2017

First Edition

www.stuckpages.com

Akim Bryant

    Beginning at the age of 18, Akim Bryant first interned for Perfect Pair Recording Studios in his hometown of East Orange, New Jersey. It's where he witnessed recording sessions by hip-hop legend Naughty-By-Nature and their R&B protégé Next. During this time, Akim was attending community college before transferring to his alma mater, William Paterson University, majoring in Communication.

    Just months before graduation, Akim got his next internship at Music Choice. Through the years, he was promoted up to management and programmed both the R&B Hits (later known as Throwback Jamz) and R&B Soul channels, taking the latter from top-20 to a top-10 channel on the service.

    As a side gig, Akim started freelance-writing to exercise his voice as a writer. Writing for him had become a hobby back at the age of 15. He loved listening to the song lyrics of his favorite artists on radio so he started to write his own versions.

    In 2007, Akim got his first gig writing album reviews for soultracks.com. That same year, he became lifestyle editor for Bleu magazine. After that, Akim wrote for GIANT, The Source and The Advocate magazines. He has also done numerous in-depth interviews

with artists such as Jasmine Sullivan, Tank and Evelyn Champagne King for the online portal soulmusic.com.

In late 2015, Black Entertainment Television (BET) approached Akim about making a return to music programming after a brief hiatus. Akim joined the BET music programming team in February 2016 to work on the launch of BET Soul (formerly VH1 Soul). It's where Akim enjoys flexing his storytelling abilities through carefully-curated video playlists, one hit after another.

Continuing to chase his dreams, Akim has completed his debut novel Stuck Pages, Vol. 1: Exposing the Heart of a Heartbreaker. It is a classic American love story seen through the eyes of a black-gay man. Stuck Pages is the coming-of-age/coming-out journey of a heart-broken heartbreaker. The main character, Quincy Simmons, graduates college and gets a dream job in the music industry only to realize the life he has may not be the life he really wanted. He's so caught up in trying to fulfill his heart that he can't see the people in front of him for who they really are. Stuck Pages is a snapshot into the life (not just lifestyle) and times of a young black-gay man who is a hopeless romantic in a rather hopeless place.

This is the first installment to the Stuck Pages trilogy. Stuck Pages, Vol. 2: The Pleasure Principle leads Quincy further down the path of decadence, while Stuck Pages, Vol. 3: How Can You Mend a Broken Heart is about redeeming his own broken heart. This series represents a new chapter in Akim's life as an author.

After years of laboring over his treasured skill of putting his thoughts in writing, Akim's long-term vision is to begin adapting his imaginative stories to stage and screen. It's also been a dream of his to create treatments for music videos that will speak to the content of the music. Music has helped to shape Akim's voice as a writer and now, more than ever, he's gained the courage to express that voice, all over the world.

Thank You!

Dear God, you are my source. You helped me to navigate this journey called life and I've bonded with some invaluable gems along the way–some of which I'd like to sincerely thank…

I love you, Ma. I don't say it often, but if there's anyone who knows my true heart, it's you.

Ricky–You are a reminder that there are people in the world who will never mean you any harm and I don't take it for granted. You make me want to be a better person.

Chris–We share the same vision. And your commitment to protecting the creative process is the reason why I was open to your business acumen. It's a blessing to know you.

David & Henry–Some say it's never too late…

Lamont, Sutan, Hassan & Winston–Camini 4 life.

Mecca, Devon, Chris D. & Will–Thank you for taking the time to help me shape this story.

Pops & his wife Sarah, my uncles and many cousins–Love you all.

And finally, I dedicate this novel to the loving memory of my grandmother Queenie, my brother Larry, my aunt Bernice, my aunt Cynt, my cousin Nikisha.

Contents

Contents

Prologue

My all-time favorite wish was to be reborn. Literally, start over and give life another try. Maybe change my name from Quincy Simmons to Ishmael Bubaka. Erase all the foolish mistakes we make out of pure ignorance and approach life's trials and tribulations with a different frame of mind because, sometimes, the more you think you know, the less you understand.

Isn't it funny how in the beginning of your life you take for granted the very things you treasure once you've come to appreciate what life is really all about? Life would be meaningless without your family, friends and loved ones.

I don't have many regrets, except those pertaining to matters of the heart. It's times like this that make me regret ever falling in love. My power has been lifted, making me feel like less than a man when men are supposed to stay strong, or, at least, that's the impression I was given from my environment. Men don't cry. Men don't behave like women. Men don't let their emotions show so, therefore, men rarely fall in love. Even though love is what I thought I wanted, I don't know anymore. I don't know how many broken hearts I can take. I thought me being a gay man would shift the odds in my favor. By definition, gay equates to happiness. But now, more than ever before, I don't know what to believe or whom I should trust.

The men in my life keep singing the same old songs. It's like the songs I grew up listening to promising endless love, dudes committing to be all the man that I need, but delivering a love

T.K.O. This is not where I ever wanted to be. I spent so much of my life suppressing that helpless little boy deep inside who quietly identified himself as the faggot so many other boys called him. So, after so much foolishness, some things have got to change.

Part One (December 2000)

No Woman, No Cry

Through my early 20s, I was blessed to have in my life two of the most beautiful women I've ever known. They're still a blessing and I don't know where I would be without them. These two ladies trust me as much as I trust them. One is, of course, the woman who raised me. She's a mother like no other in every sense. However, the other one is like the sister I never had.

Karyn Thames was a ripe 20-year-old sophomore at Rutgers University in Newark when we first met in our Western Civilization class at the start of the fall 1999 semester. We sat side by side and soon began echoing one another a lot in class, answering many of the same questions. Our instant bond felt natural and long overdue. I thought she was so drop-dead gorgeous. People always complimented her long, flowing, jet-black hair, matching eyelashes and evenly bronzed caramel skin tone, which made people ask flat out if she was mixed with something. Karyn never denied or confirmed. She enjoyed the attention, but it never got to her head. She also never seemed to have a bad day. Everyone could always count on Karyn's pearly white smile any day of the week. It was a like a tall glass of smooth sweet tea even though she had never traveled down South.

By the time the year 2000 rolled around, I was proud of myself for reaching my senior year at Rutgers after all the hours of studying I had put in up to that point. My goal of being the first in my family to complete college was so near I almost couldn't believe it was about to be a reality. It was 10:45 a.m. one morning and I had Audience and Market Analysis class in 15 minutes. It was a good thing I lived on campus. My professor was petite, yet full of spunk so no one dared to walk in the door late. Depending on what time of the month it was, some of my late fellow classmates would be told to turn right around because there would be no class for them that day. I was definitely one of her favorites though for some reason. Maybe she had a thing for black men, which went over everyone's head except for Karyn.

"Why does she keep looking at you like that?" whispered Karyn.

"Leave me alone. I'm trying to pay attention here," I responded.

She continued to badger me by saying, "Y'all need to go get a room already. I got an extra red light bulb if you need it."

"You can stick that light bulb right up your—"

I was interrupted by the professor who caught me talking during her lesson. Fortunately, she just gave me that mean look with a hint of *I know you know better.* Karyn flipped her hair from one side to the other playing off her guilt. The clock on the wall ticked away as my mind eventually started to wander as usual.

I was recalling the previous conversation I'd had with the main lady in my life over the phone the night before. Sadly, my mom was being evicted from the apartment we'd lived in since I was five-years-old. 492 Park Ave. in East Orange, New Jersey, was the only home I'd ever known. Back in the late 1980s, after having lived there on public assistance for a few years, my mother was offered the position of building manager/

superintendent. She assumed the responsibility of screening new applicants, evaluating current tenants before their leases could be renewed, keeping the land clean and tidy, and reporting necessary repairs to the maintenance crew.

The 16-family apartment complex I grew up in had been purchased by a new owner over a month before our conversation. He initially assured my mother that everything would be just fine with regards to employment and her living situation. She wouldn't have to worry about moving or finding a new job. The new owner turned out to be a liar so my mother told me that she had been apartment-hunting in the *Star-Ledger* newspaper. And despite the fact that she was out of a job, she was also not able to sign up for unemployment since the gig for all those years was under the table. I wished the timing was different. I wanted to finish school first and get a well-paying job so she could retire on my dime, never having to work another day ever again. It was all part of the fantasy, I guess.

Karyn soon snapped me out of my trance because class was over. The two of us headed to the student center to get some snacks. She greeted her male fans as I headed over to the vending machines to buy our daily dose of Drake's Funny Bones. We split it between us both. Karyn had to watch her plump hour-glass figure. Thanks to her, I was probably just as popular, but only as the pretty boy who hung out with the prettiest girl in school. My sexuality was still a major secret amongst a few others. I felt I had to keep my school life separate from my personal life, the latter of which had just begun to take off.

Not until that day did I know Karyn too had a major secret. One of her fans had snuck up from behind, using his right hand to shield her eyes while placing his left forearm across her stomach. He was one of the taller, beefier and sexier stars of Rutgers's basketball team. Even though the act seemed harmless, Karyn freaked out. She bit down on his hand like it was a chicken wing.

He screamed out, "Ah, you bitch! What the hell is wrong with you?"

She screamed back, "What the hell is wrong with you sneaking up on me? I should kick you in your nuts."

I ran over to keep her from kicking open his urethra. There was a fire in her eyes I had never seen before. Thankfully, the scene soon died down. He chose to walk off to the men's room to rinse the blood clotting up from the wound on his hand bearing her teeth marks, but not before he had called Karyn a *crazy bitch*. I had to add my two cents a little later once I got her to calm down.

"You do know that was over the top, right?" I asked.

"Seriously, not right now, I'm still pissed off," she said as we stood in the entrance of our residence hall.

"Okay, but we gotta talk about that if not today, then soon, 'cause that was completely out of line, Karyn," I said. "You know I love you. I'm just calling it like it is."

Karyn dropped her head. Tears suddenly started to flow down her face so I pulled her in against my chest. She laid her head on my shoulder. I wrapped my arm around her head, blocking her face with my hand, hoping no one in the lobby could see her breaking down. I walked her to my room, which I knew would be empty since my roommate was still in class. Once inside, she sat down on my bed as she hung her head even lower.

"Karyn, what's wrong? There has to be something I don't know about."

"This is so embarrassing, Q," she said while wiping the tears from her eyes.

I handed her my damp washcloth, which I always kept super clean because I only used it primarily for my face.

"Take your time, baby girl. I'm not going anywhere. I'm right here," I assured her.

I sat across from her on my roommate's bed because I wanted to give her some space when she muttered, "I was raped."

Those were the last words I wanted to hear from one of my favorite girls in the whole world, but I had to not be selfish and just listen.

"Damn, sometimes it feels like it was just yesterday," she said. "I know I lost it back there, but I got scared and I don't know why."

"I don't blame you, Karyn. I get it. It must still be fresh. We don't have to talk about it if it still hurts."

"It always hurts. That's the point. I can't get away from it. I keep trying to bury it so it doesn't kill me."

I paused briefly as she cried some more. I felt her pain and didn't know how to put it to an end. Was it time to stop the conversation? Or did she really need someone to talk to? I chose at that moment to take the conversation a step further.

"Do your parents know about it?" I asked.

She said, "Yeah, my dad is still blaming himself. He thought Vincent was a good guy."

"And your mom?" I asked.

"She tries to act like nothing happened, trying to be tough for me and my father but I know it affects her probably more than us."

"Wow," I said. "I really don't know what to say."

"I'm sorry, Q. This is not your deal, it's mine. I gotta handle this on my own."

"No, you don't," I said. "We've grown too close for you to keep secrets like this from me."

At that moment, I couldn't believe the words that had come out of my mouth considering all the things she had yet to know about me and my life, although I was beginning to realize that Karyn was probably the rock I needed to lean on. If she was strong enough to always wear a smile and hide such a deep, dark secret, she was definitely strong enough to deal with mine. I offered her a warm cola from the bottom of my closet and we just lay back listening to Musiq Soulchild's debut album, *Aijuswanaseing*. It was an album we discovered together and loved from start to finish. I figured it would help to shorten the distance between us regarding her pain.

A half hour later, I could tell Karyn was feeling a bit better. She broke down some of her walls and divulged a good amount of details about her relationship with her ex-boyfriend/ rapist, Vincent. Vincent was her high-school sweetheart. They met at the end of their sophomore year and dated for the following two years. Karyn was saving her virginity for him when he decided he couldn't wait any longer so he raped her on their prom night, which also happened to be their two-year anniversary. Her envious teenage girl-"friends", who were always flirting with Vincent behind her back, took advantage of the situation by spreading rumors that Karyn was drunk and probably asked for it. It took her over a year to officially tell her parents and accept that she was indeed raped by the first love of her life. Fortunately, she didn't get pregnant, but that incident broke her heart, to say the least. She hadn't dated anyone since.

Spread My Wings

"Please don't tell me you're broke," said my boy Prince who had called to harass me about going out to the club that weekend.

"Oh, here we go. Why can't you understand I'm a college student? So, of course, I'm broke," I replied.

"Yeah, yeah, yeah, I'll buy you a drink if I have to but we're going to the Warehouse tomorrow night, okay?"

He spoke the magic words. Going out to the Warehouse was not something Prince needed to convince me of. Clubbing was our chief vice so I accepted his offer to buy me a drink, then brought the conversation to a happy ending. Prince, however, seized the final moment to mention some new kid he'd met in his neighborhood of Flatbush, Brooklyn, but wouldn't tell me his name. It was basically his subtle cue that the kid must be my type—young and cute with a weapon to shoot. Even though I had not been in the gay life for long, my reputation was beginning to precede me. Prince also had a reputation himself for being the life of the party. It's how we'd originally met a year prior.

It was a scary night to remember. Having been raised in New Jersey, New York City was such a foreign place to me, although I knew I would one day make it there in some capacity. I just never expected my former babysitter, Jordan, would be my chaperone to the Big Apple. His 10-plus years of life, especially gay-life, experience served him well. I was pretty fortunate that he never abused his authority, if you know what I mean. He rather chose to be my gay mentor at a point in my life when I truly needed some guidance because I felt all alone. Like most young gays on the verge of coming out, I had brainwashed myself into believing I was the only gay boy around who wasn't such an obvious queen. Jordan sensed my loneliness so he took me on a surprise trip to NYC one day that I'll never forget.

He said he had a gig at an event in Manhattan and wanted me to tag along. A client of his had requested that he take some photos of the attendees, as my former babysitter had become a full-time freelance photographer. I shrugged my shoulders thinking it was no big deal. I had nothing better to do that day. We later pulled up in front of a large venue on 52nd Street called the Roseland Ballroom.

Everything at first glance appeared to be normal, nothing out of the ordinary. On the sidewalk, there were guys, mostly around my age, as well as some really tall chicks with bad weaves draped down their backs towering over my 5-foot-8-inch and 140-pound frame.

We stepped into the lobby where tables were lined up against the walls with random people asking for a small donation to enter what looked like a huge party. I overheard one of them say a donation was not required because it was a non-profit event. The wheels in my head were spinning and making me dizzy. Then one of the random faces looked familiar. It turned out to be the flaming queen from high school I had always tried to avoid. He was the last person I ever wanted to see, anywhere. I knew then that it was definitely a gay event and that I had been given zero warning.

With tons of shame running through my veins, I rushed inside. I could hear him calling my name out loud in disbelief.

I thought about how my whole hometown was going to be laughing at me for the rest of my life if word got out. Jordan chased me down wanting to know who that guy was calling my name. He could tell I was nervous, but he said everything would be fine. We weren't going to stay too long. Nevertheless, I was trembling in fear but did my best to not let it show. Jordan had brought me to one of the biggest and most famous gay events in the country, known as the Latex Ball, which, even to this day, has more to do with Spring Break or Freaknik than it does an awards show.

Since 1993, the House of Latex has been throwing this annual ball each summer to represent and also reach out to the underground ballroom community made up of gays, lesbians, bisexuals, and transgendered individuals living in the NYC area. I never knew it even existed until that night. I posted up to the side near the entrance, leaning against a defunct bar that was poorly lit. I was praying no one else would recognize me or, even worse, try to approach me. If it came down to it, I was close enough to the exit to make a run for the train back home to Jersey. Mama always said—*know your way home in case anything happens.*

From what I could tell about the event, there was some heated competition happening onstage, but I couldn't focus on anything except the pit of my stomach. Then before I could conjure up an escape plan, I noticed this dude come within a few feet of where I was standing by the bar. I balled up my fist in anticipation of him trying to grab or grope me. Instead, he just stood there in position for at least the next 15 minutes, glancing at me every so often out of the corner of his eye. My facial expression was stone-cold. No matter how scared I really felt, I couldn't let him know it.

"Hi," said the lone stranger.

"Hey," I replied.

"Are you here by yourself?"

"No," I said firmly.

"I'm Prince by the way," he said, extending his arm for a handshake.

I looked him dead in the eye and realized he didn't look like much of a threat whatsoever. He actually reminded me of the pretty college-boy types I went to school with. In other words, he looked a lot like me. He wore the usual uniform of a dark blue Yankees fitted cap, white tee, dark blue jeans, and all-white Air Force Ones. He was brown-skinned and about my height and weight. I dropped my guard slightly to shake his hand.

"Is this your first time here?" he asked.

"Yeah," I said. "It's my first time out, period."

"Wait—please don't tell me this is your first time out as in *gay* out."

"Yeah, it is," I responded.

"Really?" asked Prince. "And how did you find this place?"

"Umm—my former babysitter brought me here as crazy as it sounds," I said. "But he's cool though. He just didn't tell me this was where we were going."

Prince laughed at my expense and I couldn't blame him. It was a funny situation, which for the moment calmed my nerves.

"So is Prince your real name?" I asked.

"Yeah, my mom named me after Mr. *Purple Rain* himself, but no relation."

That night, meeting Prince was one of those rare interactions when you feel like you've known the person longer than your lifetime. Prince and I ranted about our mutual love for music and whether the real Prince's name is what kept him from being referred to as the true King of Pop. I later got introduced to his close circle of hot friends. They welcomed me with open arms, hearts, minds, homes, and legs. It was just the beginning of my foray into the black gay nightlife.

Prince and I became extremely close over the next year. We hung out almost every weekend, whether it was at the club or at his place in Brooklyn. Most of what we talked about had to do with dates. A date is what we gays call a new boy we're having sex with, which, only in part, might explain why they seem to always be so short-lived.

Accordingly, I had not forgotten our conversation about the dude Prince said he recently met on his block. It felt good having friends who weren't so greedy when it came to dates. If someone, either one of us met, was a better match for the other, we would work it out. That's what real friends are about.

●●●

I got to Prince's place in Brooklyn around 10 p.m. that weekend. It was following our conversation about the dude he'd mentioned to me over the phone. Since the club normally didn't close until 6 a.m., we liked to make our grand entrance a few minutes before 3 a.m. Prince opened the door to the apartment and everyone appeared to be on board; not dressed yet, but at least they were all there. Five heads were in the living room talking and watching a bootleg Usher live DVD. Four people were in the bedroom figuring out what they wanted to wear. I spotted a figure in the far corner of the room. It was Prince's roommate, Trey. The only clothing he had on was a black wife-beater and white boxer-briefs.

Trey was about 5'11" and probably weighed between 155 and 165. He had cornrows from the front to the back of his head that stretched down to his shoulder blades. He also had a tattoo of a cougar on the front of his right thigh, thick, dark eyebrows sort of like a wolf and dark-chocolate skin. He also visited the gym at least three to four days a week. We all met Trey about six months prior. He was a transplant from South Philly. Much like me, Prince bonded with Trey almost immediately, so Trey moved into one of the two spare bedrooms. It was a very spacious three-bedroom apartment overlooking the infamous Prospect Park. Prince, of course, occupied the master bedroom along with his date of the moment. I headed toward the kitchen to fix me a cocktail. I felt like I struck it rich when I bumped into a cutie I didn't recognize.

"Oh, my fault, I almost spilled my drink on you. What's going on, man?" he asked. I could tell he was interested.

"Just about to fix me a drink too—sorry if I startled you," I said.

He continued to move past me without breaking eye contact. I could only guess that he was the dude Prince had been eager I meet. I just needed to find out exactly.

"So who's the fresh piece of meat in the living room? Is that homeboy you told me you met over on Flatbush?" I pressured Prince after pulling him away from the crew of stragglers.

"Yeah, I was behind him in the store when he was buying some tampons so I looked at him kinda crazy. He noticed and said it was for his lazy-ass mom who wouldn't go to the store herself and that sparked the conversation," said Prince. "He said I seemed mad cool and he had seen me around the block before so he wanted to keep in touch. Now here he is…fitting in nicely, huh?"

From the hallway, we watched him mix well with our crowd. He was a short, super light-skinned black cutie with clear skin, oval-shaped brown eyes and wavy brown hair. He had on an all-red Coogi sweater with the matching skully halfway hanging out of the back pocket of his Diesel jeans.

"How old is he?" I inquired.

Prince said, "18, I think."

"What the hell? Shouldn't you know?" I laughed.

"He's old enough otherwise he wouldn't be here, Q, so I'll hook y'all up ASAP."

"He's hot, but nothing serious, okay?" I said. "He's probably too new to all this for me to be taking him too seriously."

"You're always over-thinking, but yeah, Q, I hear you."

"Hold up, Prince, what's his name?"

"Kevin."

It was 2 a.m. by the time we made our way out to the club. Everyone looked picture-perfect and was in the right mood. Prince let me know on the way downstairs that Kevin was interested in me as well. He was down for whatever I was down for and that was all I needed to hear. We got to the Warehouse, waited a few moments outside for the crew to gather. The 12 of us had split up into three cabs. I rode in one with Prince, Trey and another straggler. We were familiar with the doormen at the club so we never had to wait in that long line.

The Warehouse was one of the few and one of the best gay nightclubs for young black men at the turn of the 21st century.

The name was adopted in its literal sense which explained the layout. It had two stories with house music on the top level and hip-hop/R&B on the lower. In less than an hour, the floors would switch, bringing hip-hop upstairs so we could also hear our favorite hits on the upper outdoor deck because smoking, especially weed smoking, was not allowed indoors. That hazy deck was where you would find all the regular potheads. Many of whom you expected to see there at least one out of the four to five Saturdays each month. Thanks to my affiliations, I was familiar with quite a few of them. The weed habit that brought me to the deck had begun developing about three years prior. I had smoked my first blunt on my first night at college and I had no plans on quitting anytime soon.

The drinks at the Warehouse were also part of its attraction. My night was normally capped off by three Long Island iced teas and two blunts. It took two blunts since we were always sharing what we had to smoke.

The night was feeling right with the music, atmosphere and spirits all harmoniously singing the same tune. A bunch of us danced, as usual, until the last song faded out from the sound system. All I could remember after that were the club lights and then there were the traffic lights. We made it back to Brooklyn before daybreak. Kevin sat in the cab next to me the entire way and I was still drunk.

I couldn't wait for us to start deciding sleeping arrangements for the 12 of us, including a few handsome stragglers we'd gained at the club. Whether you slept in a bed or on the floor depended on your relation to the primary crew. I considered myself a part of the primary crew since I always slept in the bed with Prince. Everyone assumed we must've been having sex, but

Prince made sure to always let them know that I was different and more special to him than the boy-toys many of them were. I also wasn't the type coming around simply looking for a handout or a free place to stay so I guess that did make me different.

By 8 a.m., we were still up talking and eating a coffee table full of Mickey D's in the living room. Prince saw that Kevin's head was rested on my shoulder. Everything was moving so fast or maybe the alcohol had long since taken over. With just a look between us, Prince could tell that I would be in need of the only spare bedroom. Still, I had to confirm with Kevin.

"Are you sleeping here, Kevin, or heading home?"

"I'm too tired," he said. "I can stay if you want."

"And where do you want to sleep?" I asked.

"Wherever you're sleeping, Q," he said before moving his head from my shoulder downtown to its proper place in my lap. I felt the blood rush.

The few stragglers seemed to be a little disappointed by my connection with Kevin. I'm sure they had alternate plans for each of us. Within moments, Prince had prepared the spare bedroom for us. Kevin went in to lie down and I took a trip to the restroom for a quick birdbath in the sink. One of the stragglers was waiting out by the bathroom door when I came out. Everyone's inhibitions were dangerously low at that point.

"Are you sure you're finished in there?" he asked, referencing my use of the bathroom.

"Yeah, I am, thanks," I answered.

"You have some of the most beautiful eyes I've ever seen."

"Thanks," I said again, sounding like a broken record.

"You're welcome, sexy."

I smiled as he indeed made it pretty hard to walk away. He had a deep, even-toned, milk-chocolate complexion so he looked edible and stood over six feet tall. His thick moist lips were just begging me for a kiss. My resistance was unusual, but I believed there was something better waiting for me in the other room. Kevin, however, was not alone. Trey was keeping him company when I walked in.

"Oh, what's up, Trey?" I said, surprised by his presence.

"Nothing, man—just saying goodnight to Kevin. I thought he needed a friend, but I see you got that covered."

"You saw that a few minutes ago in the living room, right?" I asked.

"Nah, I wasn't paying attention, but y'all have fun," he said as he walked out of the room.

"Thanks, Trey," said Kevin.

"Anytime," Trey yelled back.

I stood in the doorway for a minute staring at Kevin. He wondered what I was thinking so I lied and said, "Nothing."

Kevin then removed his shirt and unbuckled his jeans. The alcohol was continuing to endure. I followed his lead. He then reached toward me from the bed to pull down my pants and along came my boxers. The door hadn't even been securely closed yet. My head went back when he took a hold of me. He had his hand full. This boy was no beginner. He pulled me into the bed like he was pulling on my leash, but then I took over.

I smothered his body with my mouth, kissing and licking everything that was initially dry. There was lots of stroking, fondling and grinding for the next 30 to 45 minutes. Soon enough, he sprayed his juice all over my chest like he was marking his territory. I soon followed. We both took a few moments to let what happened seep into our brains. It was the best sex could be without intercourse.

To break the silence, I asked Kevin, "Are you cool?" He looked me in my eyes, then turned away. "What's wrong?"

"I don't know," he said. "I don't know, Q."

"Did I do something wrong?" I asked.

"I just don't know what to say."

Kevin stared at me some more before confessing, "I want to get to know you. That's what I do know, and I know I like what you do to me, inside and out."

It was clear that he liked something about me, but I couldn't be sure what that something was. We had known each other for less than 24 hours. All I knew was that I kind of liked something about him too in spite of our three-year age difference. Maybe, I figured, he was worth taking seriously after all.

"Let's just…" I paused briefly, not wanting to rush something that was again already moving too fast.

"Just what?" he anticipated.

"Just get to know each other," I said. "Who knows what could happen?"

Kevin broke into a smile wider than the gap of a buck-toothed tramp. It was the first time someone had had that effect on me and I didn't want to lose the feeling, at least not in that moment. We cuddled in the nude, then at some point, eventually, stopped kissing and fell asleep.

Boys to Men

Semester finals were only a couple of weeks away so I couldn't yet begin to stress about being back home with Mother for the semester break. My roommate wasn't there when I got back to my dorm room after class so I went to lie down on my bed. I grabbed the lotion out of the top drawer to seize the moment.

Six minutes later, I had already cleaned up and decided to check my voicemail. I had one new message. My mother called to inform me that she had found a studio apartment a few blocks down from our soon-to-be former residence. I picked up the phone immediately to give her a call about this new place our two personalities were going to be crammed into.

"Hey boy, did you get my message?" asked Mother.

"Obviously, that's why I'm calling. How many bedrooms are there?" I inquired rudely.

"I told you in the message it's a studio apartment. Why?"

"Don't you think it's a little small for the two of us?"

She contested, "Listen boy, it's what I could find in the little time I had to look and not to mention you weren't here to help."

It was time to cease and desist because I could see the conversation going awry real fast. I said, "Okay, well, I have finals in a couple of weeks so I'll be home on the 19th."

She said, "I'll see you then."

We hung up without saying another word, which wasn't uncommon.

My mother, Ellen Simmons, is a very loving, opinionated yet guarded woman who has given her children everything she had to give. We celebrated our like-mother-like-son relationship most of my life until I turned 15 years old. My hormones were raging out of control. I had lost my grandmother on my father's side during that period. My mother was attempting to cope with my newfound attitude. It wasn't easy. I was evolving and my thoughts were beginning to vary from hers like most teenagers. One misunderstanding after another led to countless heated arguments. I had learned what buttons of hers to push and brought my dear mother to the edge of tears on a few occasions. She wouldn't dare let me bear witness though.

After our thousandth dispute, my mother sensed there was a deeper problem so she took me to visit the psychologist I had no idea she had been previously making weekly visits to. She had started attending therapy sessions about eight years prior when a brain aneurysm took the life of her first born at the age of 21. Then there I was, her fourth and last child, compounding her pain. Again, no different than any other teenager, except in this instance Dr. William Roberts was fortunately willing to volunteer his services as a favor to my mom who wouldn't have been able to pay him if she tried.

I talked to Dr. Roberts about my relationship with my mother, my father and my peers at school. The anger and depression I felt had me acting out in a major way, but it was at home where I let it all hang out. Add to that other triggers, like a lack of a bond with the man I struggled to call my father, as well as continuous bullying from some of the kids at school, and what resulted was an overflow of rage.

Before entering high school, I battled with trying to find the balance between what's masculine and what's feminine. I admittedly played with dolls as a kid, but I also liked my G.I. Joe soldiers. My voice was high-pitched, yet I still didn't necessarily swish my hips when I walked. I didn't know what it meant exactly to be a man, specifically a black man in America. I knew I was different. Still, I had no idea how far off the mark I really was at times.

There were no strong, consistent male figures around me I could look up to. My twice-divorced mother did a great job attempting to raise all her boys to be men, but she instilled in me her ideals as a strong black woman because I was much like the daughter she had never had. Of course, the boys in middle school called me a faggot and also a mama's boy. Then, family friends would whisper behind my back about my mannerisms and the feminine features I had inherited from my mother like my slanted eyes, long eyelashes and high cheekbones. I'll never forget the day one of my mother's friends said out loud that "he should have been born a girl with that face."

My three older brothers also took notice of how different I was from normal boys. I enjoyed the company of girls because I learned that boys were too intimidating. The boys wouldn't let me skip a day in school without hearing that six-letter word or its three-letter junior.

Back during my junior-high days, I would cry in private at least three times a week when I got home. I would come straight in from school and lock myself in my room for hours until I felt safe again and comfortable to just be me. My mother never really saw that weak side of me. She knew the young playful Quincy who seemed to be content with spending most of his free time indoors with his overprotective mother.

Puberty and my fear of being further ridiculed forced many changes that impacted my overall attitude toward the world. I made definitive choices to change my behavior during the summer prior to my entry into high school. The high-pitched tone of my voice needed some bass. My talk and even my walk had to be firmer. My whole outlook on life had to change. I analyzed the boys out on the block and would mimic their actions in my bedroom mirror until it felt natural. Gradually, my voice deepened after a full summer of speaking from the depths of my lungs. I developed more swagger.

The first day of school shocked a lot of people.

"Oh my God! Your voice is so different, Quincy," some chicks said in unison.

Playing the role of a victim was no longer an option for me because if they didn't kill me soon, then I was going to kill myself. I had to be ready and willing to defend my honor, sometimes by any means necessary. One fight led to another until they stopped testing me so much. I no longer felt the need to run and hide in my room after school anymore. Eventually, that God-awful six-letter word almost disintegrated, although there were still echoes from those who said it at a distance or as a "joke." Still, my friends through high school were all female. Again, with them, I felt safe.

Some boys would fool themselves into believing I was actually a pimp since I didn't appear to act like a sissy anymore. If I didn't act gay, then in their minds I must not be gay. The game was and is just that simple on a lot of levels.

Up to that point, girls were simply companions and I liked the conversation, but intimacy was a whole different story. I just stuck to dating the corny, quiet, cute girls because they would hardly ever kiss and tell so they wouldn't tell anyone that we hadn't had any sort of sexual relations whatsoever. My fraudulent reputation remained fairly intact all the way through high-school graduation.

However, it was those weekly visits to Dr. Roberts that truly saved my life. I talked through the anger and depression that had accompanied my new bold attitude. He allowed me to speak freely about almost everything in my life. However, my sexual orientation was never questioned by the good doctor so I never offered him that essential detail. I had never really taken the time to discuss it with myself. I just wanted to be normal.

Besides, Dr. Roberts was most concerned with the relationship between me and my father, Leon Simmons, who had weekend visitation rights granted to him by the court system after he separated from my mother when I was five years old. Visitation usually meant dropping me off at my grandmother's place in Jersey City while he went off to work, or we would simply spend the entire weekend locked up in his one-bedroom apartment. There were no pictures hanging on the walls because that wasn't his thing. He always kept about a half-dozen large cardboard boxes piled on the floor just in case he had to move out, which meant the closets remained empty. Everything he owned was on the floor, confined to a few corners throughout the apartment, including his bed and television.

My father also wasn't into sports so I never learned from him. Those crucial early father-son bonding years instead left me sitting in front of a 10-inch black-and-white television watching Star Trek, which was his favorite show. Any in-depth conversations were few and far between. We've never really talked about anything emotional or passionate. Whenever there was someone talking, it was typically him lecturing me about some chore I wasn't doing right, like not completely squeezing all the water out of my washcloth when I was done with it. Children should never experience this degree of extreme boredom. It messed with my mind.

My pops, which was how I started referring to him, was also a devout Sunday-school teacher at the Church of God in Christ temple in Jersey City. Yet, we never even privately discussed Bible passages. He was most religious on Sundays.

During my tumultuous years of puberty, I realized that I had individual rights so, in turn, I began to elect staying home on the weekends with my mother instead of seeing him. After some months, home was where I stayed every single weekend. I was almost 16 years old at the time. Some people in the family couldn't give me the credit I deserved. They blamed my mother for being overprotective and thought she must have brainwashed me. His late Friday afternoon pleas for me to go with him soon came to an end after a judge declared that I was old enough to make my own decisions. If I didn't want to be bothered with him, it was my choice.

Two years went by before I laid eyes on my father's face again. He had trimmed his long salt-and-pepper beard and was delivering the news about my grandmother's hospitalization. It was my sole regret that I wasn't able to see my nana much during those two years. She always cooked meals every Sunday afternoon after me, Pops, my uncles, aunts, and cousins attended church service. I loved my grandmother. We used to do everything together. I learned how to cook just by watching her.

Without being briefed on her severe condition, I walked into the intensive-care unit and there was my nana asking, "Are you the missionary coming to take me away?" Her body was present, but not her mind and soul. It broke my heart. Once she regained her coherence, she begged me to mend my relationship with my father. She said that I needed to learn how to forgive him before it was too late.

I spent that whole evening attempting to communicate with my father and help him understand it would take some time to get back what we barely had to begin with. The time had come for him to start treating me like his son, not like another one of his possessions. He agreed in theory and, of course, my nana died a few weeks later. Her dying wish had been fulfilled.

If I Ever Fall in Love

It was supposed to be our unofficial first date. Kevin and I talked ahead of time about not jinxing or rushing what we felt between us. We wouldn't call it a *first date*, it was just us hanging out and attempting to learn something new about one another, getting to know each other as friends.

My Saturday had started with a trip to the barber shop. I told my barber I needed one of those top-notch cuts. He could tell how nervous I was because, for once, he had to hold my head in place to shape my hairline. It was my usual low-cut fade, but he used the straight razor that time, making it look especially clean. My sideburns were long, thin, cutting off at my jawline. He trimmed my mustache and shadow of a goatee. I confessed, as most guys do when sitting in that brown leather, cushiony chair, that I was meeting up with someone special. He wanted to know *her* name as his crotch pressed up against my knee. He said he knew of a lot of females throughout many hoods so he might have information to help me make the best first impression. In other words, he was going to tell me whether or not she was a freak.

The barbershop is where guys can go to gossip about girls like girls gossip about guys in beauty salons. However, my girl was a guy so the conversation would've been really awkward. Instead, I just left him a good tip then rushed to Newark Penn Station to catch my train.

I didn't know why I was still shaking. Granted, I hadn't seen him since that night a week prior at Prince's spot. We had talked over the phone but made no plans for what we would do, and I didn't know what I would say once I saw his handsome face again. The walk down Market Street seemed to stretch for miles when it was only a few blocks. In pursuit of my train, I almost got hit by a speeding car running a red light. The sirens from a cop car were close behind. Even a police chase in broad daylight couldn't break my concentration though.

I wondered what two young gay men should do on an unofficial first date. It was something new for both of us. Kevin was brand new to the gay life and I was fairly new, never having taken anyone that seriously before. Love scared me to death, but I was still willing to dream.

Kevin met me on the corner of 42nd Street and 6th Avenue in Manhattan. We decided then to take a long walk through Central Park. Our money was in short supply so we kept our plans basic. We were just happy to be together.

That winter day was bright and sunny with no snow on the ground. The crisp air stood still between us. Our bubble jackets were unzipped but still keeping us warm, or maybe it was our hearts. Neither one of us could really tell the difference since it was all so unexpected.

We walked aimlessly through the park from one trail to the next. Kevin led the way, not in direction, but in conversation. He was honest with me about only wanting to have sex the night we bumped into each other in Prince's kitchen and I pled guilty to the same charge. I went on about how I was wary about dating an 18-year-old. It was a huge risk for me to open up to someone three years younger than me. Other guys wanted to get close to me before then, but none seemed to see through me like Kevin did. I didn't know if it was just a phase or infatuation or the beginning of some real love. Whatever it was, I was going along for the ride, signing away all my common sense and better judgment.

Living in or around New York can at times blind us to how beautiful the city really is. Central Park reminded us of that fact that day. During our lovers' stroll, we found some random swings that we didn't know were there. The little kids deep inside us came out to play as we hopped on them, swinging up to the sky. What were we going through? As I think back, we were so high on each other that we felt like we could fly. People walked by us staring and some even pointed like *look at the two gay boys…ha ha ha…they're so funny*. Some straight boys tried to harass us unsuccessfully. Kevin and I were on a different level.

Once we came back down to Earth, Kevin grabbed my hand, admiring the 24-karat gold band I wore on my pinky finger. It belonged to my mother. It was one of the many pieces of jewelry, some costume and some legit, she forgot she had so I kind of borrowed it without her knowledge. Kevin then looked mischievously at his high-school ring on his middle finger.

"Let's swap," he said emphatically.

"Swap what?" I responded.

"Let's swap rings, Q. I wear yours and you wear mine."

"But isn't that your high-school ring?" I asked. "Don't you want to hold onto it? Besides, my mother would kill me if she found out I not only took her ring but gave it to my *friend*."

Kevin said, "It's not permanent, just for now."

I gave in. Kevin's puppy-dog face was irresistible. I figured his high-school ring was just as valuable as my mother's ring. It was yet another risk I was willing to take with Kevin.

Roar

All while getting to know Kevin some more, semester finals had come to an end, leaving one more semester of college for me to conquer. The holiday season passed once again with less buzz than the year before. I was back at home with Mother, living in a tight studio apartment with only one room and one bath. Fortunately, we hadn't had many arguments. The lack of privacy was however an enormous shock for us both.

For me, it was tough to get a good night's rest. My mother slept on the sofa bed of her black leather sectional. There was not enough space in the new apartment for her to keep her real bed so she threw it out along with any furniture I could've mistaken as my own. She was always good for trashing stuff she herself no longer had the use for so I slept directly on the part of the sectional adjacent to the sofa bed.

On an average weekday, she would wake up around 7 a.m. to get ready for work. She found a job as a teacher's assistant for the public-school system of Montclair, New Jersey. Before making her exit, the sofa bed would be squared away and *Good Morning America* left blaring on the TV. It was her blatant signal for me to get up and make something of the morning. School robbed me of enough of my mornings so I would normally turn off the TV then roll over to go back to sleep.

My recurring dreams were often weird, but sometimes revealing. That morning, I remember they were once again filled with images you'd see on *National Geographic* or something.

Kevin and I had visited the Bronx Zoo the previous weekend. Out of all the animals we saw, I kept coming back to those tigers. They've always fascinated me ever since I was a little kid. Their penetrating eyes and definitive stripes mesmerize me, but their teeth and claws scare the hell out of me. Those are the things that keep me from getting too familiar or even owning one. Still, tigers have always calmed me. If there are such experiences like past lives, then I must've been a tiger. It was in the fourth grade when it really hit me because those dreams I was having began to manifest themselves in my real life.

Recess had just ended and my school teacher ordered everyone to line up so we could head back inside to the classroom. Every day, most students would compete to be first in line because, in some way, it made one feel as though he or she was head of the class.

This particular day, I found myself in that number-one position, but one of the school bullies didn't want to be number two. In the blink of an eye, I had been knocked down from my position flat onto the ground below. The impact tore holes in my jeans. My knees bled. It wasn't my first run-in with that bully, but I made it my last.

Something deep inside me took over as I blacked out. I heard the teacher yelling my name, which, in my head, gave me motivation. I was enraged just like a wild tiger.

The next thing I remember is being chastised while standing behind my desk in class. I turned my head toward the bully to see that his face and neck had about as many grave scratches as a tiger has stripes. My nails were stuffed with his dead skin. I slowly plucked each nail clean while the teacher, who had been one of my biggest fans, stood in judgment. She was disappointed in what I had done. She reported it to the principal who suspended me for a week. My mother wasn't bothered though because she knew in her heart that I was simply defending myself against a boy who was almost twice my puny size. It was retribution.

No Sunshine

A few Monday mornings later, following my unofficial first date with Kevin, I was awakened by a thick stack of papers landing flat on my chest.

"What is this?" my mother asked angrily.

"It looks like the phone bill to me," I said sarcastically as I sat upright. I was irritated that, once again, my sleep had been interrupted.

"It's a $375 phone bill, Quincy!"

Kevin's phone number covered almost 10 full pages of the statement from front to back. I'd had no idea long-distance charges on a landline phone were so expensive.

"So what am I supposed to do about it?" I said.

"Don't be stupid. Pay it or I'm shutting it off. That's it."

"You know I still don't have a job yet so why can't you just pay it?" I replied. "I'll pay you back when I start working again."

"What the hell is that school teaching you, boy? Like money just grows on trees, and who the hell is this person in New York you keep calling so much?" she asked.

No one in my family was aware of my sexuality, but I could tell from her tone that the question was absolutely not rhetorical. However, I still had no response so she persisted, "Is she some hoochie you met at school or one of those clubs you go to every weekend?"

I said, "Ma, please."

"You tell me or I'll call her myself," she threatened.

"His name is Kevin," I said bluntly.

She stopped in her tracks long enough to process what I had said. Mothers always know the truth, but I didn't know if she was ready to deal with it just then. Maybe it was bad timing to confess I was gay in the heat of the moment. I wanted to beg her for a response of some kind, but there was no time. Instead, she grabbed her car keys and walked out the door, slamming it behind her.

After a few minutes passed of me sitting on the sofa thinking about how selfish it was to do what I did, I went downstairs to find that her car hadn't been moved. Still, she was nowhere in sight. I thought maybe she went for a walk to clear her mind. I was about to return to the apartment when I noticed from a short distance that her car door was unlocked. I walked over and there she was lying down on the backseat with her arms raised above her head. Riddled with guilt, I sat down in the passenger seat and closed the door to shield out the noise of rush-hour traffic. She remained silent. My mother is rarely at a loss for words.

"Ma?"

"What is your issue, Quincy?" she asked. "Did you say that to hurt me?"

"No, I didn't—I was just mad and it came out," I replied.

"No, you came out—so is that how you wanted to do it? When are you going to grow up? I can't take you lashing out at me anymore. You're too old for this."

She sat up, ran her fingers through her hair, took a deep breath, then continued, "I love you, Quincy, no matter what. Some things you say and do hurt more than you know. I'm not your punching bag. I'm your mother."

"I know and I love you too, even though I don't say it much. And I've been wanting to tell you but didn't know how. This whole thing still scares me," I said.

"Well, don't fool yourself into thinking I never had a clue. I've known since you were a little boy," she happily admitted. "Do you remember when I asked you a long time ago what kind of girl you saw yourself marrying someday?"

"Um, yeah, I think I do," I said.

"I was testing you. You said you wanted someone strong and able to handle your mood swings and take charge when necessary. I accepted it back then—my baby boy is a sugar plum," she laughed.

She opened the car door, which, on top of her dark humor, relieved some of the pressure. We both stood tall. Then, she hugged me like she was indeed cradling her baby boy. My mother reminded me that day that she will always know me better than anyone else.

"Does your brother know?" she asked as we walked back upstairs.

"No, he does not," I said. "I will deal with that some other time in the future if you don't mind."

I got back upstairs and requested my mother's permission to call Kevin. She allowed it. It had been three days since Kevin and I last spoke, which broke a record for the two of us. We had been getting to know each other for over a month and I never expected him to commit the way he had.

He had also started working full-time at the Gap on 23rd St. and 8th Ave. in Manhattan. The job required him to work on weekends, which had been our personal quality time.

Nevertheless, we had made plans to see each other later that week on Friday night and I was beyond ready.

"Hello?" said Kevin, answering his home phone.

"Hey, boy, I miss hearing your voice," I replied.

"I miss you more, baby. How's it going with you and your mom in that closet?" he asked.

"She knows," I said cryptically.

"Knows what, babe?"

"Knows I'm gay and your name is Kevin."

He said, "Ha, oh really? How did that happen?"

I gave Kevin the complete story. He seemed to be happy for me although I could tell he was a bit agitated that I told my mother his name. Soon after, he changed the subject.

"Well, I can beat that," he said. "My mom didn't even go to work this morning because she quit her job."

"Quit her job? Why would she do that? Doesn't she support you and your little brother?"

"Wrong," said Kevin. "She supports my little brother now. I was told that I can take care of myself with my new job and all."

"Okay, that's crazy, but at least she's not putting your independent ass out on the street," I said with a nice round of laughs. "So are we still on for Friday night?"

"I don't get off work until 10, but I still want to see you. I need to come home, shower, change my clothes, then I guess we can meet up 'round midnight."

"Do you want to go see a movie or get something to eat?" I asked. "We gotta pick one or the other unless you paying for everything with your new job and all."

Kevin almost choked on his spit before responding, "I'll probably just want to chill over at Prince's again. I'm going to be dumb tired. I'll let him know we got the spare room when I see him on Thursday. We're going out to Suspects."

Suspects was a down-low, trendy hole-in-the-wall in the West Village. There was never enough space for all the people they liked to cram into the railroad-style bar each week. I was sure they had dozens of fire-code violations, but it was all about the drinks and the cute dates. There was also the V.I.P. section upstairs in the attic where smoking of almost any substance was allowed.

"You be easy at Suspects, Kevin. Don't talk to strangers, okay?"

"Only if they look like you," he said. "I'll be too high and drunk to know the difference."

"Real funny, fool, talk to you later," I said before hanging up.

●●●

I spent most of the week trying to figure out how I was going to support myself financially for the next semester of school and beyond. Money was dwindling and my mother was no longer a reliable source of income, especially since she had a $400 phone bill to pay down. She gave what she had when she could give it, but those times were becoming less frequent.

Over the previous months, I had been calling Sean Wilkinson concerning a paid internship. Sean was the programming director of WUGH, which spun the best hip-hop and R&B music in the country. Russell and I met Sean in Manhattan at a *Billboard* magazine panel discussion called "How to Break into the Music Industry." Russell was, at the time, my only close, straight-male best friend whom I had met at Rutgers. Sean gave each of us his business card and I had kept in contact with him ever since.

The following week I was scheduled for an informal appointment with Sean to discuss my qualifications for the internship. One of the current interns was leaving to pursue her dreams as an actress. It was one of those rare opportunities of a lifetime that I just couldn't let pass me by.

●●●

Finally, Friday had arrived. Kevin and I had made plans to see a movie, grab a bite to eat, then head to Prince's place for a nightcap. My patience was wearing thin as the hours dragged by without any real sense of my urgency. I figured it was about time to give Kevin a call for final confirmation, but it went to voicemail. I imagined he was extra busy at work assisting some hopeless teenage girls who wouldn't have a clue that he was involved with another dude. However, there was still no word from him just an hour away from our time to meet.

"So what do you have planned tonight?" my mother asked.

"I'm going out with Kevin so I probably won't make it back 'til the morning," I responded.

"Where will you be sleeping if that's the case?"

"Please don't ask me too many personal questions, Mother," I demanded.

"Watch your tone when you're speaking to your mother. I don't know what you're trying to hide because I've been there and done it all before you were born."

I said, "Well, I'm sure you didn't run around telling everybody about it either."

I always had to have the last word. Soon, it was 11:30 p.m. and four voicemails later. The store had closed over an hour earlier and my mother had already fallen asleep. Kevin and I had agreed we would meet at midnight, but hadn't discussed a specific location so I couldn't assume he would be waiting for me on some lonely street corner. What had begun as concern had transformed into heavy disappointment. I was also angry because I hated to be disappointed. A phone call seemed so trivial to me yet I was still on hold essentially. It wasn't until 20 minutes after midnight when his cell finally rang out.

"Hello?" he said, sounding drowsy.

"Kevin?"

"Yeah, baby—I'm so sorry. I closed my eyes for a few seconds and I guess I fell asleep. What time is it?"

"Don't worry about it. Go back to sleep," I said with a defeated tone.

"Alright," he said. "Goodnight, babe."

I couldn't believe he hung up so quickly. He should've recognized from the tone of my voice that I didn't want him to go back to sleep. I wanted to see him, feel him and continue falling for him. The state-to-state thing was beginning to take its toll. I wish I would've known better. Kevin also had to work that Saturday and Sunday so there would likely be another week of anticipation before I could see him again.

●●●

Saturday morning was so sunny, but, for me, so dreary. My boy, Roman, called early to see if I wanted to ride with him up to Willowbrook Mall in Wayne, N.J. Roman had been another one of my closest friends since I had chosen to forfeit my sexual attraction to him about a year earlier. The decision wasn't easy. It was very difficult for almost anyone, gay or straight, to resist him. He was absolutely a complete package. However, he did have an ego to match. I guess Roman was just like a supermodel in that way. He was a light-skinned, hazel-eyed black man with a face that appeared to be sculpted by the best plastic surgeons Los Angeles had to offer, but his 6-foot-2-inch slim frame was all natural. Even the jet-black waves in his hair didn't need much besides some water, grease and a hairbrush.

Roman knew that a shopping trip would ease my mind a bit so we spent the whole day in and out of stores. He kept encouraging me to waste the rest of my available credit on a complete outfit for the club that night. Roman said it would make me feel better to get out, especially since Kevin hadn't called me the whole day.

I got dressed at his mom's place where he lived. Roman's sexuality was no secret to her because he had been in the lifestyle since he was 12 years old. It was at that time when he met my former babysitter, Jordan, who was about 10 years older than Roman. Like he had later done with me, Jordan taught Roman everything there was to know about being gay, black and proud. Jordan was also well-known on the ballroom scene. The oftentimes superficial and materialistic sub-culture within the black and Latino gay communities can be quite intense when you have a 10's-across-the-board face and body like Roman's. The ballroom *kids* take themselves very seriously to the point of bitter rivalry.

They compete in balls, like the Latex Ball, where multiples crews, or houses, as they're called, strive to be the best and the fiercest. Each competition consists of categories such as

Butch in Drag (a boy who looks like a boy, but also looks good dressed as a girl), Sex Siren (a boy like Roman who strips down to his underwear for the judges and everyone in attendance to gawk at), and Voguing Fem (a boy like the ones you'd see in an old-school Madonna video) in which members from each house battle for cash and prizes.

Jordan had walked in almost every ballroom category and later introduced Roman to the scene at that tender age. Roman got addicted to winning multiple categories because that face of his was the greatest. He, of course, lost sight of what the real world was like and had to get readjusted through high school where the straights will give you a rude awakening. Those straight boys, as well as his jealous ballroom competitors, kept him fighting. It was one knock-down, drag-out after another. Luckily, he was always a natural self-defender, meaning he could kick some serious ass when necessary.

●●●

Roman found a parking spot that night around the corner from the Warehouse. We had been drinking on the way over, which was the only way we knew how to party. We passed by security. While on our way up to the outdoor deck, I ran right into Kevin on the stairs. My head started spinning. He wrapped his arms around my neck and planted kisses all over my face.

"What are you doing here, baby?" he asked.

"What are you doing here, Kevin? I thought you would be too tired to hang out tonight with work and everything."

"I came out with some friends. They wanted to celebrate my first full week on the new job." For some reason, I didn't bring up the fact that he and I had yet to celebrate. I just settled. He then said, "Come on so I can introduce you to them."

"Why haven't you called me all day?" I asked as he pulled me by my left arm up the stairs. Roman had already disappeared into the crowd as usual. "Did you even think about me?"

Kevin replied, "Of course I did. I've been working all day with no break so I couldn't reach out to you."

I thought maybe I was overreacting so I decided to put a smile on my face. Again, I just settled. Kevin introduced me to each of his five friends before having been dragged onto the dance floor. There was no question he was happy to see me.

"I haven't even had a drink yet," I said.

He then handed me his half-empty cup of vodka and orange juice as he slowly turned his back to me without breaking physical contact. I could finally see him and feel him, but was growing cautious of falling in love with him. He moved my hand down to his inner thigh and he instinctively pressed his body up against mine even harder. I thought about backing away since I was wearing my new Sean John sweatpants. Instead I guzzled down his drink and threw the cup on the floor. I pulled Kevin closer. He had me willing to do many things in that moment.

About three drinks and 30 songs later, the lights came up. His friends had been standing nearby watching us dance most of the time. Kevin kissed me goodbye, fondled me a bit, then I was off to search for Roman.

In a back corner of the club, there was Roman surrounded by four other pretty boys. They were trying to convince Roman to join them for the rest of the night/morning. He mentioned to them that he hadn't come alone so that's when I stepped forward to introduce myself. The invitation soon turned into a sexual proposition for the two of us. Roman was anxiously leaving the decision up to me. Out of the corner of my eye, I saw Kevin waving goodbye from the opposite end of the floor so I reluctantly had to decline their offer.

The Beautiful Ones

It was one of the best days of my life. The informal meeting I had at the radio station went better than expected. Sean took a long glance at my resume, then had me speak to a few of his colleagues, which made this informal meeting feel more like an interview as the hours crept by. They were all smiles. I knew that had to be a good sign. By the end of it, I was offered the internship at WUGH and my first day on the job was going to be the following Monday. It was going to be a challenge balancing work, school and a progressive love life, but it was what had to be done if I intended to be successful.

I spread the good news to my family and friends, including Jordan, which turned out to be perfect timing because one of his clients wanted to fly him and three guests out to Vegas to photograph the grand reopening of the Blue Moon Resort. It was a four-star hotel strictly for men, with a clothing-optional policy anywhere on the gated premises.

There was no time though to plan when we were going. The reopening was scheduled for that weekend so Jordan, Roman and I had to decide quickly on who the fourth wheel would be. I thought of bringing Kevin along, but talked myself out of it. We wanted it to be a fun, no-holds-barred trip. It was by no means a lovers' retreat. Roman then suggested we take his ex-boyfriend Shane along for the trip. Jordan and I ignored that little voice deep inside both of us saying *hell no*. We had nothing against Shane. We had nothing against the fact that they were in transition to becoming friends. We instead didn't trust Roman's fragile ego. They had only split up their nearly year-long relationship a couple of months prior so their resentment toward one another was still green.

Shane had been pursuing a relationship with Roman for years before they officially met face-to-face at some ball. They were competing against each other in the Sex Siren category and, of course, Roman won, but Shane was not a distant second. Shane was also one beautiful man. He stood about 5'8", had a gym rat's hard body of about 160 pounds. His round ass always had a hard time cooperating with his fitted jeans so he sagged a lot. In addition to his forearm tattoo sleeves, Shane also changed his hair color like the wind changes women's hairstyles. For the trip to Vegas, he dyed his own hair honey blond, which was cut into a low Caesar, to contrast his bronze skin tone.

At the beginning of their relationship, the dynamically sexy duo shut every club down when they would go out. Roman always gave his model fever to his admirers while Shane came off as a Hollywood misfit. They not only turned heads, they started heated conversations.

However, behind all that glitter and gold, there was an ugly truth. Some believe lovers are supposed to support one another in their endeavors and not feel threatened by the other's achievements. Both Roman and Shane were guilty of the latter so they fought at least once every other week. I don't know if it was their goal to take away the other's beauty, but it sure seemed that way.

Jordan and I never witnessed the fights between them out at the clubs or elsewhere. I think Roman thought too highly of us to let us see him get so weak. We would, however, hear about it in the streets from mutual friends who were rightfully concerned that someone might end up in jail one day for murder.

Most of their battles happened in private after they chose to move in together about six months into their relationship. Roman had even given Shane a broken arm once, while Shane had blackened Roman's eye on a few occasions. Theirs was the type of "love" I had always refused to settle for. To me, love is an emotion, not a weapon.

In spite of all that history, Jordan, Roman, Shane, and I were off to Vegas for one memorable weekend. Thankfully, my brother let me borrow some spending cash, but Kevin wasn't too happy when I told him about our weekend trip. He said, "They don't call it Sin City for nothing, Q. You better not cheat on me." Indeed, it was my first trip out of town with friends, putting our new relationship to the test. I told Kevin he had no reason not to trust me. He had my heart.

That four-and-a-half-hour Vegas flight was so smooth. We got seats near each other. We just talked about all the things we wanted to do when we got there, like gamble, of course, and hit up every buffet in town. Unfortunately, the elaborate stage-show productions couldn't fit into our tight budgets.

The plane captain made the happy announcement that the record-high temperatures in the 80's would carry through the entire weekend. Once we arrived at the Blue Moon, I think all of us quickly realized that our set plans were likely going to change. The sexy Justin Timberlake look-alike in his cherry red mankini and all-white hi-top Chuck Taylors behind the front desk checked us in. He handed over the keys to our rooms.

Jordan and I shared a room on the first floor, two doors down from the sauna. Roman and Shane got a double on the second level, overlooking the swimming pool. There were naked white men left and right. Some were as old as the Founding Fathers. Others were as young and ripe as Chippendales dancers. It was no surprise that we were the only black men at the resort, which meant we got a lot of attention.

Jordan started working immediately after we dropped our bags off in our rooms and changed into our swimsuits. I threw on some horizontally striped, black-and-white swim trunks. Roman and Shane wore matching royal blue Speedo briefs and Jordan covered up in his usual white tee and below-the-knee jean shorts.

Jordan took photos of the hot guys passing us by in the hallway. Most of them barely even saw the flashing camera because they were so busy staring at Roman, Shane and myself—in that particular order. By the time we made it to the pool, it was as if we were some out-of-town celebrities. Not only were we the only black guys, but we didn't lug our standoffish Jersey attitudes on the plane with us. Again, it was supposed to be a fun, no-holds-barred mini-vacation. Besides, nudity can be quite disarming.

We just chilled by the pool, taking in the sights of the fine naked white men getting soaked. The sun soon set so the hotel transformed the pool into a dance floor. A sturdy yet transparent platform came out of one end of the pool, locking itself into the other end, making it seem like everyone was dancing on water. The DJ played every pop artist from Pink to NSYNC. Still, half the crowd was naked and partying like rock stars.

Then, around midnight, we suddenly weren't the only black men anymore. At least a dozen more joined the party. Two out of the dozen stripped down naked, disappearing into the crowd. All of them were invited by different people so they didn't really know each other, as Roman and I had first assumed.

Roman was talking in my ear, plotting which one he was going after since we had a long night ahead of us. He made eye contact with his first choice, the one whom had come to the party with a single friend. Roman spent the next hour flirting with him from across the pool. Since Kevin had warned me to be good, I did my best to ignore any of the other hot boys there. I did entertain some of the fogies though. There was a group of them by the open bar seizing every chance they got to talk to some of the younger guys who had drinking habits. I was one of those guys. They politely flirted while I politely indulged.

Inevitably, after more than two hours of drinking, I had changed my mind about ignoring the hot boys throughout the party. We all had a change of mind, actually, except for Jordan. We could always lean on Jordan to be our sitter. Roman changed his mind about the dude from across the pool since he had lost his attention. Roman just chose the center of the platform to burn a hole in while dancing. He was so drunk that he didn't realize that his dude from across the pool had changed his mind about me.

I could see it in his eyes. He no longer wanted Roman. He wanted me so I kept thinking and reminding myself of Kevin's smile, his style and his little skinny muscular legs I loved so much. Those thoughts distracted me from the temptation I felt on what happened to be the first night of our weekend getaway. I didn't know how much longer I would be able to resist, especially if the second night turned out to be hotter than the first.

While Shane and I headed over to the bar for our fifth drink, the dude and his friend approached us both from behind. Both of these dudes were sexy. They looked a little like Andre 3000 and Ludacris, one was dark-skinned and his caramel-toned friend appeared to be Dominican. They stood pressing right up against our bare backs. The party had become pretty crowded, which meant the bar was backed up so it was within reason that after a few drinks they felt the need to get that close to us. With only two bartenders, it might have been hard to be seen and heard.

Still, their throbbing swimsuit bulges were beyond necessary. I had to shake dude immediately even if Shane wasn't going to follow my lead. I grabbed my drink, then joined Roman on the dance floor. Roman still didn't have a clue about what was happening until Shane brought the Dominican dude to the dance floor. Then, the dark-skinned dude Roman was after walked up and started grinding on my hip to the beat of Jagged Edge's "Let's Get Married (Remix)." Roman rolled his eyes at me. I couldn't tell if he was being playful or dead serious. He just buckled down and danced even harder.

Another hour had passed. Shane and I were still freaking the two friends on the dance floor. I had stopped torturing myself with guilt. I was out of town with two of my closest friends in the whole world so why not enjoy it. However, the more Shane and I enjoyed it, the more outrageous Roman became.

Roman had pulled his Speedo down so far that his pubes and half of his butt-crack were on full display. It was like he was in competition mode. He kept dancing up next to anyone who showed him the least bit of attention. His pool of onlookers grew smaller and smaller the drunker he got. It was embarrassing. Jordan eventually decided it was time to put an end to the night before things got out of control. Unfortunately, he was a little too late for that. Roman went from being frustrated to furious.

Shane and his new friend had deserted the party while we weren't looking. We could only assume they went to the hotel room for the after party. I was still poolside with the dark-skinned guy having a friendly conversation, which was as innocent as it could be considering we'd lost count of how many drinks we'd had. Jordan soon grabbed me by my arm up out of the lounge chair saying he needed help with Roman, who was by then trying to break down the door to his hotel room.

"Come out here, Shane! I just want to talk to you and your Vegas whore. Now open the door!" screamed Roman.

There was nothing Roman really wanted to discuss. We all knew as soon as Shane opened that door, Roman was going in ablaze. Jordan tried talking some sense to him, but the alcohol pumping through his veins was deafening. The hotel staff asked if they should call the police. Jordan said no. I insisted yes. I couldn't believe Roman was blacking out. He was doing exactly what he promised he wouldn't do. If it came down to Roman spending the night in jail so the three of us could enjoy the rest of our getaway, then it's whatever. Jordan talked the staff out of it though.

Fed up, I backslapped Roman across his face followed by me shoving him halfway down the hall until he shifted his rage from Shane to me. He then started yelling at me and Jordan for always sticking up for his ex. He called us traitors.

Just then, a cleaning lady, making her rounds, entered the hallway to clean the rooms on the second level. Roman grabbed her spray bottle of bleach, aimed it at my face and pulled the trigger. I shut my eyes a millisecond before the chemical could have potentially blinded me. Jordan ran toward us because I'm sure he could feel the pressure building, but I had already exploded.

I picked up the cleaning lady's vacuum cleaner and swung it at Roman one good time before Jordan could stop me. Roman broke the impact with his forearm, but I knew I at least broke skin. The cleaning lady wasn't that spooked by the whole incident. She instead ran into the bathroom of one of the rooms to wet a washcloth. She used that cloth to wipe the bleach from my face as Jordan kept me restrained from behind with both of my arms strapped at my sides. Roman had run off down the stairwell, probably realizing he went too far.

I couldn't believe it. I had always treated Roman like a blood brother. Maybe the alcohol had a bigger effect than I was willing to admit, but it was a major turning point in our friendship. Jordan tried to convince me that Roman's rage was more directed at Shane than either one of us.

"How can you say that?" I asked. "His evil ass was looking directly at us."

He replied, "Q, he's a Gemini just like you. That was his evil drunk side talking. The normal Roman loves us just as much as we love him."

"Well, I'm actually hating him a lot right now," I said.

"Yeah, maybe so right now, he can do some ugly things, but I'm in love with him regardless," Jordan confided.

"Wait, what did you just say?"

Jordan's head dropped. He tried mumbling his words, but I forced him to speak up. He confessed that he had been in love with Roman long before I came into the picture. He'd never said anything because he was scared it might send Roman running away. As much as Roman seeks constant love and attention, he really doesn't know how to handle it. Jordan made me promise never to tell him, which was going to be easy since I had planned on ending my friendship with Roman for good.

The next day Roman sobered up and attempted to apologize. Jordan gladly accepted, but I couldn't. I couldn't look him in the eye. I couldn't even acknowledge his presence. For the rest of the weekend, I just pretended Roman didn't exist. All four of us walked the Vegas strip, ate at a few buffets and tanned some more by the hotel's pool. I made sure that my path never crossed with his. Not once did I speak to Roman. Shane had also accepted his apology, which for him was probably one out of a million times. I couldn't let it slide so easily. I just wanted what happened in Vegas to permanently stay in Vegas.

●●●

"Damn, so why wasn't I invited?" asked Karyn after I told her about my trip to Vegas with the boys.

The four of us flew right into Newark airport late Sunday afternoon. Before considering taking a nap, I met Karyn at the school cafeteria for dinner. It was the start of my last semester toward my undergraduate degree. Karyn and I had a lot of catching up to do since we barely got a chance to speak over the semester break.

Of course, I had to tell a white lie to my homegirl. I told her Jordan, Roman, Shane, and I went for a friend-of-a-friend's bachelor party, which was no place for a single female. She believed me. I also lied about the fight, telling her it was over a girl Roman and Shane wanted so Jordan and I got caught in the crossfire.

"Well, I'm glad I missed the drama. Sounds like my therapist would have a field day with your boy Roman," she said.

"Your therapist? What does that mean?" I asked.

"It means what I just said, Q. I had to go talk to someone about my issues. We've only done one session so far, but I'm definitely getting it out of my system. That talk we had before the break opened my eyes. I can't do this by myself and asking for help doesn't mean I'm as weak as I felt that night my life changed," said Karyn.

"Congrats, beautiful, I think you're doing the right thing. Therapy definitely helped me climb out of my hole back in the day," I confided.

It was yet another piece of my puzzle Karyn didn't know existed. I explained how severely depressed I was as a teenager, going so far as to swallow a handful of my mom's pain pills because I wanted to die. My life back then felt like a burden, not a true gift from God. The only peace I found was within the four walls of my bedroom with the door shut, when the fact is that's not actual peace. It's more like fear. Fear grows in isolation, but shrivels up and dies in the light of day. While sitting across the table from each other, I could tell Karyn's fears had begun to fade because she was glowing more than ever before.

"And my counselor wants to bring in my mom and dad too at some point," said Karyn. "She said, as my guardians, they've probably been affected just as much as I have by the whole thing."

"Yeah, that's probably right," I said.

"But enough about me and enough about your Sin City shenanigans, I'm supposed to be helping you celebrate your new internship. Are you excited or nervous?" Karyn asked.

"Oh my God, I can't wait. I was listening to WUGH before I left the dorm to meet you. They announced Whitney is in town and might stop by the station to talk about her new album dropping later this year."

Karyn said, "I don't even want to hear about it if she's a complete mess."

"Oh, yes, you do," I teased.

"Okay, you're right. I want all the juicy details down to how crooked her wig looked on her pretty little head," she laughed. "But, not to change the subject, but I got a personal question for you that I've always wanted to ask since we became friends."

"Should I prepare to be offended now or what?" I joked.

"Stop it. Seriously though, you're the only guy I've ever been this close to besides my dad of course," she said. "I just want to know, why are you single?"

It was the question every eligible man or woman hates to hear. How does anyone respond?

"Why do you think I'm single, Karyn?" I asked.

"I don't get it," she said. "If we hadn't become friends first and you were about three inches taller, I would've been all over you. I still dream, I mean, think about it though, to be honest. I mean, you're a cutie and you got a cute little slim frame with those piercing eyes."

"Wait, back that up. You said you still dream about me?" I quizzed.

"Oh, boy, did I say that?" she responded.

"You've been dreaming about all this manliness, huh? What were your dreams about? Were we having sex, Karyn?" I said right before I started shaking my head.

"Well, we were getting to know each other a lot better than we do now and that's all I'm willing to say."

"Awkward!" I cried out, successfully dodging her question. We just laughed, finished eating dinner, then headed back to the dorms to rest up. Classes were beginning the next day. We needed all our energy to cope with the new professors and decide whether or not we wanted to drop any classes.

After getting back to my room, I checked my voicemail for any messages. There was one from Kevin. He had called just minutes before I left for my flight to Vegas. At the beginning of the message, there were about five seconds of silence followed by him simply saying, "I guess you thought I was joking when I said I didn't want you to go."

The bass in Kevin's voice was normally a turn-on, except in that instance. He said nothing more in the message. He just hung up. I prepared myself for what was going to be our first real argument if he believed I wasn't supposed to go to Vegas with my friends because he said so. That's not the way my mother raised me.

Even though I've never been afraid of an argument, I hate getting into them with someone I don't want to lose. Kevin was becoming a significant part of my life. I hoped my trip to Vegas would not put that in jeopardy. I picked up and put down the phone over and over again. His was one of the few phone numbers I knew by heart. In my head, I kept running through some of the things I figured he would say. I was trying to be prepared for something that would come out of left field. I also made a conscious effort to check my ego at the dial tone.

"Hey," said Kevin nonchalantly after answering my call one ring away from being picked up by the answering machine.

"Hey," I responded. "Miss me?"

"Umm, I guess. I've been keeping myself busy though."

"Doing what?" I asked.

"Family stuff, working," he said. "How was your trip?"

"It was cool. Me and Roman got into it big time Friday night. I probably won't be speaking to him ever again." Kevin didn't respond. He seemed to be preoccupied so I asked him, "Are you okay? Do you feel like talking?"

"What do you want to talk about, Q?"

"Well, I got your voicemail from Friday," I said. "Are you mad I went?"

Again, Kevin didn't respond. I assumed something in the background was holding his attention more than me. I thought I had heard a stranger's voice, but he said it was his little brother playing around too much.

"Kevin, are you okay?" I asked with a bit more concern.

"Why do you keep asking me that? You've been gone the whole weekend living it up in Vegas with your friends, no call, no nothing," he said.

"Babe, it was barely two days and I've gone weekends before without hearing from you so why are you buggin'?"

"You're right, I'm buggin'," he agreed sarcastically. "Can I go now? I got something to do."

"Kevin, what's wrong? Don't you miss me? I miss you like crazy. I'm sorry I didn't call you from Vegas, but that fight I had with Roman killed it for me. I couldn't even think straight."

Kevin said, "Nah, it's cool. I just had a bad weekend. It's probably 'cause I missed you. But I really do have to go. Hit me up tomorrow when you get out of class. I'll be in a better mood to talk then. I promise."

However, I wasn't in the best of moods to fall asleep that night. I thought it was possible that Kevin did have a rough weekend too. All I could do, all that was within my power to do was to force myself to sleep on it and pray that my first day at WUGH would make my troubles with Kevin disappear, even if only temporarily.

First Time Together

Am I ready for the real world? That's the question random teachers, family, friends, and strangers kept asking me. It was my senior year in college. It was my first week of my last semester. It was the first week of my internship and I began to worry. I needed a real job. The internship wouldn't pay the rent. I couldn't return to that tight studio apartment with my mom.

My new boss, Sean, couldn't promise me fast growth at WUGH. Basically, someone else would have to quit or be fired in order for a full-time position to open up. He said, "It's just not in the budget right now." I hung onto the final two words of his statement, thinking maybe it was a test because so much of life is about timing. I was still very new to the station so I knew I had a few months to prove my loyalty and worth to Sean. I had to make him dismiss any doubts he may have had about me and understand that I could be his wingman while we navigated the shark-infested waters of the music industry. Sean needed a soldier just as much as I needed a well-paying job.

Then, while walking from one class to the next, in the midst of this contemplation of my life, I saw a blast from my past appear on campus. He was looking down at some pamphlet in his hand so he didn't see me. Instead of fleeing, I froze. My mind shut down. My heart changed its beat. It was someone I figured I would never see again even though we went to high school together only one town away. He represented the reason why I accepted being gay after hating myself for years.

Gabriel Watson was his name. He was a freshman at Clifford J. Scott High School during my senior year. I was a 17-year-old boy with needs. I wanted to feel myself up against another boy and I wanted it before I graduated, heading off to college. It was my mission.

I wouldn't exactly call my first childhood sexual experiences exciting, but most, if not all, were with girls who seemed to know more about what they wanted to do. I was technically a male virgin though. The idea of man-on-man sex preoccupied my mind, but it scared me up until then. I said to myself, even if it happened only once, I *cannot leave high school never having had an experience with another dude.*

Gabriel was my target. He caught my eye with his slim frame, dark-chocolate skin and slightly less-than-masculine ways. We used to run into each other in the hallways, in the library and we shared the same guidance counselor. I made it obvious only to him that I was staring at him. It was the type of look where you almost want to smile, but you don't. Gabriel noticed every time. He also would nervously stare back when he could or had the courage to. After a few weeks, the game paid off one day.

Gabriel was seated in the magazine section of the library when I walked in the door past the turnstile. The chair next to him was vacant so I went over and sat down. I could tell from the look on his face that he was happy to see me as well as apprehensive.

About halfway between class bells, I decided to push the envelope farther. I seduced him like a paid stripper. With a magazine in one hand, I reached down under my t-shirt with my other hand to expose some skin. His eyes were glued. Then

I rubbed my hand across my stomach, exposing more skin. His bottom jaw hung low. The eye contact between us spoke volumes so, without saying a word, I handed him a torn sheet of notebook paper with my phone number written on it.

Gabriel, at the time, lived at home with his single father who worked early afternoon-to-evening shifts on weekdays. After a few intense, detailed conversations over the phone, we arranged the appropriate date and time to have some fun.

We both skipped all classes that day. I imagined us getting right down to business once I crossed the threshold. There was, however, a slight delay of action since he wanted to sit in the living room and talk about Missy Elliott's new video that had just premiered on BET. Sex was my only interest so I voiced it. He smiled as he led me by the hand to his bedroom.

As soon as we reached his bed, he turned around to kiss me. It was my first time kissing another dude. I felt years of frustration drift up toward the ceiling, beyond the sky, out of range. Our clothes couldn't come off fast enough. We just continued gasping for air. I tasted every part of his naked body as he lay flat on his back. The tone of his chocolate-brown skin and the symmetry of his adorable face drove me insane. We panted like two dogs in heat. Inexplicably, I pushed myself deep inside him without taking a moment to think about the pain, while he buried his dry screams in his oversized pillow. We then swapped positions and that's when I realized that thin line between pleasure and pain. I found my face in that same pillow, but our passion kept us both motivated. Our simultaneous, self-induced climaxes left us in a state of shock. Gabriel soon got up to get a towel to clean up the mess we had compiled. In that moment after it was all over, I wondered about what I had been so afraid of for so long.

The sight of Gabriel on the Rutgers campus brought back all those memories. But why was he there? At the end of that episode with Gabriel, he dropped those three words about something I couldn't accept so I ran. The split wasn't amicable. I personally wasn't ready to give him my heart. I wasn't prepared to fall in love with a dude. He was heartbroken, to say the least, then graduation day came and off our communication went.

My mistake was thinking I could share that information with Kevin. I called him almost immediately after seeing Gabriel. Gabriel was my past. Kevin was my future so I didn't anticipate Kevin getting jealous.

"Yay—your ex now gets to see you more than I do," he said sarcastically. "I'm so happy for you, Q."

No matter how much I tried to explain my juvenile past with Gabriel, Kevin still played the victim. I then tried to tell him about how Whitney, who was scheduled to visit the station earlier in the week, had canceled. He flipped it, saying Whitney probably wanted to spend time with her man instead of working. Kevin implied that I could stand to learn something from my childhood icon. He was definitely doing a great job at being my personal Bobby Brown. I know it was all coming from a good place. He missed me. That was the bottom line. I just wished he had the guts to simply say so.

Without a doubt, my disappointment with Kevin was rivaled by my disappointment with not being able to meet one of my favorite singers of all time. Whitney Houston is one of the reasons why I fell in love with music. Her instrument of a voice and pure sound was like nothing I had ever heard before.

Then I learned she was born in Newark and raised in East Orange just like me. She was my hometown hero. She became America's pop princess, who later married the bad boy of R&B, Bobby Brown. I never quite understood why everyone was so unhappy about her falling in love. To me, she looked content like there was nothing she wouldn't do for her man, even if it meant jeopardizing her career. Sadly enough, that's exactly what happened. Whitney lost her damn mind by the late '90s so her cancellation wasn't surprising, just disappointing as all hell.

As if my first week wasn't disturbing enough, I got a sad phone call from my mother before I got ready for bed. She dropped the bomb that her Aunt Ruby had passed away late the night before. Unbeknownst to me, Aunt Ruby had been admitted to Newark's Beth Israel Hospital over two weeks prior. Cancer in her lungs and complications from type 2 diabetes claimed her life.

Still, my mother's voice never cracked. There was no awkward silence. Before I could take a breath and ask her how she was taking the news, she confided that the family had always rumored that her aunt was actually her real mother. I thought about how, if that's the truth, I had never gotten to know my maternal grandmother.

In the backwoods of early 1950s Bogalusa, Louisiana, having a child out of wedlock was considered one of the greatest sins under God and just flat out humiliating. Many young, unwed pregnant girls would simply hand over their parental rights to an older family member to avoid the ridicule. My mother's family was no exception.

My mother was raised by her neurotic and abusive grandmother. She never knew her biological mother, or even her father, for that matter. Aunt Ruby never said a word about it though to anyone before she died. We were left to drive ourselves crazy wondering whether the truth would've made a difference in our lives, in our family. It was also a wonder how my mother was handling the death of the only family member she wholeheartedly loved and trusted.

The funeral, later that week, was set on a cloudy and windy Thursday afternoon. It rained all morning until the exact start of the service. It was at that moment when the sun broke through so we knew it was a peaceful sign of God. Aunt Ruby was missed, even though I never got the chance to know her as well as my older brothers. Seeing her lie in that casket was the first time I saw my resemblance in her face.

My brother DJ trailed behind our mother most of the morning in case she collapsed like she had during the burial of her first born, whose plot was just a few yards away from Aunt Ruby's. I cried only when she cried, although she seemed more angry than sad. Maybe she was angry that they didn't have enough time together. Maybe all the time they spent together seemed like a total waste since she never really got to know her as a mother, only as a loving aunt.

In my mind, I reminisced over my past selfish behavior while living under my mother's roof as a teenager and into my 20s. We battled for control that neither one of us could stand to lose. All at once, shame, embarrassment and regret showed me my ugly reflection in the puddles of the burial ground. I turned toward my mother. I whispered in her ear, apologizing for the trouble I had caused her over the years. She erupted with tears, for once. It was necessary.

We all then watched Aunt Ruby's mahogany-wood casket drop six feet deep into the damp soil. My brother and I had to carry our mother back to the limo. Her heart was heavy.

Every relative of ours soon walked off toward their respective rides. No one, not one of them, even said goodbye. We received no calls about a repast. Our lives went on. It made me angry how cruel life was for my mother. I never wanted her to ever come close to losing her strength, or possibly her sanity. I simply prayed that my mother had shed enough tears that gloomy afternoon.

Georgie Porgie

I love to wander. It gives me time to just think and after a couple of months into my internship and school, I had a lot to think about. My main concern was whether I would find a real, paying job following graduation day. The goal was to avoid returning to my mother's studio apartment. Staying on campus got me too used to having my own space, in spite of there being a roommate.

My day at work had ended. Kevin and I were still dating and I really wanted to see his face. Every other conversation had become an argument, but we refused to give back the rings we had exchanged on our first date. Something worth fighting for should never be a chore. I felt just as strong for him as I had the day we'd first met. Were those feelings reciprocated though? I had my doubts and would sometimes blame myself for his wavering lack of interest. With work and school, there was little time for Kevin. Many nights I fell asleep thinking about what Kevin was up to. Eighteen year olds are not known to live boring lives.

However, that day, I decided to wander in his direction, paying him a visit at his job. Stepping into the Gap on 23rd Street in Manhattan was going to be a challenge since I loved to shop, loved to shop at the Gap, but couldn't afford to buy even a pair of socks.

Kevin was posted at the store entrance greeting customers when I walked in. From the look of surprise on his face, I could tell he was as happy to see me as I was to see him. We wanted to kiss, but didn't want to attract needless attention so we hugged briefly, like most men do who are friends, not boyfriends.

"Don't you belong in Jersey?" he said sarcastically.

"I escaped to come see you," I joked.

"Yeah, yeah, you don't love me, you just love my doggystyle."

It was a Snoop Dogg reference from the '90s that made me appreciate his often dirty sense of humor.

"Stop it. You know how I feel about you, now come on, let's take a walk. Tell your boss you need a break," I told him.

Kevin disappeared behind a door that read Employees Only. He returned after a minute, signaling with a head nod that he was ready to go. We walked down 8th Avenue all smiles because we were happy to be side by side. We admired some oversized muffins on display in a coffee-shop window. We willfully passed by a number of clothing boutiques, not venturing inside since we had to save our money for our regular weekend date night. At the time, I was still slightly disappointed that I hadn't been able to see him the weekend prior. His excuse had been that his cousin was in from out of town. I had suggested we all hang out together, but my request had been denied. Nevertheless, he was my boyfriend.

"How was work today?" he asked.

"It was cool. Nothing special. No artist visits. Pretty quiet except for Sean trying to scream on me for scratching one of his precious CDs."

"And you shut him down, didn't you, babe?"

I confirmed, "You know I did. He's so damn forgetful. I reminded him that I told him it was scratched before I asked him to listen to it."

"He's an asshole," said Kevin.

"Nah, he means well, for the most part."

More small talk ensued. Then, in the next part of the conversation, Kevin slapped me in the face, figuratively, of course.

"So when are we getting married, Kevin?" I asked in jest after staring dizzily into his eyes.

"Never," he responded matter-of-factly.

"Damn, did you have to say it like that? It was a joke."

"If you say so."

"What does that mean?" I asked. Kevin pretended like he didn't hear me. "Hello?"

"Oh boy, Q, what?"

"Why are you with me, Kevin? Why am I here right now?"

"Honestly?" he asked as if my questions were rhetorical.

"No, I want you to lie to me. What the hell is wrong with you, Kevin?"

"I'm just having some fun," he finally said while shrugging his shoulders.

"At my expense, huh?"

"What?" Kevin said yet again.

"Nothing, I don't want to talk about it anymore. Don't you have to go back to work?"

I said goodbye to Kevin as he ran up the avenue, headed back to his job. He gave me some food for thought and I wasted no time filling up. I had so many more questions I wanted to ask him, but I was afraid of the answers. He was my first love and, to that love, I felt like a slave, even if it was not meant to last.

Best Man

Like a brother was how I always described Russell Sims. From day one, we hit it off like we'd known each other our entire lives. He was the one who encouraged me to approach and stay in touch with WUGH PD Sean Wilkinson for the internship I eventually achieved. Russ, in an unexpected way, filled the void left wide open by my blood brothers. There was nearly nothing sexual about us becoming the best of friends. He showed up at a time when I was overdue for a strong example of what it means to be a man, the kind of man I wanted to be. He was independent, brave, conscious, and humble. I was grateful for Russ. He respected me man to man even though he suspected I was one of the gays soon after we first met.

It was the beginning of my freshman year at Rutgers. I was on my own for the first time in life. There were a ton of mistakes destiny set forth, such as partying almost every night on campus like there were no classes or responsibilities the next day and spending too much time thinking about what sex would be like with half of the basketball team.

On the first night of the school year, my suitemates paraded the halls on the floor of our dorm, inviting all the seemingly cool people to the smoke cipher they were having. How my suitemates felt so secure about inviting some complete strangers to a party of people all doing drugs, mainly smoking weed, I have no clue, but they pulled it off.

About a dozen dudes were crammed into their room. I kept the door to my adjacent room locked because I didn't feel as secure as my suitemates. They had turned off the lights, then cut on the black light, closed the windows, shut the curtains, and stuffed the crack under the room's door with a damp bath towel. Supposedly, the dampness would help absorb some of the smoke.

For the most part, everyone just smoked weed while a few other dudes branched out, popping ecstasy pills or tabs of acid. One guy offered me a tab. I did my best to hold back on letting the disgust show on my face. Russ, sitting across from me on the opposite bed, noticed and got a good chuckle out of it. He was the most aware of what was going on because he wasn't into drugs or alcohol. In fact, he was a bit of a cornball at first glance. He wore these black-frame prescription eyeglasses and dressed as if he shopped off JCPenney's clearance rack, but he was ultimately cool.

All the dudes in the room kept mixing and bouncing from one conversation to the next. I thought for a second that it was odd how no girls had shown up, but they were probably just being cautious. My suitemates either gave you the impression that they were going to legitimately run this town or violently run up in your house. I learned that semester how cool they really were though, considering how much we used to borrow so much from each other, including money, that whole school year.

That same first night, the one who looked like a 6-foot-2-inch replica of Taye Diggs gave me a shotgun I'll never forget. The shotgun was not an actual lethal weapon, although it caused some internal trauma. Already shirtless, my dark-chocolate suitemate squatted down in front of me, leaning forward, waiting for me to meet him halfway. He closed his eyes, turned the blunt around placing the lit end inside his mouth. Between my puckered lips, he blew. Our mouths were less than a half inch apart and, once again, I caught Russ chuckling at me. I could tell he wasn't doing so to embarrass me. He wanted me to know, all in one look, that he had figured out my secret.

Russ was the first person I ever came out to. It didn't happen that first night we met. It happened a few weeks later. Russ had this mind game he would play, in which he would bring up sexual subjects and leave open traps in the conversation for me to fall into a confession about what I truly craved. Knowing I could no longer lie to someone who made it clear he lacked judgment, I told him my truth.

"Dude, why'd you wait to tell me?" he asked as we sat in his car outside of the dorm. "You know I knew weeks ago."

"Yeah, I know. You're the first person who knows for sure though so you can't tell no one, okay?"

Russ said, "That's not me, dude. I have a gay uncle so I know through him it's not easy. I got your back regardless."

After that, Russ and I talked about the ways of the world. The world would always remind me of my blackness so being gay made life that much more complicated. He understood my process of self-awareness and acceptance. I had to figure out who I was in relation to the rest of the world. Some people, like Russ, would be supportive while many others would rather see me die. Through it all, I chose to live and, after the nightmares, I chose to fantasize.

"From time to time, I still think about what life would be like if I were straight," I said to Russ.

"But you're gay, Q."

"I know, man. I'm just sayin'."

Russ said, "Sounds like you just want to be normal."

"Something like that, if only for a day, just fit in," I confessed. "Have sex with a girl and it not feel like a chore, not feel so empty."

"Dude," said Russ, taken off guard, "for you to say sex with a chick feels empty proves you are g-g-gay, but I believe, God makes no mistakes. People do though all the time."

"Do you think I'm making a mistake?" I asked.

"That's none of my business. But just be happy, dude. It's your life. If slobbing up dudes makes you happy even though it makes me sick to my stomach," he joked, "then do you! Life is too short to be worried about what other people think."

"Even if those other people happen to be your family?"

Russ replied, "Yo, my uncle went through the same thing about 10 years ago when he finally came out the closet. It took my mom a minute to accept it but now his boyfriend is like a part of the family."

"So let me ask you…"

"Ask me what, Q? I don't think I like the sound of this already."

"Have you ever had thoughts about being with another man?" I asked.

"Ah shit, I knew you would go there eventually," he said.

Russ sat straight up in the driver's seat of his burgundy 1997 Mazda 626 coupe bracing himself to be bold. He ran his hand down his long, scruffy face before his moment of truth.

"You don't have to answer me, ya know," I said.

"Nah, I can be honest. You've been honest with me so it's the least I could do in return, and, yes, I have had some thoughts before."

"Like hardcore thoughts?" I asked.

"No! Oh my God, this is crazy. I can't believe I'm telling you this," continued Russ. "I have only noticed when a dude is good-looking, then, I think to myself, *if I was a chick, I'd do him.*"

I screamed out laughing at the realest confession I had heard up until that point. My respect for him cemented. Out of curiosity, I asked, "Did you think that about me?"

"No, dude," he said with verbal regurgitation, but backtracked a little. "Okay, maybe I did for a hot super brief second, but we are definitely into two different things."

After some nervous laughter, I set that topic to rest simply by saying, "I hear you."

●●●

Three years and one semester later, Russ and I were facing graduation. Karyn was a year behind us so she couldn't relate to how excited we were. It was the middle of April and the cold weather was beginning to give us a break. Russ wanted to make a trip home for the weekend to be better prepared for graduation the following month. His parents had to get his tuxedo. Russ also had to make sure his parents weren't inviting the whole town because he didn't want to be embarrassed like he said he was at his high-school graduation. They sounded like they loved their son to no end so I tagged along for the ride.

Russ was always so cool to be around. He could fit in with almost any crowd on campus, from the college thugs to the preppy scholars, but I had assumed his family had struggled financially most of his life much like mine had. I was dead wrong.

We left campus before dawn that Saturday. His parents usually rose along with the sun so they were expecting us. Soon after we hit the turnpike, I fell asleep. I thought we had gotten lost when I woke up to what looked to me like a scene out of *Leave It to Beaver*. There was one picket-fence after another. Every house had its own garage and no house stood out from the rest. It was like the quintessential suburban neighborhood.

Russ was raised in the town of Hammonton, down in South Jersey, right outside of Atlantic City. His parents bought their four-bedroom Victorian home a year before their first born, a.k.a. Russ, came along. They were the first African-Americans to own a house on the block. They were also the first ones to build a massive treehouse for their kids. It sat balanced along the branches of two trees that appeared to be reaching for one another, like yearning for an embrace. The trees were located in the woods just beyond their backyard. It was the other side of Jersey, opposed to the one I was used to.

Russ was one of only five black students in his high-school class of 1997. Based on that, Russ dealt with daily taunts since integration was still somewhat of a dirty word to the neighborhood. After about a half dozen black eyes he administered, Russ figured his best defense would be maintaining a 4.0 grade-point average. It landed him at the top of his class all four years, resulting in a full scholarship to attend Rutgers, which was his father's alma mater. Finding out he had a free ride at Rutgers didn't intimidate me or make me jealous.

I was proud of him. Then, I had the opportunity to meet his mom, dad and younger sister.

It was 7:30 in the morning and the whole family was in the kitchen preparing breakfast. I smelled bacon, eggs, pancakes, oatmeal, and coffee from the front door. I loved breakfast food, but hated early mornings. We all sat down at the dining-room table to eat. They even had hot chocolate with marshmallows and cinnamon. Russ's family was spoiling me in a way I'd never experienced in my own family. Envy could have crept into my mind to ruin the whole day, but I felt so comfortable in their home. I felt like I was at home so I helped myself to seconds. Russ went for thirds.

When the hall clock struck noon, everyone in the house was ready to take a nap. Russ and I stripped down to our boxers and were watching the movie *X-Men*, playing on HBO. It was just the two of us in his bedroom with the door locked. Everyone else had retreated to their corresponding bedrooms. Russ's legs kept distracting me at the corner of my eye. He had runner's legs from his days of running track in high school. I forced myself to focus on the television in front of me. Magneto was performing as usual.

My concentration broke after Russ continued kicking me. He wanted to play. The little boys in our hearts wanted to play. It began with me punching him in the shoulder whenever he would kick me with one of his long, stocky and hairy legs. Russ escalated the situation by standing his six-foot, 185-pound body straight up on the bed, then dropping his limp elbow down on top of my bare chest.

Getting physical was never a problem with me. The hood I grew up in required it. There was always some random dude testing me, whether it was on the playground or on the block. Many times I came out on top. Sometimes I did not. Still, the older I got, the stronger I knew I had to be.

I started working out regularly in high school. Push-ups and squats were the routine as most men are only concerned with keeping the upper body tight. By the time I made it to college, I doubled up on the reps and added in sit-ups to my routine. I wasn't bulging out of control. I was just able to get physical without feeling weak or getting too winded so Russ had to work harder at beating me than he'd originally thought.

That day, I had something to prove. I had to show him that skinny doesn't mean fragile. We pulled, tugged and tumbled all over his bed, ending up on the floor at times. He kept trying to secure a headlock, but I broke free again and again. That was one of the advantages of being slim. One of the disadvantages, however, was not being able to hide my arousal under a layer of belly fat or between two plump thighs.

"Dude, what is that sticking me?" asked Russ suspiciously.

"I told you to stop 10 minutes ago," I replied. "I can't always control him. He can be a beast when provoked."

"Yeah, let's quit this now and finish watching this damn movie," he said while shaking his head in slow motion, but I couldn't tell if it was out of disgust, disappointment or wonder.

Ain't Nobody

Go on, girl was the lick that started it all for me. I was too young for *Off the Wall* and *Thriller* so my first memory of Michael Jackson in his full element came in 1987 when his third solo album, *Bad*, dropped. "The Way You Make Me Feel" will always be my No. 1 karaoke pick, but Michael had an arsenal of hits I could call my absolute favorites ("Billie Jean," "Remember the Time," "I Wanna Be Where You Are," and "Break of Dawn"). Then, there was the King of Pop's only competitor in the battle for his throne.

My first memory of Prince came about during his "purple" reign. Even though I was too young to understand what was going on in the movie, I knew "Purple Rain" and "When Doves Cry" would live on forever. Some songs define some people's lives in that way. Later on, after more exposure, I fell in love with "Do Me, Baby" and "Controversy." I learned that people had grown to worship Prince while others idolized Michael.

By April of 2001, fame had taken its toll on both entertainers. In most people's eyes, MJ had turned into a plastic freak and Prince had become a religious hermit. I never judged them though. I just kept living for their music. That's all that mattered to me. I think that's all that mattered to most real fans, including the likes of Usher, Alicia Keys, Justin Timberlake, and Chris Brown, which is why a party pitting the music of two of the most influential artists in history against one another was so genius.

Brooklyn-born DJ Spinna started the party in the late 1990s. It was originally called Soul Slam and Spinna spun the hits of Michael Jackson and Prince, as well as any music they influenced or were a part of. We heard classics from The Jackson 5, Jermaine Jackson and SWV's "Right Here (Human Nature)," straight to The Time, Sheila E. and Chaka Khan's "I Feel For You." The popularity of Soul Slam grew from year to year.

Kevin, my boy Prince and I swung through Pepper's Lounge on the Lower East Side to celebrate our all-time favorite performers alongside NYC's vanguard. Spinna even shouted me out on the microphone since he recognized me from WUGH. He did visit the station pretty often. Spinna and my boss Sean, who had initially told me about the event, were friends. The shout-out made Kevin and my boy Prince feel like VIPs for the few hours we spent dancing like it was "1999."

I saw Q-Tip that night dancing amongst the regular crowd because the vibe and energy in the place was just that chilled. The dim, yellowish lighting did make it hard to recognize him though unless someone was just as observant as I have always been. In reality, I'd just rather hang back and, like a wild cat, keep an eye on the scene than engage.

While skimming over the heads in the crowd, I noticed the then-fairly-unknown actor Anthony Mackie was there. This was about a year or two before his breakout feature role in the indie film *Brother to Brother*. In it, he played a black gay artist/writer struggling with homophobia and racism. His performance was as authentic as his persona in real life. We'd brushed shoulders back at R&B singer/songwriter Jimmy Cozier's release party about a month prior. Many gays later assumed Anthony must be gay for playing that role, but that was like me saying I was straight simply because I played that character for the majority of my life. I wish sexuality was that straight forward.

Our night did not end there though. The three of us planned to make it uptown to the Warehouse around one o'clock in the morning. The rest of our Brooklyn crew was on their way up and I was also looking forward to seeing a part of my Jersey clan. Jordan set out to make a rare appearance at the club to celebrate his 30th birthday. Of course, Roman would be at his side. I still had not spoken to Roman since he sprayed bleach in my face back in Vegas. How could I forgive someone who at the heart of it had tried to blind me? He was supposed to be my friend. Even though I missed him, I couldn't move past the idea of a close friend doing something that vicious to me. Both Kevin and Prince echoed Jordan. They all wanted us to make up, but I suspected they would not have felt so strongly if he wasn't so gorgeous.

While leaving Spinna's party and finishing off my fourth vodka and orange juice of the night, Kevin jumped in front of me, planting the quickest kiss we ever had on my lips. He turned back around just in time because he was about to bang the back of his head against the glass door. That would've been a mood killer so then I grabbed his ass from behind. Not many people were watching us long enough to see what happened, but I did lock eyes with one girl who happened to be coming in the door at just the right moment. Her boyfriend was a few feet behind so he didn't see anything. She shyly smiled at me. I breathed a sigh.

Kevin, Prince and I lit up a blunt on the way to the train station. Usually, in NYC, as long as you stay on the move, you won't get caught up.

"So what are you going to say to Roman?" asked Prince.

"I don't have anything to say to him. If he got something he wants to say to me, it better begin with an apology," I insisted.

"Isn't being from Jersey enough of a reason to feel sorry for him?" Kevin joked, then gave a high five to Prince. I rolled my eyes since I knew it wasn't going to be the last Jersey crack of the night.

We jumped on the 2 train headed uptown. I sat in between Kevin and Prince as they continued hounding me with questions. I wanted to ask why they were so interested in me making up with Roman, but the answer was as obvious as the two thirsty, shameless queens sitting across from us. They stared at us the entire 30-minute ride from the Lower East Side to the Bronx. It was creepy, but not unusual.

"But, babe, I still don't get why he would be so mad at y'all for something his ex did," said Kevin.

Prince and I locked eyes. Prince knew I had not told Kevin the complete truth about the trip. I didn't tell Kevin that I was also preoccupied, that our friendship probably would've survived that weekend if I had stayed by Roman's side. Looking back, I can see that he needed me as a friend since he was nowhere near being over Shane.

"He was drunk, Kevin," I said. "What else can I say?"

Prince, being a true friend, followed up by saying, "Yeah, that dude turns into a fool when he's wasted. I can't take it, but I know a few people who have."

"Oh, like who?" asked Kevin. "Did he beat it up or get beat down?"

"Wait, why would you ask that?" I said.

"Right, fall back, boo-boo," Prince said to Kevin while laughing. "Q will knock you. But, yeah, I heard Roman gives you whatever you ask for especially when he's twisted."

"Well, we all know you're not much different," I said to Prince before immediately changing the subject.

Prince and Kevin had crossed the line. Roman was no longer a friend to me, but it still made me uncomfortable hearing Prince dump on him while Kevin melted in his seat for him as if I wasn't there.

We made it to the corner of East 140th Street and Grand Concourse where the thirsty queens from the train were headed too. It's not that they were deformed in the face or anything. The three of them were very much on point. They looked like they were plucked from Destiny's Child's troupe of backup dancers so, if they hadn't been staring so hard, we wouldn't have felt so creepy about their attraction to us. Kevin kept getting closer and closer to me, trying to make it obvious that we were together since a large part of their attention was directed at me. Prince avoided eye contact with them at all costs because he was feeling asexual that night. Also a Gemini, Prince was a moody son of a bitch. Eventually, we were able to escape into the crowd outside the entrance of the club. Again, security knew our faces, not to mention, Prince had blown one of the undercover detectives supervising the pedestrian muscle-heads posing as security. The DTs kept many of us from getting robbed by security's sticky fingers. It didn't happen often, but getting robbed by security happened.

Once inside the lobby, they followed protocol and patted us down from head to toe. Fortunately, all of us arrived without weapons. The crowd was too thick to just ease through. We had to push and shove our way past the boys grinding on each other to the beat of Lil' Kim's "Crush on You." Our goal was to reach the stretch bar upstairs where our entourages would be waiting for us. At the top of the stairs to the right, we tripped over the feet of Prince's Brooklyn set crowding the entry to the main dance floor. Hugs and kisses on cheeks went around, then Kevin and I left them behind to look for the birthday boy.

We squeezed our way through the maze on the dance floor, out the first doorway on the left. Facing the stretch bar, we scanned it starting on the right, and there was Jordan and Roman with a beautiful pale-faced black woman standing tall in between them. Their backs were pressed up against the cedar wood. Her fiery red, high ponytail that she kept sweeping from one shoulder to the other grazed the very tip of her shredded 7 For All Mankind jeans. With the jeans, she wore a crisp, white button-down shirt. The sleeves were rolled up and every button down the front hung loose. Like leaves on a tree, her breasts seemed to float in air. From 20 feet back, the woman had the curves, the tenderness and the femininity, but she wasn't born a woman.

The closer we got, our jaws began to drop because Kevin and I realized, almost at the same time, that she was a man. The gays classify her as a *fem queen*. It's every fem queen's intention to look like the real thing even though lots of them fail miserably. Her pearly, off-white, smooth skin felt softer than mine as I shook her hand. Jordan introduced her as Michelle Piper, or just simply, Shelly. It wasn't the name her mother gave her at birth. I later learned that she was a huge Michelle Pfeiffer fan so she adopted the name, but adjusted the last name to be more relevant to what she did best, laying pipe.

During that time, I was still naïve. Whenever I would see some straight-looking pretty thug with a fem queen, I assumed the fem queen was also ladylike in bed. Michelle Piper was not that kind of lady though. Any fine, thuggish dude Shelly was normally with had to be a *size king* for his top-heavy queen.

It was Jordan's 30th birthday. Shelly, also 30 years old, was there to celebrate. They grew up together in the Vailsburg section of Newark. She was there early on when Jordan started mentoring a teenage-Roman in the Ball competitions. Both Shelly and Jordan had reached legendary status for not only winning every category, but for also surviving all the drama of living hard and sometimes dying young.

I looked to Shelly's left, meeting eyes with Roman. I smiled politely. Then, I went to her right to give Jordan his birthday hug.

"Bitch, don't start, say hi to your brother," Jordan said, whispering in my ear.

"Hi," I said to Roman.

"Hey Q, what's up, can I get a hug too?" said Roman stretching out his arms.

As I hesitated, Kevin pushed me from behind right into Roman's chest. The animosity I breathed life into for months dissipated. I hugged him back. The night was getting off to a great start in spite of how it would end.

Prince had taken a Brooklyn-crew break to wish Jordan a happy birthday, buying him his first drink of the night. Everyone socialized at that point, making small talk about boys, boys, more boys, and sometimes pieces of our lives. Not long into the night, Roman had collected dozens of compliments. Half of them were for his shredded outfit on drugs. We could never accuse him of being shy. The man walked out of his hood into the club wearing a sleeveless, shredded and studded raw denim jacket by G-Star with no shirt underneath. His G-Star jeans were punched full of jagged holes, but the holes stopped just short of exposing Roman to everyone at waist-level.

I left Jordan and Roman at the bar to go dance with Kevin and his friends. They were at the far end of the dance floor, in the back corner by the restrooms. Regulars knew it was the best spot to see faces. The club's laser-light show, in an otherwise pitch-black room, made us look like ghosts, silhouettes crashing into each other. The bright light of the restrooms hit some of them like a ton of bricks. On top of that, the boys normally approached the bathroom from the left toward where the bar was located. Standing to the right changed the nature of the bright lights. The rays shone like a thick white screen behind which no face could be seen, just more silhouettes in the crowd.

That was where we were. I had Kevin's back pressed hard against the wall as I grinded on his pelvis. It was all done to the beat. Every so often, we'd switch up the rhythm. His 18-year-old friends watched us move. Kevin smiled at them so I did the same, not realizing how the 18-year-old mind works. The slightest bit of attention I gave them could cause trouble. Kevin had a maturity that his friends lacked. Still, they all fit in with each other, light-skinned, skinny, Michael Jordan on their feet, and a fitted cap to match in color.

The drinks kept flowing all night so our inhibitions were soon on empty. Kevin and I danced in that corner of the club like it was only the two of us, until it wasn't anymore. One of the dudes from the train ride uptown had been standing a little too close by watching us. It was as if we were in his shadow. No matter how many dirty looks we shot at him, he wouldn't go away. We did our best to ignore him until he decided to speak directly to me.

"You need a real man," he confidently said without screaming above the music.

"What did he say?" asked Kevin who was beginning to lose his patience.

"Nothing," I replied. "He's not worth it."

At that point, I thought it would be best to separate myself from Kevin since I was the common denominator and go look for the birthday boy. Jordan and Shelly were still posted up by the bar having one drink after another. Roman had disappeared though. Our best guess was that he had attracted the attention of some petite and pretty boy-toy willing to be used for sex, or he was feeding off the hate of some jealous dudes somewhere on the premises. Roman liked to flaunt his narcissism in the face of whoever was willing to watch. He could afford to. He was always willing to be a lover or a fighter. What I found out that night was that Kevin was part of the same breed as Roman.

While waiting at the bar to order myself another drink, the bartender kept looking up at me, grinning. She grabbed a medium-sized plastic cup, dipped it into the ice below, poured about two ounces of Patron and twice as much pineapple juice. She then pinched a lime wedge over the cup. I licked my lips lusting for that drink, but was not ready to pay that $22 premium price plus tip. The bartender continued giving me eye contact before she walked toward me and said, "The guy, in that black studded leather, bought this for you." I smiled on the inside because I couldn't let that dude from the train know he had gotten to me.

"I can't take this," I said to the bartender.

"Why not? You got a boyfriend?" she asked.

"Yes, I do."

"Do you love him?" she then asked. "Listen, I only ask 'cause I know that man down there. He likes you and wants to get to know you better. So if you don't love your boyfriend, then you should give my boy a shot, or at the very least, take the drink, baby."

I didn't say another word. I wrapped my five fingers around the base of the cup, pulled it up to my lips and took a sip. I was drowning in the alcohol when Kevin walked up behind me, tapping me on the shoulder.

"What's that?" Kevin asked, referring to the type of drink.

"It's Patron," I said simply.

"Damn, babe, I thought you didn't have money."

"He didn't buy it," said the incendiary bartender fighting for her friend's honor.

Kevin asked me directly, "Who bought it?"

"Kevin, chill out, let's just go find Roman," I said. "He's probably downstairs."

"Yeah, he's probably downstairs loose as a goose. Go on, honey," said Jordan, pushing us in the direction of the stairs because he also could feel the tension rising. Unfortunately, to get to the staircase, we had to pass the boy from the train standing with his two friends. I left the drink he bought me sitting on the bar, but that didn't change the fact that I still had the taste of the juice on my tongue. Kevin could probably smell it on my breath, driving him insane with rage. I put my arm around his neck as he glared down homeboy. All of us further drowning in the alcohol, the boy winked his right eye at me and Kevin lost it.

He spun around full circle to our left, dipping out from under my arm like a B-boy. Before I could blink, Kevin was running chest-high at the boy whose back was eventually slammed up against the hardwood of the bar. People started screaming trying to get out of the way. I tried breaking them up, but couldn't get close enough without getting hit. Kevin had knocked the boy to the floor, climbing on top of him, pounding his face with his fists.

For a moment, I stood in shock. There were two men fighting in the club over me and it was shamefully exciting until Kevin's friends, Prince and the Brooklyn crew all started jumping the boy and his outnumbered friends. Blood dripped on the floor. Jordan, Shelly, security, and Roman, who appeared out of nowhere like a superhero, helped me put out the human inferno. The fumes were steadily rising from the tops of their heads. My boyfriend was pinned to the floor by three bouncers. His bottom lip was split in the process. The boy he mauled had a swollen-shut black eye and some missing teeth. He just kept spitting more blood on the floor.

The cops were never called. Even the detectives hanging outside never came in. They only did so if they had to use their weapons, which never happened. We could be violent, but were too focused on getting between the sheets than getting shot and killed. That night was no exception.

After everyone was kicked out of the club, each set 30 minutes apart, Kevin, Prince and I sidelined from the birthday celebration. Kevin and I had sex again in Prince's spare bedroom in Brooklyn. We didn't care if they heard us. I didn't care about anything except him that late night. I believed Kevin was my little loyal pit bull and I was the only one who could feed him without getting bit. I believed he loved me as much as I loved him. Any doubts I had about us I laid to rest, so when Jordan kept texting my phone saying Kevin was not worth it, I turned my phone off. Kevin had my undivided attention.

Blackberry Molasses

"He's a homo!" screamed my boss Sean as I opened the frosted-glass door to the station's green room. On TV, the headline flashed. It was something about a shooting in a nightclub over the weekend. I sat down in the farthest corner shaking anonymous hands along the way. They were all too involved in their conversation to tell me their names so I slouched down in my chair after I heard one of them say, "Those dudes been mad suspect from day one." I felt like everyone was looking right at me just then, but, in reality, they'd forgotten I had entered the room. No noise was coming from my cozy, suspect corner.

Harlem-bred rapper Kid Twist, famous for always eating a small bag of some bright-colored candy during interviews, was arrested at the SoHo Grand Hotel downtown on West Broadway. The report said they had turned the penthouse into a strip club until Kid Twist threatened to kick some dudes out of the party. Those dudes pulled a gun. One of Kid Twist's friends, also known as up-and-coming rapper Bling, pulled his own, then shots were fired and a couple of bystanders were the only ones who got hit. Others were hurt in the stampede of bodies trying to squeeze through a handful of exits. Fortunately, no one was killed.

Some witnesses from inside the party said shots started flying after a couple of dudes called Kid Twist a homo to his face out of envy because they couldn't get any action from the strippers. Ironically, Kid Twist was credited as the wordsmith behind the no homo trend. Saying no homo allowed any straight man to say something only a gay man would say simply by capping it off with no homo. According to Sean and his industry friends, they coined the phrase to distract fans from the truth.

"Fuckin' homo-thug-faggots goin' to jail," said one of Sean's friends, laughing as if he had just told a knock-knock joke. They all burst out into laughter, but not in a million years would I ever find the humor.

"But come on, why else would they wear them pink furs and purple shoes? That's some true homo shit," said another friend of Sean's.

Even if I wanted to go to war with their hatred, I wouldn't have won and I would've stood the chance of losing everything in the process, so I compromised. I had gotten used to compromising. It wasn't the first time and definitely was not the last. At the very least, I knew where I stood with them. It was at a distance.

This pack of alpha males gave me a flashback of the boys I used to lust after in junior high. To make it to high school from junior high, all students had to take and complete both a gym class and a swim course. Throughout my childhood, I had gotten comfortable being surrounded by half-naked black and Latino boys in the gym locker room. There was a shower, but no one ever used it because we rarely broke a sweat in class. That's also why no one ever stripped down past their underwear.

Swim class, on the other hand, separated the big boys from the little boys. We were a bunch of seventh and eighth graders learning how to swim, but we learned so much more about each other. After climbing out of the pool at the end of class, the girls went their way into their locker room while I fell in line behind the boys into ours. Anyone passing through the locker room from the poolside had to walk through the showers to get to the lockers. Immediately, two or three of the alpha-male types would peel off their soaking wet shorts as soon as they hit the doorway. The showers would fill up with bodies from wall to wall. Almost half of the boys would be completely nude. I did my best not to look, until my very last day of swim class.

When that day came, the horseplay was at an all-time high. Wild boys kept streaking through the locker room and occasionally out into the main hallway where the teachers were. One of them kept palming my ass playfully. He made a routine of it that entire school year. Whether we were in the gym locker room or in the showers after swim class, his stealthy hands were offensive. My gross reaction never seemed to bother him though and I didn't know well enough back then to know that he must've liked something about me or my assets. I was naïve. In my mind, he was a spy trying to dig up my deepest secrets.

All the wild-boy behavior couldn't distract me from the five most popular boys in my class. I was surrounded by them. They had found their way to my otherwise empty bench after taking their showers. Wrapped in towels, they barely acknowledged me while each of them pulled the clothes they were about to put on out of their lockers.

One by one, I watched them release their towels, then stand nude long enough for the curious to see. There stood mister pretty-boy with a muscular body well beyond his years. Mister pretty-boy had turned a lot of the girls I went to school with into groupies, but, if only they knew, it was skinny Puerto Rican Dave who was the heavyweight champion of the entire class.

Those boys grew up. They could have been sitting right in front of me in that conference room and I would not have known the difference. Sean and his friends were like those boys in grown-up bodies. I never knew what to say to them or even how to interact with the boys from swim class so not much had changed in adulthood, except there being a paycheck involved. The money, I figured, would overcompensate. Still, every insult, whether directed at me or my kind, burned and left a scar deep in my mind.

Joy and Pain

Back on campus, I told a hundred lies. People who knew me knew how much I loved music. They knew I was interning at the hottest radio station on the planet. Everyone, including Karyn, thought I was living on the edge of fame and I liked it that way. Details can complicate matters. It felt good to know that they wanted the best for me so the lie was worth the reward, never mind the consequences. I didn't want to tell Karyn that her five-star confidant was just beginning to breathe life into his deepest desires while working alongside men who would blackball me if I even hinted at those desires.

Karyn meant a lot to me. She was next on my list of people I had to tell, but I was aiming for after I graduated in case things between us changed. Gays never came up in our conversations. If they did, I can't recall.

"So let's just agree if we are both still single by 25, we'll make a baby, you and I," she paused before mumbling, "at the very least."

Of course, I had to ask her to repeat herself to make sure I heard correctly. She sighed, "I said, if we are both single at 25…"

"Yeah, yeah, yeah," I said interrupting her. "So you want to have my babies?"

"I want to have a baby. And if not you, then your brother will do," she said. "He's like the six-foot version of you."

"There you go with the short jokes again."

I hated those short jokes. Somewhere along the way through junior high, most of the boys sprouted up above me, then started calling me short, little man or, the biggest insult of them all, big man. Karyn pleasured herself by plucking at the strings of my insecurity. In the meantime, as she kept pushing the issue, I rolled the blunt we were going to smoke under a half roof of one of the abandoned buildings Rutgers had recently bought.

The building on the corner of Central and University Avenues had been abandoned for decades. It was the type of old, Victorian-style, red-brick building that would cost more to renovate than it would to build something from scratch. Its half-moon roof sagged like an autumn leaf. The walls still reeked of the fire that nearly burned the building to the ground. Many of us stoners were lucky enough to have those four tie-dye-like walls for shelter.

"Feels like we've traveled back in time," said Karyn.

"I just hope we don't see anything crazy in here," I responded.

"Like what, ghosts?" she asked.

I answered, "Ghosts, spirits, killers, midgets."

"Oh Jesus," she said rolling her eyes.

"Yeah, now would not be a good time for Him either," I said, "unless He's here to save us."

It was ultra quiet in that place and, of course, the rumors persisted about it being haunted. Nothing was ever documented, but I will never deny the supernatural. Karyn must have sensed my fear.

"Q, talk to me. What's on your mind?" she said before laying her head on my shoulder. "Wait, why aren't you wearing your mother's ring?"

"Um, I lost it," I lied. "It's probably somewhere in a pile of clothes. I don't know. I'm sure it'll turn up again soon."

"It had better. You know your mother will finish you if she finds out you lost her wedding band."

"Whatever, you know you always wanted it for yourself," I said. "And why are you thinking about having my baby anyway? Don't you want to be married first?"

"I don't know if I can trust another man like that again," she confessed.

"I get it. How has therapy been?" I asked.

She said, "I quit. I've done enough crying. It's time to move on. But the one thing I can't seem to shake that might sound sick is…"

Karyn paused midsentence. The weed was just starting to kick in making us feel light-headed and heavy-hearted.

"Go on, I'm listening," I said not prepared for the words to follow.

"I still kinda miss him, Q. Oh my God—I swear I will not cry right now. Please don't think I'm crazy for saying that."

"Karyn, you have every right to feel how you feel. You trusted him. You fell in love with him and he—"

"Raped me—the one guy I wanted to spend the rest of my life with, raped me," she said. "Therapy did at least that much. I can actually say it out loud and not break down."

"I'm proud of you."

Karyn's head never left my shoulder. We continued talking about what was in her heart when, out of nowhere, the rain began falling down on us through the sagging roof. By then, the blunt had been finished. It was a light yet steady rain that felt refreshing. There was no need to run indoors. We stayed put. To lighten the mood, I decided to tell Karyn that WUGH was not my first internship.

"Yeah, my first one only lasted a couple of weeks 'cause I got fired," I said. "Or actually Playa got me fired."

"Playa? Who is that?" she asked.

"Playa was that R&B group Timbaland produced back in '98. I think 'Cheers 2 U' was their biggest song."

"I don't remember them. What did they look like?" she asked. "Were they cute?"

I said, "They were cute enough and could sing, write and produce their own stuff."

"So how did they get you fired?"

"Well, I was interning at the studio in East Orange where they recorded their debut album. The studio was also where Naughty By Nature would record all of their music back then. The group Next also recorded their debut album there. It was crazy," I said. "But Playa had come through looking for some smoke. They asked me if I knew where to get some before they started recording."

"They were in your hood," Karyn acknowledged.

"You know it," I confirmed. "I went out to Dodd Street, copped it, then went back to the studio. Static had already started tweaking some of the tracks they were going to record. Black and Smokey were waiting out in the seating area with the papers ready. Black broke up the weed faster than anyone I had ever seen. We smoked and I thought nothing of it since we were in the hood and I had seen so many other artists come through and smoke before they went into the studio."

Karyn then wanted to know, "Did your boss smoke too?"

"Nah, he always stayed level-headed. But I was 17 years old going on 18. I didn't know that getting high and dealing with studio equipment was not a good combination especially since I had just started smoking weed. I almost burned the place down."

"Oh my God, what did you do?" said Karyn, laughing.

"Oh, it so wasn't funny to me then. It was embarrassing. He told me to go home and he never let me come back."

"But what happened? Something caught on fire?" inquired Karyn.

"I plugged the wrong adapter into the wrong unit, sparks started flying, my boss was screaming something at me but I was too high to make sense of it. It was despicable."

"Oh man, thank you for being so funny, Q," she laughed.

The rain continued to drizzle down on us. We got up and went back to the dorm. As people ran past us to gain shelter, trying not to get wet, Karyn and I felt nothing but joy because we were definitely in each other's prayers.

Funny Feelings

I took a walk to the train, then to a bus to see Kevin in Brooklyn one last time the week before graduation. All finals were done. The university couldn't pay me enough to take another test. I wanted that degree, I wanted my future and I wanted it all with Kevin by my side.

Of course, he showed up almost an hour late even though he lived just a few train stops away. We planned to grab some cheesecake from Junior's Restaurant. It was his treat. He said he wanted me to feel like a king for my graduation. He said he was proud of what I was about to become. He said a lot of things out of the corner of his mouth.

Almost six months to the day I first saw his handsome face in Prince's kitchen, Kevin still had that same effect on me. I couldn't look him straight in the eye without cracking a smile. I loved the way he made me feel, but Jordan and Roman thought I was blinded by the thought of being in love. I guess that's why I blackmailed them both to maintain some boundaries. Jordan had that sincere secret love for Roman, and Roman probably had a warrant out for his arrest thanks to all the stuff he stole from the hotel back in Vegas so they backed off.

While we sat at the table, Kevin's phone kept ringing. I imagined him ignoring every single one of my calls as he ignored each call that came in. I sat and wondered for a moment why I had to be the one always picking up the phone, making plans and saying what I meant. We would never see each other if I were as passive.

"I told you we would make it," said Kevin, acknowledging how far we'd come in our relationship. "You thought I was too young, remember?"

"I remember," I said. "I also remember you said you wanted to get to know me. Do you think you know me by now?"

"Q, I know you better than you think I do. And I've told you before that I'm not here to hurt you. I'm actually proud of you for finishing college. I hope I can too."

"Of course, you can, but you have to apply first. What are you waiting for?" I asked.

"Okay, Q, you know it all," he responded while gesturing to the waitress so we could place our orders.

The waitress made her entrance and her exit. I didn't want to say another word that could ruin the type of moment we needed to have. Swallowing my pride, I asked Kevin how his little brother was doing. They had stopped speaking to each other the week prior. The little green monster also known as his little brother had uncovered the truth about his happy family. His father was not Kevin's father.

"I still can't believe that little bastard would hate on his own brother," said Kevin as he shook his head.

"But wait, aren't you the bastard though?" I said jokingly to keep his mood positive.

"That's why I like you. You always got jokes."

Kevin's origins date back to a nightclub during the early 1980s when his mother was 14 years old. She wasn't a virgin and she was developed beyond her years. Even if the bouncers knew she wasn't of age, it was a different time. The question was more geared toward whether they gave a damn. That night, they didn't care that she had wandered into the club, got pulled into a dark corner and forced to have sex.

It wasn't rape because she never cried out. She thought the perpetrator, about 18 to 19 years old, was cute and she was not an angel. The pregnancy came as a surprise, but Kevin's soon-to-be-mom lucked out. She had just started dating this 16-year-old so she lied to him about him being the father until her second born came along. With a new baby he could know for sure was his, he accepted responsibility for both of her boys.

They lived happily ever after until Kevin's little brother overheard his parents arguing about it late one night. The next morning following their fight was when Kevin and his little brother had their own fight.

"Yeah, I just don't know what I'm going to do. Will I have to move out? I don't know," said Kevin.

"You won't have to move out," I said sternly. "Stop it. Your parents, both of your parents, still love you Kevin. I know you know that."

I wished he knew how I really felt about him. Still, he was right. He needed to hear it from his whole family like I need to hear it from him. We'd been together for six months and had never mentioned those three words to each other. What were we doing?

"Since we're talking families, how is yours? Your mom cool?" asked Kevin.

"Yeah, everybody is good. No complaints," I replied.

"Heard from your brothers lately?"

"Nope," I said flatly.

After a few seconds of silence, he said, "Okay, I'm trying to talk to you and you're shutting down on me, Q."

"No, I'm not. I just don't want to talk about what you want to talk about right now."

"Well, are your brothers coming to your graduation?"

"They were invited. I'm sure DJ will come, but Dino, who knows?"

Kevin asked, "Do you want me to meet them?"

"Why wouldn't I? Do you want to meet them? Are you ready for that?" I countered.

"I guess I am. It's crazy though. I keep thinking about your mom losing her first born like that."

"Yeah, I think about it a lot too," I said. "But this is our lives. I was only 10 years old when she got that call from Larry's father. My mom just sat completely still like her whole body went numb. Everything after that point changed."

"In what way, babe?" Kevin asked.

"Larry had been the glue holding us together. After he passed, DJ and Dino just kept disappearing more and more. I felt like an only child then. DJ came around a few times a year, if that much. Dino was out in the streets 'cause that's where his friends were. Mom was done chasing after both of them. We all fell apart, dropping like a house of cards."

"Okay babe, this is depressing," Kevin said. "Let's change the subject. What do you want to do the night of your graduation?"

"Blow you."

"Okay, after that?"

"Wait four minutes and blow you again?" I said as if he was quizzing me.

"I suggest we go to Twilight and get twisted," said Kevin.

"And what's so special about that Kevin?"

"You've never been and I'm so sick of the Warehouse. It'll be a different crowd, a more mixed crowd."

"I don't know. We'll see. If I have something better to do, then you're just going to have to go with your friends who I'm sure will be there anyway," I said. "You see them more than you see me."

Kevin dodged yet another one of my slick comments, paid for the meal and barely held the door for me as he walked out of Junior's ahead of me. He gave me a long kiss goodnight. There was no trip to Prince's apartment. Kevin had to work in the morning and I had to finish spending time with those people on campus I would likely never see again after I got my degree.

Heartless

There was nothing the operator could say or do to fix my line. The dial tone was on a continuous loop. I hated it. That sound never disturbed me so much before the night Kevin hung up on me. What did I do so wrong?

It was the night before graduation and I wasn't in the mood to celebrate. It took everything in me not to break down. I kept calling and calling and calling his phone, but he never answered. In fact, he did answer a few times only to hang up on me again and again. Alone in my dorm with less than 12 hours before one of the biggest successes of my life and Kevin was the one failure I gave all my attention to. Despite how hard I tried to ignore it, my heart was broken. I couldn't sleep whatsoever.

I called Prince who also couldn't reach Kevin. Prince told me, "Go to sleep, Quincy. His phone probably died or maybe he fell asleep. You know how he is."

I knew better. I knew me trying to convince Kevin to take some responsibility for getting fired from his job at the Gap earlier that day was not a good idea. He responded as if I were the enemy, like he never trusted me from the start.

Even though I couldn't sleep, I shared my pillow with the phone, hoping it would ring. By daybreak, my phone was useless. I missed calls from my mom, Jordan and Prince congratulating me on my big day. It didn't bother me because I knew I would see them after the ceremony.

At some point, I figured Kevin would fade away or be overshadowed by the moment I shook hands with the president of the university on that stage. I wasn't foolish enough to deny myself that much. One of those missed calls that morning came from Kevin. He left a voicemail I didn't see until after I walked off stage and greeted my family and friends. I hesitated listening to the message. I held it until we reached the local diner for some food and drinks. While in the bathroom, in a stall with the door locked shut, I listened to Kevin's dedication song to me. It was "Where I Wanna Be" by Donell Jones. He played what I could guess was supposed to be the most relevant part of the one of the biggest ballads of that year. Those lyrics I had heard before, but never in that way. I cried. Sitting on the toilet of some New Jersey diner, I pushed back the remaining tears and got up to go join the people who would never hurt me like that.

●●●

Everyone, at once, screamed, "Surprise!"

Prince had arranged a surprise graduation party for me that night in Brooklyn. I showed up not having a clue about the party. Jordan and Roman, I thought, were just tagging along, but they knew the whole time. At first glance, it appeared everyone I had ever met through Prince was in the house, excluding Kevin. There was catered soul food. Prince bought loads of alcohol and, of course, the weed was being passed around. Later in the night, we all would start to make moves toward Twilight, the new nightclub in midtown Manhattan that wasn't exclusively gay, but gay enough.

Then, my second surprise of the night came in the form of a beautiful woman. There Karyn was staring at me from across the room. My mind raced through a thousand questions.

What was she doing there? How did she make it to Flatbush, Brooklyn, without me? Lastly, what would I say since she must've known the one secret I had been hiding since the day I met her?

"Don't think I never had a clue," Karyn said echoing my mother's sentiments.

"Then why didn't you say something?" I teased.

"I should slap you for keeping this from me, Q. Like seriously? What were you thinking?"

"He wasn't thinking, sweetie. He was scared," said Jordan walking up behind Karyn to my defense.

"But why?" asked Karyn. "After everything I've told you about my life, why would you be scared?"

"I don't know. It's complicated, Karyn."

"Um, is this a party or what? What is going on over here?" asked Prince also coming to my defense. "Did I make a mistake inviting her?"

"Oh, that's how she got here. Thanks, Prince, for the heads up," I said sarcastically.

Prince said, "It's called a surprise, Q. You don't get a heads up. Besides, I knew you were never going to introduce her to us so I introduced myself."

"Listen, Q, I want you to enjoy yourself tonight and we will talk about this later. And no matter what, know that I love you," said Karyn looking deep into my eyes.

Laughter filled the rooms. If anyone was not having fun, we couldn't tell. Prince introduced me to so many sexy, hot boys. After finishing one conversation, I would get pulled by my arm or the back of my neck into another. Kevin had faded away into the background of my thoughts.

Karyn said, "Wow, Prince is such a…"

"…a whore," I said.

"Really, Q?" she laughed. "You are a mess, but what about you?"

"I have a boyfriend," I hoped still.

"Now I really wanna kick you in the nuts or smash this drink right in your face, but I know these queens in here will probably jump me for it," she reasoned.

"And throw you down the garbage chute with the rest of the trash," I joked. "No, but seriously, we do have to have a talk. Not tonight though. I need this distraction."

"Wait, so you and Prince ever mess around?"

"No, not at all. I mean he probably wanted to when we met, but my closest friends are like brothers to me, like you're my sister, in my mind," I answered.

"But he is a cutie. Actually, most of the boys in here are fine as hell and not one would want me."

"That's a lie. Switch-hitters do exist. They go back and forth from front to back," I said.

"Yeah, one of my homegirls actually just finished dealing with one," said Karyn. "He was calling the dude from her phone and that's how she found out. His dumb ass."

We bowed and shook our heads in unison, then sipped on our drinks with our eyes closed. Deeper into the music blasting through the apartment we became. I was a college graduate. It had hit me hard in that moment, which made me start dancing in the middle of the floor. Jordan, Roman, Prince, and Karyn fell in line. We wound our hips and stomped our kicks until the time had come for us to begin getting dressed for the club.

It was Karyn's official first time going to a gay club. Jordan brought his car for the sake of us conveniently getting home after our night out. Prince revealed yet another surprise for me in the bedroom before we left. He had a dozen ecstasy pills wrapped in a sheet of paper towel, lying in the palm of his hand. Some of them like Karyn and Roman took half a pill, while others, like me, swallowed a whole one. We had all heard the media reports about the new club drug hitting urban nightclubs throughout New York City. We took the chance and didn't look back.

Twilight was, as expected, buzzing from the sidewalk to every crowded bar on its three levels. The pills had not taken any effect on us until after most of us finished our first drink. I lifted my head and noticed that we all had formed a circle in the middle of the dance floor. Our arms rested on each other's shoulders. We looked high and I, for sure, felt super high.

This moderately sexy Puerto Rican with chiseled dark eyebrows kept motioning his hand up and down my spine. The mini-vibrations awoke a special part of me, but ironically I wasn't interested in having sex. It wasn't on my brain. I just wanted to feel and be felt, touch and be touched, love and be loved.

The DJ played those records like an angel with a harp. Each strike of the bass made its mark like single rays of the sun. We branded the dance floor *cloud nine*. Suddenly, I had the urge to urinate, which turned into a long trek for the restroom. Halfway between points, I ran into Kevin, or, in fact, he nearly ran into me. He brushed right by me so fast I had trouble determining if he even saw me. There was no line for the bathroom so I entered the first empty stall. Urinals can be too inviting for that type of atmosphere. On my final drip, the unlocked door was pushed open and in stepped Kevin, locking the door behind him. My high was partially blown.

"What the fuck?" I yelled.

"You tell me. Why are you here, to check up on me?" he asked.

"Actually, Prince threw me a surprise party in Brooklyn then we decided to come here."

"He didn't tell me about a party," he said as if he cared.

"Why would he, Kevin? It seems we're done, aren't we?"

"Prince is my friend too," he said.

"Is that what this is about? You barged your way into a stall to tell me that Prince should've invited you? And you still didn't answer my question. What happened? Is this really over?"

Kevin didn't say a word. He turned around to escape the question, but not before extending his sharp elbow deep into my stomach. It could have been an accident under different circumstances so I couldn't resist screaming, "Fuck you, Kevin."

He responded by back-kicking the door hard enough that it smacked me dead in the face. A few bathroom-cruising sissies chuckled. The stars in my eyes soon dissipated, then I lost control. Kevin must've taken me for a punk as he had his back turned exiting the bathroom. I shoved him up against the wall with just enough force to convey how mad I was. He swung his body around, bent over, then charged at me like the raging bull he was. I slammed my knee into his pretty face, which forced him into an upright position for an inevitable fistfight because wrestling seriously was not my thing.

We hit each other repeatedly until Prince rushed in to break us apart. Kevin had a bloody cut over his left eye and his face was beet red. I took a glimpse in the mirror on my right to realize how visibly upset I was, but not a scratch. I was, however, having difficulty catching each breath. It had been years since my last panic attack and I believed that was what I was experiencing. Kevin had run out of the bathroom, directly into the arms of a bouncer. As I dropped to my knees, I tried to remain calm and catch my breath.

"Someone call an ambulance," Prince shouted.

Karyn was whispering something in my ear I couldn't quite understand. From the thumping of the club floor to my throbbing pulse, there was so much commotion. One of the bouncers lifted me up into his arms and carried me downstairs curbside for the ambulance. It felt like I was tripping. I was concerned about my mother killing me if she found out how the night of my college graduation ended.

The oxygen mask got me breathing normally again. The police were standing by waiting for their opportunity to question me about the night's events. Thankfully, all of our illegal drugs had already been flushed by word of the club owner before the authorities arrived. Nonetheless, I was facing a possible assault on a minor charge since Kevin's 17th birthday wasn't for another week. Kevin had lied to me about his age. He lied to everyone.

I wished I had taken my last breath. That lie cut long and deep. Who was the real Kevin? I didn't know him as well as I thought I had. The officers, though, elected not to ask me any more questions since they believed I had been misled. Kevin could've been a repeat offender.

As planned, Jordan drove us home and Karyn was still in shock. As best I could, I explained to her my dealings with Kevin up to that point.

"Why would he lie to you about his age though?" she asked.

"I wish I knew, Karyn," I said.

"Listen, people lie, people of all ages lie to get what they want," said Jordan. "He knew exactly what he was doing. Ain't that right, Roman?"

"Fuck you, bitch," Roman said sternly.

Roman did happen to be unusually quiet about the whole topic.

"Did you lie too about being 18?" I asked Roman.

"Sure did," he confirmed.

"Why would you do that?"

Roman said, "Your Kevin is better suited to answer that since he was the one who played you for a fool for the past six months."

"Bitch, pull over," I said angrily to Jordan.

"Both of you bitches, cut it out," Jordan said as he intervened. "Everyone got their issues, including you, Q. Kevin got the best of you and now you mad and feeling evil. Take what happened tonight in stride - learn from this shit 'cause life goes on, honey."

Our uniform silence gave Jordan the entire acknowledgement he needed. His words were stuck in our heads. I soon laid my head down to sleep on my mother's couch in that cramped studio apartment. She rolled her eyes at me as I barely beat the sun home. My reality seemed to remind me that I had *grown up*. Those were the resounding words I had heard the whole week. It was time to *grow up and be a man*, as if I had any idea what that meant.

Part Two (June 2002)

Journal Entry #143

Sunday, June 30, 2002
10:42 p.m.

It's been a full year since I graduated from college and a whole year since Kevin deserted me. I started this journal because of him. My pride is on the page where the world can't see how I let him get the best of me. The past comes back to haunt me every now and then, but for the most part, I have moved on with my life. I think and feel differently than I did back then. One major difference in my life is the fact that I'm not living at home with my mother anymore. It was all unexpected. She said things I didn't like and I'm sure I said things she took a little too personally. Maybe it was wrong to try to criticize her after she sacrificed her whole life for her boys and then had to lose one to God. In reality, I've only begun to understand the kinds of sacrifices she's had to make to raise four boys with little to no help from their fathers. She was only 14 when she first got married. Her grandmother thought the boy next door was a good match. It's the way it worked deep in the South in those days. However, she hated that boy so they fought like cats and dogs until it ended. After two kids and six years of fighting, she walked away from him. She said it was the first time she couldn't stand to look at herself in the mirror. But she had two kids in the process that would still need to know their father. Very little was done to make it a smooth transition from having two parents down to just one. Still, she did the best she could do. But my two oldest brothers grew up resenting her for walking away. In their eyes, she seemed to be the one in control, rejecting the father they loved. It didn't help that he used his money to buy their love. Then my mother's family made things worse by telling them stuff like "your mother doesn't want you boys to be happy" and whispering "your mother hates you boys 'cause she hates your father." They thought it was a game. No one took it seriously except my brothers. So my mother just got tougher on them as they tried to rebel later on in their teenage years. From what I can tell, it scared them—she scared them and she didn't soften up until she had me. But before me, she had Henry, whose father changed his number and left town when our mother told him she was pregnant. But Mommy had fallen in love with him even though they had only known each other for like two weeks. His name was Dean so she nicknamed his son Dino. For like the first 10 years of my life, I thought Dino was his real name, not Henry. And I don't think I've ever called him Henry. Dino turned out to be diagnosed as bipolar, or so the doctors said. It did explain a lot, but it was too little too late. He was too far gone at 16, never mind at 30 years old. He was always that problem child in school and at home so my mother put him out before he could finish high school. Dino lived on the streets whenever DJ or friends of his couldn't house him. Actually, it's something we all have in common as brothers, being put out of the house by our hardcore mother. Still, I always felt different because I felt like they knew I was the one she wanted to do right by even though she still made mistakes. My mother was a different mother from theirs. My brothers saw me get away with murder, especially as a teenager. I probably got beat like five times in my life when they couldn't have kept count. We were definitely half-brothers. My mother has always hated that term. My friends growing up thought I had it made. I was my father's only child and the baby on my mother's side, which normally translates into a spoiled brat. But after she put my brothers out, I was lonely and fell into myself. So I suddenly had to be independent. My mother was the only real support I had. It wasn't perfect, but then my pops was more selfish than me and he didn't care about keeping any of the promises he made to his only child. For example, he told me far in advance that money would not be a problem for me in college. Of course, he lied yet again. I only forced myself to ask him for money because tuition was due before I could start my senior year. I was flat broke and so was my mother. My pops then said he never made that promise to me and that I needed to get a job. I broke down over the phone. Just thinking about it takes me there every single time. I was in my room down on both knees screaming like someone had stabbed me in the back of my head with a knife. I felt no real pain, but I was hurt. I just kept screaming and crying. Thank God my mother was home. There's no telling what I would've done all alone. Like I was a baby, she got down on the floor and rocked me to sleep. She was trembling more than I was. The next day, I couldn't believe I had lost it like that. I was drained. I finally got up off the floor. The only thing I knew for sure was that I never wanted to feel like that again. I never wanted to feel that helpless. I had to toughen up and I made myself a promise I refused to break—never again will I allow myself to be that helpless. My mother had reached out to my brothers' father who wrote a check so I could finish school without interruption. I even had enough left over to buy books. I was blessed. And still, my pops does not get it. So I haven't called him Daddy in over 10 years and I guess it hasn't bothered him enough to ask why.

Didn't Cha Know

My roommate, Ron, was seated on the couch in the living room as I came into the apartment after nine long hours that day and five long days at work that week. The path into the apartment still seemed unfamiliar. My name hadn't been officially added to the lease or the mailbox. It was my new home. It was my first time living on my own. I was independent. My mom and I had not spoken a word to each other in over a month. We were on speaking terms, just not heavily.

"How was work?" asked Ron.

"Work was work," I responded. "And how was your day?"

Ron was on disability from his employer. It was some sort of medical issue I couldn't see with my naked eye, but he said it was legit.

"My day was cool," he replied. "I changed the towels in your bathroom and made up your bed."

"Thanks, Ron," I said suspiciously.

Ron was kind enough to let me move into the guest bedroom of his two-bed/two-bath apartment located near downtown Newark, N.J. It was ghetto, but you wouldn't have been able to tell from the inside of the place. The black cherry-wood pillars on either side of the living-room entrance helped to elevate the experience. Ron was responsible for all the interior design, including the guest bedroom. He had passion. He said he wanted me to feel completely at home since we had become roommates. I was struggling to cope with the concept. I didn't even have my own phone line yet.

"Did I get any calls?" I asked.

"Nope, it's been pretty quiet all day."

I was beginning to get sick of that textbook response. My messages were almost never delivered and due to his frequent online guests during the day and night, things weren't all that quiet either.

"So what do you have planned for the weekend?" he asked.

"I have a date," I said.

"Another one, you whore?"

"Yes, another one. If you can have four to five online dates a week, then my one date every other week should not be an issue. What are your wild plans for the weekend?"

"Actually," said Ron. "There's only one person I'm involved with right now and we'll be hanging out here all weekend, watching movies and fucking. You can join us if your date is wack."

Ron and I used to date soon after Jordan introduced us to one another. Older men were just easier for me to talk to. Ron claimed he was only five years older than me, but according to Jordan who was in his early 30s at the time, Ron told that lie to all of his dates. Jordan said Ron was five years older than him. The two of them grew up together on Prince Street in Newark in the same housing project that blanketed about a dozen city blocks.

I rebounded from Kevin directly onto Ron. I needed a distraction and he was there. Those first two weeks were fun. Anything I wanted he was willing to go out of his way to get for me. The bliss ended right before the holiday season. Ron was moving really fast. I lost my motivation to keep up. Jordan had told me about how Ron had bought me about a bunch of

Christmas gifts, ranging from a new leather coat to three pairs of sneakers. There was no way I could accept those gifts feeling the way I did so I came clean, over the phone. We argued. He pleaded. He wanted to know what was wrong with him or was there something wrong with me since I wouldn't let him just love me. With no real choice in the matter, he came to terms with my decision, but only after he held me hostage in Branch Brook Park.

The park is the largest in Essex County, stretching from one end of Newark, NJ's largest city, to the next. Trapped in his car with childproof locks, Ron kept driving and turning left, then right, then right, then left again until we were too deep for me to access a busy road back home. As far as he was concerned, I was the perfect man for him. His ex-boyfriend shattered his heart so he felt as though God was granting him another chance. Every time I tried to open the car door, he would extend that arm from his six-foot, three-inch frame to pull me back in and shut the door.

I hated hurting people that much because I knew how it felt to have your heart broken. I wanted to dislocate Ron's jaw with blunt trauma, but I knew he would only forgive me for it. Instead, I began to rock back and forth in the passenger seat. There was nothing left to say. His words began to fade. Ron could soon see the tears well up in my eyes. Once again, I allowed myself to feel helpless. He must've seen me begin to torture myself because I heard him apologizing. At that point, he let me go and I walked over five miles home. Oddly, we wound up as, not just roommates, but also like friends.

"Hello?" I said after answering the home phone.

"Hey baby. How are you?" Karyn asked from the other end.

"I'm good, lady. I just had to deflect another one of Ron's sexual advances," I said once I dragged the base to my bedroom and shut the door.

"Is he seriously trying to take advantage of the situation?"

"It's more so him putting out different types of bait waiting to see which one works best," I said. "But he's harmless, trust me."

Karyn said, "Yeah, well, if your mother wasn't such a stone cold…"

"Take it easy, Karyn," I said interrupting her. "She's been through a lot and it's taken me a while to figure that out. I had a long talk about her with my brother DJ. He basically said she's not the same person she used to be, but for him and Dino some things are hard to forget."

"Just when I was perfecting my mother-bashing bit, you had to go get a brand-new attitude. You're so all about you right now it's not even funny," she joked.

"Whatever. Why did you call here to begin with?" I asked while giggling.

"How's WUGH treating you?"

"It's cool. I thought things would be different once they hired me full-time after graduation, but I'm not really learning much. My boss Sean is either too busy or can't be found."

"How often do you get to speak with him?" she asked.

"About once a day," I said. "He does look out for me from time to time, sort of like a big brother."

"Well, you be careful over there," she said.

"What is that supposed to mean?"

"I remember what you told me the last time we talked. Sean gets a lot of free stuff. In his position, it may be a little suspect," she said in response.

"I don't know about that. But what's up with you this weekend?"

"I got plans," she replied.

"Are you finally using that gym membership I bought you?" I laughed.

"I have a date," she said. "Thank you."

"Really, with who?" I asked Karyn, who hadn't dated anyone since she was raped.

"Russ."

"Russ who?" I asked in my high-pitched voice.

"You know who I'm talking about, Q."

"Wow, when did this happen and where have I been?"

She said, "He was there with you at my graduation a few months ago, remember? We exchanged info and have been keeping in touch since then."

"Damn, Karyn, I have a confession to make," I said. "Russ and I have been having sex since the day we met."

It sounded as if she dropped the phone yet was quick to respond.

"What the hell are you talking about, Quincy?"

She sounded extremely annoyed on the verge of going ballistic. This was how I sometimes got the best laughs.

I said, "Nah, he's straight. I almost got him confused with this other dude who looked like him. Silly me, but please tell me what does it look like?"

She laughed out loud then said, "Juicy and thick, but sex is not an option just yet if you must know. I just like to play with it."

"I understand, all in due time. I'm proud of you because that's truly a good man. We've been friends for awhile and he's always treated women right."

"Are you seeing anyone right now?" asked Karyn.

"Oh yeah, for sure, you know how I do. His name is Mitch. He was at my surprise graduation party last year. At the time, if you remember, he was in that relationship with Trey."

"You're in trouble," said Karyn. "You're taking other people's men now?"

"No, I'm not. They broke up before I even knew he had a thing for me."

She asked, "Wait, was it the tall one with the tattoos kissing in the corner that night?"

"Yup. Unforgettable, huh?" I asked.

"He looked like a purse snatcher until his white pearls fell out his mouth."

"Huh? Why would you say that?" I said laughing uncontrollably.

"I mean, he's a really nice person instead of the thug he appears to be. That's a good catch, Quincy."

"Ditto," I replied.

The conversation ended with the usual—a promise to make time to see one another soon. Karyn was continuing her education in graduate school. She was going for a master's degree in communication. Her family would have it no other way.

●●●

Night fell on that following Saturday and I was running late. Mitch already called once to let me know that he would be browsing some stores on 34th Street until I got dressed and met up with him. The cab was on its way to drop me off at the train station. I stood outside to wait. In the blink of an eye, I saw a shadowy figure in the dark of night positioned across the street, beside the light pole. People were out and about at all hours of the night around there so it didn't disturb me much, although he seemed to be staring in my direction.

The cab pulled up and as I was making my way to the curb, I heard my name being called. The voice was soaked in desperation. Sure enough, it was Gabriel. I hadn't seen Gabriel since spotting him on campus that day over a year ago. He wanted to talk so I told him to get in the cab with me because I had no time to spare.

"What's up, boy? Long time no see—how have you been and most importantly what are you doing around this part of town?" I asked.

He said, "My uncle lives a few blocks away on Summit Ave. I thought my eyes were deceiving me when I saw your face from across the street. Where are you headed?"

"Downtown to catch the train—don't worry, I'll pay for your ride back if you were going to visit your uncle."

"Why? Where exactly are you going?" asked Gabriel more directly.

"I'm meeting a friend on 34th street."

"What kind of friend? You can be honest with me, Quincy."

I said, "It's someone I've been dating for a few weeks."

"I love you, Quincy," Gabriel said as the cab made its final turn before pulling in front of the train station.

I lost count of my money and I believe I gave the driver more than I intended. Gabriel stepped out. From the look in his eyes, he seemed to be telling me the truth.

"Gabriel, why were you on the Rutgers campus about a year ago?"

"I contemplated going to Rutgers but eventually changed my mind," he said.

"Why?" I asked.

"Because I thought I wanted to be close to you. I wanted a future with you. I've never met anyone else like you. I thought this shit in my heart, in my spirit would fade but it hasn't. Is there something wrong with me, Quincy?"

I told him, "I didn't pursue a relationship with you because there was something wrong with me. I wasn't ready at the time. I still hated the fact that I was attracted to boys. It made me sick to my stomach. Sex with another guy was about as far as I willing to go at that time."

"So what about now?" he responded.

"What about now? I'm not the same person I used to be and I'm sure you're not either. Besides, I'm going to meet up with someone I care a lot about."

"Oh. You know, I guess this was all a big waste of time," he said sadly while hanging his head.

"Don't think of it like that but don't hang on to the past. Gotta let it go. I definitely have."

"Okay, well, I won't bother you again," Gabriel said. "Have a good life, Mr. Simmons."

"Gabriel, take care. Here's money for that cab ride back, like I promised."

Gabriel slid his hand down mine from the wrist to the tips of my fingers while collecting the cash. I smiled, then he walked away.

Mitch had been waiting about an hour for me to show up. His temperament wouldn't allow him to be upset.

"Sorry it took me so long. I ran into an ex of mine on the way here," I said.

"Really?" said Mitch who was a man of very few words.

"Yeah, he confessed that he's still in love with me."

"Really? What did you tell him?" he asked.

"Basically, I told him to move on because I sure have. I guess he really meant what he said when he told me back then he loved me."

Come to think of it and unbeknownst to me, Mitch also had feelings for me long before our impromptu drunken kiss the month before. I thought he had always been threatened by me while he was with Trey. Trey and I grew closer as friends after Kevin and I broke up. Trey's boyfriend before Mitch had done nearly the same thing as Kevin. Although, I still can't accept Kevin lied about his age and cheated on me.

One day a couple of months prior to my breakup with Kevin, I visited my clique of friends in Brooklyn who were then officially known as the Rude Boyz. There, I found a hand-drawn sketch of myself lying on the floor in Prince's bedroom. The sketch was drawn using a headshot I had given to Prince when we first met. Mitch was the sketch artist. I had misread his energy the whole time. Soon after I discovered the sketch, Mitch and Trey broke up. Trey substituted his relationship with a life of even heavier clubbing. He also had been busted more than once kissing random strangers at the house parties the Rude Boyz promoted.

So four weeks to the day of their split, I found myself lip-locked with Mitch during one of those infamous house parties. Respectfully, I approached Trey at the end of the night to gain clearance because I wanted to see if dating Mitch would work out. I didn't want to pursue something I knew would hurt Trey. I got what I wanted and so there I stood with this tall, sexy black man who was much more interested in me than I was in him.

He could have been my soul mate for all I knew. Though, it entered my mind that I had been in that predicament before experiencing that same feeling of fulfillment. I didn't want to think about how it would come to an end, but I couldn't help myself. Each step he took equaled about two of mine. We were moving somewhat fast. Everything was fine though as long as we kept moving so we kept moving right on to see Spider-Man, then we grabbed a bite to eat.

The smile on my face helped me to plant my feet on the floor for the first time the next morning. Mitch was still sleeping and totally stretched out flat on his back. He kicked off the covers at some point overnight so there he lay as his nude body rippled like the ocean. He was built like no one I had ever dated—like one of those dudes playing basketball on the courts up in Harlem. His tattoos covered his wavy arms.

I kept rewinding in my head what had happened some six hours prior. I damn near lost all breath control because I wanted his bare flesh in my mouth. It was like he made me want him just that much. Testing the boundaries of our insatiability was what led to Mitch falling asleep and spending the night. He really couldn't leave my side so we cuddled together.

Unfortunately, there weren't any deep conversations considering our differences.

Mitch was three-and-a-half years older than me, living in his older sister's basement, not paying rent and cutting hair for money at a local barbershop in Brooklyn. He told his fellow barbers that a girl had put that glow on his face. That girl happened to be me. Mitch hadn't told them he was gay.

Mitch was the quiet shy type that you should only want to sleep with, but yet there I was. It was as if I was waiting for things between us to change. I was hoping the man would turn over out of his sleep and tell me about his past, present and future. Instead, he woke up without saying a word and went to take a leak, just like a man, so I lay back down to sleep a bit longer.

Hours later, Mitch had already gone home. Ron and his weekend guest were watching television in the living room. I could smell sex in the air. The two of them had been up to something or just finishing, which would have explained why they were in their underwear.

"What's up, Q?" Ron asked.

"Just getting a snack from the kitchen," I replied.

"Quincy, this is my boy, Nathan."

"Nice to meet you, Nathan," I said and he politely reciprocated the comment.

I couldn't help but notice Nathan's subtle interest he had just discovered in me. It's always in the eyes. We also shook hands so I felt it in his grip as I pulled away. Nathan definitely had some demons that Ron was oblivious to.

By 10 p.m. that Sunday night, I had positioned myself completely nude in the center of my bed. The window, on my right, was open wide without any curtains. I didn't mind if my neighbors wanted to be nosy. I lit four toasted almond-scented pillar candles and put one in each corner of the room. That was all the light I needed. Sade's "Love is Stronger than Pride" bounced off the walls. I got sent into a trance when Anita Baker's "Giving You the Best that I Got" also played during WUGH's Quiet Storm block of music.

With hip-hop on the rise, my old soul still craved the classics like the music my mother listened to while I was growing up. She collected piles of cassette tapes during the 1980s and that became my playground as a child. I didn't know what the songs meant, but I could feel them. Music makes one feel. Not much else goes into good music.

A steady rainfall outside was dampening my windowsill. I burst out of my slight trance laughing at the thought of me rubbing my skinny naked ass on the windowpane. The neighbors would have had a fit. Instead, I walked up to the full-length mirror hanging on the closet door and sang along to Erykah Badu's "Didn't Cha Know," which was one of my favorite songs of all time.

The words told my story about being confused about what I really wanted out of life. Where was I headed and do I go full force or proceed with caution? To wrap up the night, I dropped down to the floor for my daily routine of push-ups, squats, calf-raises, sit-ups, and whatever else I had the energy for. As most gay men, I had to preserve the sexy. Once I lay back down, the night had indeed ended in a trance, a trance-like sleep.

Fairy Tales

Another routine Monday had begun. The week led off
with a visit by the queen of hip-hop soul. Mary J. Blige had
a new album due in stores while the autumn leaves fell from
the trees. The station was on edge. There were three separate
pre-production meetings to prepare for the interview. It was my
assigned duty to escort Mary and her entourage to the green
room once they arrived. My potential misused, but the difficult
task was attempting to converse with people whose six-figure
salaries had forced them to forget what we had in common,
like being a human being. I just reminded myself to be nice.
Sean took a moment out of his busy day to inquire about the
five extra minutes it had taken me to get to work that morning.
Before I could respond, his phone rang. It was in regards to
Mary so the moment was cut short.

Mary was expected to be in the building soon. I made my
way to the lobby. The elevator doors parted and out stepped
a big dude who was followed by another big dude. A small
female then appeared followed by Mary J. Blige, followed by
three more average-sized dudes. They must have tested the
elevator's capacity from the looks of it. I quickly extended my
hand as a greeting, but was barely acknowledged. The small
female stepped forward out of the shadows to greet Sean who
was then standing to my left. Sean introduced me to the crew.

"Everybody this is Quincy and he'll lead you to the green
room now," said Sean. While walking, one of the average-sized
dudes stepped forward to break the ice.

"Hey, what's up? Quincy, right?"

"Yeah, are you with the label?" I responded.

"Yeah, sort of—they call me Monty. I handle promotions, but independently of the label."

Independent music promoters are hired as a helping hand/ contractor to the record company. It's also a huge loophole for payola. Often times, indie promoters will offer a music programmer something of value in exchange for airplay. The label pretends to turn a blind eye.

"How long have you been here at WUGH?" he further inquired.

"A little over a year," I replied.

"Ah, so you're a newbie. Do you like it?"

I said, "Hell, yeah. I never expected to wind up programming for one of the top radio stations in the country; it's definitely official. Music is one of my passions."

"Passion, huh," he said while briefly staring me right in the eye. "Listen, do you have a business card or something?"

I thought twice for some odd reason, then responded, "As long as you plan to make use of it."

Monty and I were now seated side by side on the couch in the music-infested green room. No one could eavesdrop. His body language was as subtle as mine. We just appeared to be shooting the breeze although I believed we were both aware that we needed to begin networking outside of one another. We were bordering on suspicion in an industry that overflows with it. By the time I caught up with the chemistry racing between us, Monty had already walked out of the room. I needed a moment to get my thoughts back in order as nature was calling.

While answering its call, Dove, one of the station's premier on-air personalities, asked Mary all the right questions during the interview. The respect they have for one another was undeniable. They were like two old friends catching up on new times. Mary's manager alerted the crew of the time on the clock. Their busy schedule had them on a serious grind. Instead of leaving the way they came, they chose to exit out the back through the freight entrance. It was one celebrity down and so many more to go.

●●●

It took a little less than three weeks into the month of October for Mary J. Blige's new album to be certified platinum, selling over a million copies. The record label was hosting her platinum party at the Hammerstein Ballroom and I was prepared for something crazy to happen because that's the way the industry functions.

The industry party of the year was due to start in less than an hour. My boy, Russ, was spending some time away from his girlfriend, Karyn, to coordinate the party. Russ's passion for party promotion and planning seemed to be innate. Back in college, he was the reason why our school became known as one of the top party schools in North Jersey and the administration didn't mind the cash flow. Consequently, Russ was promoting after parties for various awards shows as well as private music-industry events. He was indeed a great catch for Karyn.

I showed up to the 12,000-square-foot venue just 30 minutes before Mary and her entourage entered the building. Once inside, I brushed and bumped shoulders with Puffy, Jay-Z,

Lil' Kim, and Queen Latifah. It was all so overwhelming. My boss Sean was in attendance with his fellow industry execs. He nodded in my direction before pulling his usual disappearing act. It made me feel like I was back in high school again, being picked last for some sports team in gym class.

"Having a good time?" asked Monty with the palm of his right hand caught in the arch of my back.

"Um," I paused, feeling confused. "Yeah, I think so."

He said, "You don't sound too sure about that."

"I'm unsure about a few things right now."

His aggression was out of bounds so I assumed he was intoxicated.

"Are you unsure about what I want from you, Q?"

"Are you drunk?" I asked.

"Why? You want me to get you a drink?"

I responded graciously. Monty wasn't interested in my drink preference though. Within five minutes, he had returned with an Incredible Hulk, which was the ghetto drink of choice at the turn of the century. It was made up of one-half Hpnotiq and one-half Hennessy. He brought me a tall glass as opposed to the sea of 12-ounce plastic cups in everyone else's hands. I alerted Monty to all the females who had taken notice that we were the only men, together, drinking from real glasses.

"These bitches are about fucking and spending money," replied Monty. "What the fuck I care what they think about two grown men drinking out of a glass? Come on now, Q."

I thought to myself that they could also be suspicious of us. I asked him, "So how many drinks have you had?"

"About six or so, but listen—let's get out of here."

"And go where, Monty? I've only been here for less than an hour."

"Your boss won't know. His attention is always focused on what's in front of him and that's it," said Monty who definitely knew what he was talking about.

I said, "But I have to work in the morning."

"Me too," he concluded.

Monty and I then walked a few blocks west to escape the crowd before hopping into a cab together. I had no more reservations.

"Take us to 116th and St. Nick," he directed.

"That's where you live?" I asked.

"All day, been living in Harlem for two years, but born and raised in Bedford-Stuyvesant, the livest one."

The cab driver swerved in and out of lanes. He cursed the brazen pedestrians in the crosswalk and screamed at almost every other vehicle on the road. I've always despised their kind. They overcharge, discriminate and abuse. I shouldn't let their behavior get next to me, but it does at times.

"What are you thinking about?" asked Monty.

"Nothing," I lied. "Do you have smoke?"

"Upstairs in my condo," he said as we exited the cab in front of a high-rise residential building complete with a doorman. Once we made it inside his two-bedroom condo, Monty wasted little time getting comfortable. He stripped down to his boxer briefs then sat on the living-room couch to begin rolling a joint.

"Make yourself at home, Q," he said. "The bar is well-stocked and the bathroom is down the hall."

I took the liberty of removing my shoes so I could dig my feet deep into the beige shag carpet. He cut the big screen on.

After a quick rinse in the bathroom sink, I asked him for a tour of the place. Monty lit the joint then informed me that he had a roommate. There was hesitation on his part.

His kitchen and bathroom were covered in stainless steel from the appliances to the showerhead. Chandeliers hung above the coffee table and in the hallway. The third door on the right was opened. It was Monty's master bedroom. His queen-size bed was unmade. Dirty clothes littered the floor, closet and dresser. I asked Monty if he had a female roommate and my suspicion was confirmed. His messy room was inconsistent with the rest of the clean condo. Nervously, I pulled back the comforter on his bed then smiled. At least the sheets were spotless. Monty was simply untidy.

He then moved swiftly to my backside to kiss me on my neck. Before I could respond, he pushed me down onto the bed. I moaned and groaned with every bite from his passionate mouth. He felt so strong. We wrestled heart to heart and I was losing immensely. Monty broke away from me to grab a condom. The lubrication appeared at the last possible second before I clinched the sheets. He took his time digging into me like a turtle in the sand. Never had it felt so good going in, then out, then back in again. His kiss was pacifying. His sex allowed me to forget my worries and thank him by the time it was over.

"Why are you thanking me?" he said with a chuckle as he searched for a clean towel.

"Because you cared enough to take your time. Maybe next time, I can use that same technique when I do you."

Monty cringed. He delivered a swift response. "Nah, man, I'm not with that."

Everything I was feeling then came to a screeching halt. I felt naked from the inside out so I got fully dressed as fast as I could, but the sense of vulnerability wouldn't subside. I couldn't find the right words to express what I was feeling and why I was getting mad.

"Are you okay?" he asked.

"I'm going to head home."

"To Jersey? Why? You can leave for work from here in the morning. I'll give you a change of clothes."

It turns out that Monty was a top. We took time to talk about our preferences before I still carried out my decision to bail. Once again, I set myself up for the fall. Everything I used to believe about this lifestyle was not the reality of it. I had a lot to learn. I started off expecting some immediate gratification after spending so much of my life trying to hide who I was. I never considered sexual compatibility would be such a big deal in this new life.

These odd societal labels exist in the gay community. There are tops like Monty who refuse to be penetrated and bottoms unlike myself who couldn't care less to use their penis. I came into this lifestyle thinking that being fully versatile, enjoying the best of both worlds, was the universal preference. However, there are also versatile-tops with only a slight preference for receiving and versatile-bottoms with a slight preference for giving. Some of us are openly gay while others choose to keep their sex lives private or on the down low.

Then there are the bisexuals and lesbians. Many straight women unwittingly date bisexual men. However, I believe the overwhelming stigma of having sexual relations with both men and women can sometimes force the door to close shut on a way of life many straight and even some gay people would call being greedy. Again, it's the assumption that someone would actually choose to be attracted to both sexes and want to face the legion of naysayers. Lesbians, though, experience life on a different plane. In a man's world, the rules change. Girl-on-girl action is as innocent as two girls brushing each other's hair. I don't have any lesbian friends. I wouldn't even know where to find them since our interests are so different.

The two-hour trip home in the cold that night through a flurry of fresh snowflakes was exhausting. I was sitting upright at my desk within the following two hours. I spent much of the day just trying to get Monty off my mind, which proved to be more difficult than expected.

●●●

It was business as usual that day. The commute back home from work was nothing new. I had trouble sleeping while standing up on the crowded train. There were bodies everywhere and many appeared to be on an undeniable mission. The bills must be paid. For every minute that passed, I was that much closer to lying my head down on my pillow after not getting much sleep thanks to Monty.

Drug addicts and their suppliers were actively pounding the mid-autumn snow on the pavement. There was a trail of debris from the shoveled sidewalk to the elevator, which normally meant someone had either moved in or out of the building. My sole destination was apartment #234. I noticed that the elevator was also filled with the strange debris. I wondered how long it would take the superintendent to clean up the mess. Ironically, the people who either moved in or out had similar taste to mine. There was a Matrix DVD lodged in the railing of the staircase. I lifted my eyes slowly to witness the trail of debris lead directly to Ron's apartment.

The door was pulled shut, but unlocked. Ron's shiny hardwood floors were bruised and everything of value had been stolen. I ran in disbelief from one room to the next tripping over underwear, shattered picture frames and disheveled magazines. A draft from the open window in Ron's bedroom answered most of my nagging questions. It was the only window with a fire escape. They climbed in, then they walked out. They robbed us in broad daylight. So much of what I worked for went with them.

The police report was lengthy and Ron wanted to find them before they could begin selling off our stuff. He made phone calls to his cousins, his older brother and a private investigator.

Over the next few months, his date, Nathan, watched Ron obsess over finding the petty thieves. Eventually, Nathan grew tired of being ignored and never came back. Ron was unfazed by everything at the time except the robbery. I focused in on replacing what little possessions I had lost, which wasn't very difficult for a recent college graduate with barely a roof over his head. Ron, however, was starting to make me believe there was more to what he was looking for.

Jordan told me to mind my business and focus on moving out into my own place. That was my goal. I needed to stand up in my own skin feeling like I had won, like I had beat the odds. Living with Ron was my stepping stone toward greatness because I wanted to have much of what he had. From the apartment to his brand-new Mazda 626, I admired him as a man. It wasn't until months later when I felt the need to withdraw that pedestal.

Journal Entry #249

Thursday, March 27, 2003
4:00 a.m.

Spring is finally in the air after another long cold winter, but I am exhausted. We spent almost 17 hours on a shoot with Nas. Our video team shadowed him all day and night for The Formula—the online show featuring a different rapper every month. Nas didn't hold back one bit. He was raw and captivating. We first caught him rolling out of bed in his custom Gucci boxers. I don't know how we managed to get that footage. And to say he's sexy is an understatement. But he is a man with a strong head on his shoulders. Nas then gave us a glimpse into his creative process by spitting some new verses off the top of his head. Still, he was in his underwear making it hard for me to do my job. The shots after that were of the Queensbridge rep arriving on the set of his latest music video. There were groupies everywhere. They just kept flowing like the Moet that seemed to be on tap—even the production crew had a few drinks. All the girls there, of course, wanted to have sex with one of the most gifted lyricists of our generation. I can imagine how they feel. By the end, Nas had to escape the groupies. Some of them actually chased his limo down the block hoping to still get a piece of him. It was crazy. Our producer continued to interview him in the car until we got to the next location. His record label had thrown him a surprise birthday party at Webster Hall. That didn't end 'til 3 a.m. and, of course, I ran into Monty there. Monty and I are on another level now. I mean, we haven't really talked about what we're doing and how seriously to take it, but I like him. Plus, he's a freak in between the sheets. He's taught me a lot. I didn't know I could do half the things I've done so far. My tongue alone is a deadly weapon now. But besides that, dude is just funny and beyond cool. The real funny thing is when it comes to business, he don't play. We don't mix our business with pleasure. If we're working, whether it's at a party or some conference, we don't talk about how we feel. But outside of work, we're all over each other. I can't believe it's been like five months 'cause it feels like five minutes. His roommate disturbs me though. How do you share an apartment with a girl you used to date? And it bothers me I still haven't been introduced to either one of his two sons. Maybe they're too young to meet Daddy's boyfriend. So I ignore all of it. He rarely talks about them so I rarely bring it up. And I can't believe his roommate has no clue Monty is bisexual or that him and I have been more than just homies. She's a fool. It's that simple. But when I saw Monty at the party, we kept our cool. Most of these industry heads call us the dynamic duo, but they don't have a clue about how we really do. As long as it's not dangling in someone's face, they don't question. They always assume straight. It works in our favor most of the time like it did tonight. The party was so dope. Monty and I blended with the crowd. We danced, separately. The looks we gave each other like every 15 minutes said all that needed to be said. Unfortunately, I couldn't head uptown with him to fuck like we usually do, drunk after the party. We both agreed to give it a break tonight. And I'm thinking about calling out of work in the morning. I just need some sleep, some time to sleep. Goodnight.

6:32 a.m.

 Stuck Pages, Vol. 1: Exposing the Heart of a Heartbreaker

P.S. This is the first week I haven't gotten a call from Mitch. I guess he's giving up. What can I say? I just didn't feel it with him. Sex became ordinary when that used to be the main attraction. I got over it. I wish him well. But Monty feels comfortable and something tells me Monty has a lot more to give.

Is It a Crime

"Ron, can you get the door? I hear someone knocking, but I need to use the bathroom real quick," I shouted from the hallway.

Ron's room was closer to the door so he responded quicker when someone visited. I sat down on the toilet to prepare myself for a massive undertaking. I had indeed called out that day.

Suddenly, the bathroom door got kicked in. Good thing the toilet was positioned like five feet away from the door. Two masked thugs stood in front of me while one held a gun to Ron's temple. The other trigger-happy goon pointed his pistol at me and made a point of telling me that he would shoot me in my pretty face if I tried anything stupid.

"Where the fuck is the money?" the gunman demanded.

"I don't know what money you're talking about. I just live here," I said with both hands raised to the sky, my underwear touching the floor and my heart banging against my ribcage.

"Where's the box, stretch?" said gunman No. 2 even though he was just as tall as Ron.

However, Ron didn't say a word back. He was asked again and again and still no response. Did he have a death wish? Next thing I knew, gunman No. 2 ordered Ron to strip off all his clothes. Of course, he refused so they pistol-whipped him into submission. I still couldn't move. I could see the killer in their eyes. After Ron removed his clothes, my pretty-face shooter inquired again about the location of the mysterious box. Ron seemed to choke on his blood for a moment before screaming out loud, "I know who you are!"

The thugs raged. It was almost as if they forgot I was there because they both bent Ron's naked body over at the waist to take more than just the box they were not leaving without. Dear God, why was I still frozen? It was still too easy for me to get shot. I would have had to take at least five long steps to stop them so I pleaded, "What are y'all doing? Ron, tell them where the box is, please."

"I know who they are and they can't have shit," Ron challenged.

"Yo, shut the fuck up, kid! Ron is right. This shit here is personal," said gunman No. 2 before penetrating Ron.

My shock morphed into disgust over the next 20 minutes. It was humiliating to have to watch. Ron was sodomized and urinated on. They were determined one at a time to rip his body apart although Ron never buckled. I wished he would scream bloody murder. Instead, he grunted angrily until they finished themselves off inside his wounds. They used my bath towel to wipe themselves clean. There was no relief for Ron though. He just dripped fluids like a leaky faucet. He was deep in a daze. The tears started flowing through his wrathful grimace. No man, whether gay or straight, likes to feel that helpless.

The gunmen tore through the apartment in search of the mysterious box. They soon found it hidden under Ron's bed beneath a trap door of some kind. Not a word was spoken between the two of us in that crime scene of a bathroom as the thieves ran out of the building into the dark city streets. All of it had to be extremely personal because they barely looked in my direction except to ensure I wasn't trying to escape from my isolating corner. Finally, I felt safe enough to move. Gently, I lay my hand on Ron's shoulder and he jumped up from his kneeling position with total fury before realizing it was me.

"Leave me alone," he barked.

"Do you want me to call the cops, Ron? God, what is going on here?"

"It's my fault."

"Why would you say that?" I asked.

"I have AIDS, Quincy, and that was my ex-boyfriend."

I was blown away. Speechless couldn't have begun to describe my reaction. Ron continued, "I messed up and gave him the virus. That's why him and his new boyfriend robbed us before, trying to scare me. But they were looking for the money. That's why they came back."

"Why didn't you tell me this before, Ron?"

"I didn't think they would come back," he defended.

Here I thought Ron was valuing his life by not resisting the rape when, in fact, he had neglected to value the life of his ex. In an attempt to flee the scene, Ron slipped and crashed back down to his knees. He sobbed like he should, like any grown man in his position would. Again, I couldn't find the words. Nothing mattered.

And two hours later, still nothing mattered. Nonetheless, Ron managed to climb into his bed. The sheets stuck to his body like glue. I checked on him every 10 to 15 minutes for the next couple of hours until I fell asleep. The cops were never called and it was probably for the best since Ron had committed a crime himself. His debt, however, was repaid in the most heinous way. I suspected his ex also knew that I once dated Ron too. Fortunately, I dodged a bullet or two of his with some latex condoms. That was one chilling night. No one can imagine the nightmares we both had that night.

Work had called me 30 minutes prior to me waking up the next morning. Sean questioned me repeatedly about my lateness, especially on the day of a scheduled field shoot. What was I supposed to tell him? I was supposed to be the programming lead present for B-roll footage of R. Kelly arriving at Kennedy airport over an hour earlier. I had overslept. Sean warned that he didn't want the producer calling the shots for that particular shoot. The two of them almost never saw eye to eye. I ran out the door, as soon as I completely woke up, neglecting to check on Ron. I made a mental note to give him a call later that afternoon. My job was most important.

Luckily, R. Kelly's plane was delayed an hour and 15 minutes so I pretty much made it to the shoot on time. Mini-crisis averted, but there was yet another one right around the corner. The R&B superstar didn't want to be filmed. His management wanted to reschedule for the afternoon when he'd had a moment to settle in at the hotel. Artists can be very moody. I called Sean and he was livid after not being able to change their minds. It forced him to rework his vision for some new online music video countdown show he had been planning on his own.

Back at the station, Sean wanted to meet one on one. It was not the time to tell him what I went through the night before. Would he have even begun to understand? So I just zoned out during his rant about it being my fault they wanted to cancel. He always stopped short of throwing things because I think he could sense I was not as docile as I sometimes appeared to be.

He made jokes all the time about me being from dirty Jersey and the bricks of Newark.

The fact remained that I was doing far more good than bad. Despite our positions, there was no way I could convince an artist like R. Kelly to do something he seriously was not going to do. He flaked on his own label when it comes to album deadlines so what would make WUGH any different?

My calls to Ron all afternoon went unanswered. I couldn't expect him to want to speak to me or anyone. I imagined his brain was splitting at the seams. Thank God it was Friday. The whole weekend would be dedicated to me serving Ron whatever he wanted, except for pity sex. Still, his phone continued to ring and ring. Four voicemail messages later and home was only a few blocks away.

For good reason, I felt uncomfortable in my neighborhood, in my skin. I kept scanning the parking lots and alleyways for strange figures. It was probably paranoia or something like that. I pushed through it all and landed on our doormat. I unlocked the door, opened it, then just stood there in disbelief. My eyes scanned the apartment sending unwanted messages to my brain. All the furniture and electronics were gone. Only this time, it felt different. Ron should have been there, but he was not and neither was anything he owned. My personal stuff was intact this time and there was this letter taped to the wall where his oval-shaped mirror used to hang:

Yeah, it's me. Here I sit alone in my room with you on my mind, not knowing what to say or how to say it. As you already know, I have very strong and sincere feelings for you and I am dying to show them to you. But there has been one thing holding me back and that's you. I write you this letter to express to you these deep emotions I have inside of me. I don't know if you noticed, but every time I'm in your presence I turn into a 12-year-old who has a crush on the prettiest girl in class (not that I think you are a girl). Most of the time, I'm at a loss for words. Quincy, before I met you, I was content on chillin' with myself being that I had just got out of a two-year relationship with my crazy trigger-happy ex. You've impressed me with your character, personality, honesty, sexy smile, and those beautiful eyes. When I look into those eyes, all I can see is me doing everything possible to make you happy. Your presence once gave me joy, but after last night all I can see is shame...shame for who you think I am now. There's something I've never told anyone since we or rather YOU decided that we can only be friends. Since that day and every day after, I cried for you. I prayed for you. I know you may not feel the same about me, but I feel differently. I feel like you have been holding back your true feelings. The feelings I have for you are what everyone in this lifestyle searches their entire lives for. Most never find it. Remember when I told you how music plays a big part in my life? So the fact that you love music too means the world to me. You mean the world to me, Quincy, which is why I had to leave for Atlanta. I don't know when I'm coming back. Please don't contact me unless your feelings change and you don't believe I am the person you saw last night. There's definitely more to my story. Anyway, I'm sure you'll find another "friend" to stay with. You keep being you. Don't let anyone change you for that's the Q I fell in love with. Until we see each other again… You're #1 fan, Ron.

Most of the mystery was solved. I could only assume the virus had taken a turn for the worse since he was on disability from work. And I couldn't blame him for wanting to escape me. I saw the dark side of him, serving as a reminder of the pain he went through the night before. It was time to pick myself up and find a new place to stay. I couldn't afford to have those goons return to finish the job. The first phone call I made was to Karyn.

"Hello?" said Karyn.

"Hey lady…"

"What's wrong, babe. You sound down."

"I am, but I'm fine. I just need a new place to stay," I said.

"Why? I thought Ron was behaving himself."

"I don't know how else to say this, but Ron was raped last night, Karyn."

There was silence on the other end. Maybe Karyn was not the right person to call in that moment. It had been about four or five years since her tragic ordeal with Vincent. I said, "I'm sorry, Karyn. You're the first person I thought to call. It was stupid of me."

"No. No worries. I'm fine. You can talk to me. What happened, Quincy?"

After struggling to divulge all the sordid details, Karyn remained strong. In a hurry to redirect the conversation, she insisted that I call Russ and move in with him as soon as possible.

She said, "I'm sure he will be glad to help out one of his best friends and you should make that happen tonight. I won't be able to sleep while you're still in that apartment."

"I hear you. Let me hit him up now. I'll call you back in a few."

Before disconnecting, Karyn finished by saying, "Q, I love you. I'm glad nothing happened to you."

"Love you too, Karyn," I said, fighting back tears. "I can't wait to see you again."

Russ picked up his phone right away and, without hesitation, drove over to help me pack. That's what friends do. Russ actually lived closer to the train station so my commute to work was cut by 10 to 15 minutes.

"It's time for a celebration, homie," said Russ after we lugged in my last box of belongings, mainly clothes.

"And what are we celebrating?" I asked. "I feel like shit."

"Come on, man, you're okay. Dudes never touched you. Ron did what was best for the both of you and one of my best friends is now my new roommate. There's plenty to celebrate if you ask me."

I watched Russ run around like a brazen streaker at a soccer game. There was alcohol on his mind. He kept the vodka in his room for some reason and found two clean mugs stashed away in a closet since the sink was filled with dirty dishes. He was definitely not as clean as Ron. While he mixed drinks, I called Karyn to place her mind at ease. I also took a moment to relax. Russ soon reappeared with two light-colored drinks. Thank God it was Friday.

"So, mi casa, su casa. We can share the rent and all utilities, which is another reason to celebrate. More money in my pocket," said Russ happily.

We both laughed and talked until Russ passed out on the couch from having too much liquor. I decided to stay up to greet the sun. I dug into my box full of toiletries to grab a bar of soap. My funk had gone from smelly to offensive. About 10 minutes into my shower, Russ walked in without knocking to take a leak.

"Do you want to replace these clear curtains at some point?" I asked out of pure curiosity, not insecurity.

"Nah, does it bother you?"

"Not really. I'm not that shy," I replied.

"And neither am I. We're two grown-ass men up in here. I'm going back to sleep, dude. Peace."

It was going to be a new and interesting arrangement.

Somebody Else's Guy

The scene was pure pandemonium. People were running and pushing each other out of the way. Women and children didn't stand a chance. It was survival of the fittest to the nth degree. A bloody, pale-faced Asian man screamed, "We can't stop it!" They were all in some cramped local shopping mall where all the stores had been closed to avoid costly damage. People were behaving like animals in a zoo during a 7.5-magnitude earthquake, but, in fact, there was only one large animal in the midst of the terror.

A large and wildly aggressive tiger was on a rampage, destroying whatever and whomever it came into contact with. Blood began to flow from every puncture wound in the thick crowd. No one could escape.

As frightening as it seemed, it was just a dream I'd had the previous night. I woke up butt-naked, drenched in body sweat. Drool soaked my pillow and my heart was pounding for at least the next ten minutes. My mind kept recalling the whole sequence over and over.

Strangely, I wasn't running in fear of the tiger because I was the tiger. Now how was I supposed to interpret that? Only God knows. Anyway, Monty's roommate had called and left a voicemail earlier in the day saying she had something to ask me. I hoped she was not expecting an invite to the housewarming party Russ and I were throwing that night, a couple of months after I moved in. We wanted to keep it small and intimate so the guest list was closed.

"Hey, Nicole, I got your message. How is everything?"

"Everything is fine. Can you talk seriously for a moment though? It's about Montero," she said, always calling him by his official first name.

"Yeah, I got a moment. What's the problem?" I asked.

"I don't know if it's a problem, but you were the first person I thought to call. Is your boy gay?"

It further proved how foolish she was since I was the first person she thought of regarding this question.

"Wow, okay, that's a deep one. Why would you ask that?" I said, needing more time to pull a lie together.

"Well, he has this new friend he's been obsessing over a bit. Supposedly, the guy is a singer who just got signed to Def Jam Records and there's just something fishy about him."

Nicole's gaydar was warped beyond repair. For whatever reason, she still didn't suspect my ongoing relationship with Monty. Besides, who was this new guy I hadn't heard anything about?

"Monty is a grown man, Nicole, so you should ask him yourself," I said. "I've never seen him get weird with another dude before so that does sound a bit crazy."

This was indeed the truth.

"Okay, you're right. I'll ask him when he gets in tonight if he comes home at all. I figured I'd ask you since you're one of my favorite friends of his. You always keep it real, babe."

Well, that night I planned on keeping it real by digging into Monty's ass about his new friend.

●●●

It was party time. The guests had begun to arrive. I'd already had about two shots of Patron while waiting for my entourage to get there. Karyn was there, of course, but I couldn't hog all her time. Russ was in love and couldn't separate himself from her for too long. Russ's younger sister also came up from South Jersey. I doubted many of his straight friends would've been willing to party with me and my rowdy gay bunch, or maybe he didn't invite them as he'd said he had. I understood though. Just because he was accepting of my sexuality didn't mean every other straight man would be.

Before I knew it though, everyone I invited actually showed up. I was in awe of my people—Karyn, Prince, Jordan, Roman, and even Shane. My big brother DJ also came through to show his love and support. However, Karyn, Russ, and I were the only ones aware of why my living situation with Ron had come to an abrupt end. Not everyone needs to know everything.

Surprisingly, Monty had the nerve to bring his new artist friend with him too. He had no clue what the night had in store. The Gemini in me was feeling especially messy and there was no turning back.

"So Chewbacca…" I said, noticing the long mane Monty's friend had hanging down his back.

"It's Bootnocka," he said while rolling his eyes.

"Yeah—mm-hmm—so how long have you known Monty?"

"About two weeks."

"And how did y'all meet?" I asked.

"My manager introduced us. Monty is helping to promote my debut album coming out on Def Jam."

I looked Bootnocka up and down. I didn't care if he noticed. It did seem to make him feel a bit tense until we caught eye contact. He was a cutie despite those fly-away split ends. Monty had pretty good taste. Bootnocka looked like he belonged in the Marley family. At a bit more than average height, you could tell he worked out. All he needed was the proper stylist to really boost his image.

"Why are you staring at me like that, homie?" he asked while laughing nervously.

"I'm still trying to figure it out," I replied with a clever smirk, then walked away.

My brother and I bumped into each other outside the kitchen. DJ had been spending most of the time talking to Russ and Karyn, which was, of course, where he felt more comfortable.

I asked, "Are you cool, bro? I'm really glad you came through. I appreciate it."

"Anything for my little bro," he said before putting me in a headlock and rubbing his knuckles across my freshly brushed waves.

"Get off of me," I screamed.

"Ha ha, your friends are cool too so far. I would snatch up that honey over there if it wasn't for your roommate."

He was referring to Karyn. I responded, "Yeah, that's my homegirl. She's a great friend and is right where she needs to be. You can't handle that. Anyway, what have you been up to? It's been months since the last time I saw you. Have you spoken to Mommy lately?"

"Nah, she hung up on me last time over some bullshit. I'm too old for her to still treat me like a little boy."

"Okay, but why did she hang up?" I asked, knowing our mother and that she had her reasons I was sure.

"Some shit about not calling her on Larry's birthday," he said. "I had to work."

I just looked at him with my usual little-brother-playing-big-brother expression. He had always been resistant to Mommy for reasons I had yet to understand. All of it preceded me. However, I couldn't sympathize with a grown-ass man behaving like a child around his mother. She could be a she-devil at times, but she was also the woman who gave birth to us. We owed her more than she owed us at that point. I wished my brothers would have gotten that.

"Okay, so when did the party move to my bedroom?" I joked, continuing my social rounds. Jordan, Shane, Roman, and Prince were all sprawled on my bed with drinks in hand.

"Q, come in, we're about to play truth or dare," said Prince, the messiest one of them all. "Roman, truth or dare?"

"Wow, straight for the throat huh, Prince?" I said. We all laughed. I could tell Roman was apprehensive. Nevertheless, he replied, "Truth."

"Boo—you're a punk," screamed his ex-boyfriend Shane. They appeared to be good friends finally. I hoped there was no resurgence of drunk Roman that night because if there was, I would have lost my mind.

"How many people in this room have you had sex with?" Prince inquired.

There was a hush over us all. We weren't sure about Roman's response. He was well sought after and could be very accommodating if he liked you in return.

"Three," said Roman referring to his relations a long time ago with Jordan and with Prince and, of course, his relationship with Shane. In the gay community, there are only about two to three degrees of separation versus the six degrees in the straight world so his response wasn't entirely surprising.

"Hey, what's going on in here?" said Bootnocka as he entered the room. Roman then changed his response to "four."

Monty soon followed Bootnocka, so I turned to Roman to ask, "Five?"

"No, it's still four, bitch," said Roman after punching me in the chest.

"I had to ask," I said while laughing.

"Wait. Hold up. What are y'all counting?" asked Bootnocka.

"The number of people Roman has had sex with in this room," I offered with delight.

He looked toward Roman before stating, "Oh, what the hell. The cat's out the bag now and I'm too drunk to kill it."

Bootnocka then leaned back against the wall and grabbed his crotch. Monty appeared to be surprised by his new friend's behavior. So much so that he rushed back out to the living room for some straight conversation. Jordan motioned Bootnocka to come have a seat on my bed.

"So who else besides me?" asked Bootnocka, regarding the number of people Roman had slept with.

"That wasn't the original question, besides it's my turn," said Roman. "Quincy, truth or dare?"

Unfortunately, I tended to become more daring when I drank so the fitting choice was, without a doubt, dare.

"I dare you to strip naked and run through the apartment." I shouted, "But my brother is out there."

We were hysterical at that point. Bootnocka had his eyes glued to me. Jordan was in the corner halfway covering his face with his hands. Shane and Roman seemed to have the best seats in the house, positioned right underneath me.

"Eeewww, you have hair on your ass," said Shane jokingly in his 15-year-old girl voice.

"Stop staring at it. I'm going to make this quick and I'm cupping my meat the whole way, thank you," I said.

Bootnocka got up to open the door and I ran through the hall into the kitchen where Russ's little sister was fixing a sandwich. I almost slipped on the turn from the kitchen into the living room. Russ jumped to his feet in the midst of a fist pump. Karyn screamed out loud then wouldn't stop laughing. Monty held his head in shame, but he had no right to judge me. Luckily, my brother had already snuck out of the party so there was no emotional trauma on that front. It was just some good ole streaking fun. I got dressed as quickly as possible. Bootnocka handed me each piece of my clothing, one by one, even down to my gray, reflective, crocodile Nike Dunks.

"Mm-hmm, Quincy and lover boy, come back over here so we can continue this game," said Jordan with his usual shady tone that always made me laugh.

"Yeah, it's my go," I said.

"Make it a hot one, honey," said Prince.

By then, Monty was in the room, standing by the door like he was ready to make a mad dash again if necessary. Russ and Karyn were in his room doing God knows what and Russ's sister was preparing to fall asleep on the living room couch watching television.

"Monty, are you playing?" I asked.

"Nope, just watching," he said.

"Anyway—Bootnocka, truth or dare?"

"Truth."

Jordan hopped up, clapped his hands twice like he was in church, then said, "Come on, people—this is a game for the daring. Truth is for pussies."

"Okay, then I'll take dare," said Bootnocka, changing the game.

"Amen," said Jordan and Shane in churchlike unison.

"I dare you to French kiss everyone in this room including Monty," I demanded.

Monty immediately ran to the bathroom. He looked angry, but so was I secretly. Bootnocka was not just a friend of his. Still, he hadn't come clean with me. The dare presented was well received by everyone else in the room though. Jordan bounced to the front of the line and straddled Bootnocka as he lay pinned to the mattress. We all hollered in amusement.

Roman then took position. This one was guaranteed to be even hotter. Bootnocka stood face to face with Roman and the moment began. Bootnocka caressed the back of Roman's head in a way that I'm sure seemed familiar to Roman. I had to get to the bottom of that story later.

Shane, who's more my height, was picked up in the air like a video ho by Bootnocka to execute their kiss. Prince chose to lie across the bed while Bootnocka did the straddling this time. About two minutes later, he turned to me. I was last, but definitely not least. However, Bootnocka simply stated, "I want to catch you when you least expect it. I'll let you know when I'm ready."

What could I have said in response to that? Absolutely nothing—I just blushed, then it was time to return to the game. Bootnocka, oddly enough, dared Roman to tell us all how they had originally met. The alcohol was doing wonders. Roman reluctantly admitted that they'd met online.

KillEve.com is like the Facebook of gay debauchery. Nearly every profile reads something like an escort ad. Guys strictly looking for just friendship are usually new to the site so they soon wind up getting with the program or ultimately deleting their accounts. I have an account with some racy pictures, but I have always refused to show my face. It's mainly a voyeuristic thing for me.

As for Roman, he puts it to more physical use. Roman confessed that they had sex the night they met and never saw each other again. This is how many undercover dudes like Bootnocka operate. What I wanted to know was who gave up the booty. Roman was the extreme pretty-boy type, yet he was pretty aggressive in bed, according to Shane. Bootnocka didn't come off as submissive so their rendezvous intrigued me.

About half past 3 a.m., I was awakened by a kiss. Bootnocka called it. I did not expect it at all. I looked around the room and realized that we all must've passed out soon after the game. There was indeed a ton of liquor flowing through our veins. Jordan, Roman and Shane found their spots on the floor on top of a couple of blankets. Roman was too damn pretty to snore like he did. Prince was sleeping next to me in my bed. I supposed Bootnocka had joined Monty in the living room at some point then snuck away to lock lips with me. The kiss was one I could never forget.

I then pulled him into the bathroom for some privacy, trying not to wake Monty in the living room. Unwittingly, we left the door ajar. Bootnocka kept rubbing up against me during our kiss and I could tell he was super excited. I reached down his pants to see if it was real. Not only was it real, it also had a smooth cut. Bootnocka was sexy all over.

I couldn't resist so I gave it a taste, leaving no area dry. He continued to let out an endless sigh. I quit before he could finish. He didn't know me well enough for all of that. It was in the nick of time too. Monty had just awakened to tell Bootnocka that it was time to go. He didn't suspect a thing. Jordan also soon woke up to take Roman and Shane home. I asked him to drop Prince off at the train station. I glanced over at my housewarming gifts on the coffee table. From the steak knives to the artwork, their love was felt.

Journal Entry #303

Friday, June 13, 2003
7:35 p.m.

It's been an absolutely crazy week at work after that crazy housewarming. My clueless yet slick boss Sean got fired from WUGH for taking money and other goods to play songs. It is actually against the law to do so. Sean defended himself by saying he never played a song solely based on the money. He would always say, "A hit speaks for itself." Then he turned the other cheek and said the labels and promoters are supposed to invest in their projects. I read online on some industry sites that Sean received over a half-million dollars' worth of stuff. And he was always taking a vacation somewhere with or without his family during his five-year stint at WUGH. Payola is wrong, but someone needs to recognize that the industry was built on payola. Back in the '50s, labels had no choice but to pay stations to get their records on air. Yeah, eventually, the law caught up to the practice and now independent promoters, like Monty, are hired to alleviate some of that suspicion. Basically, if one of them gets caught then the label can just scapegoat him. The labels have a product to sell and the stations help them sell it. It's give and take. And one can't exist without the other so the payments usually serve as a monetary thank you. The screwed-up part is it eliminates those players who can't afford to pay. Indie labels or even the local talent gets shut out of the process. That's what radio was also built to do—represent their community. Instead, now they wind up representing the interests of the major record labels—a huge disservice to music overall. But Sean knows a lot of people and has some great relationships so I'm sure he'll bounce back and end up at some other major-market station in the country. That's another thing about this industry or maybe any industry. One top exec just gets shuffled around from one label to the next, chasing that big money whether they were fired or not. All this shadiness would have pushed me away from music if it wasn't for perks, like going to concerts for free and drinking for free at all these listening parties and album-release parties and after-the-after-after-party parties. Last night, I was talking to Prince on the phone about the whole situation at work when he told me Trey is now dating Kevin. Is this payback? I date Mitch so Trey goes off and dates my ex? Karma is a truly bitch. It's been a while since me and Kevin broke up. I refuse to let them see me sweat, even though it does make me mad. Kevin did a number on me. I wish I knew exactly how I should feel about this instead of how I feel now. I wish I didn't blame myself for what went wrong. I feel stupid sometimes the way I allowed Kevin to play me. Anyway, Trey can have him. He can have Mitch too for that matter.

And to top it all off, I bumped into Gabriel again in my new neighborhood. He still looks the same—skinny, so damn cute, that chocolate skin, jet-black hair, and always a pair of some straight-out-the-box sneakers on his feet. The question I had was why was I bumping into this dude again just steps away my building? Of course, I asked him. Gabriel said that his father lives in this building too. He's been here for almost a year now so he was visiting. I felt a lump in my throat. When he was telling me this, I kept looking the building up and down as if it had done me wrong. What are the chances of me moving into this raggedy ass building where his father lives and how often will I run into Gabriel? I was thinking out loud and he responded quickly. He said, "I will see you as often as I need to." A taxi pulled up just then and Gabriel was out. That dude is really starting to creep me out.

Stronger

Our family reunion was taking place that day at Liberty State Park in Jersey City. My mom had received the invitation two months earlier. We did not make it though. She said she wasn't in the mood to deal with their bullshit. I really couldn't argue much because I never had the chance to bond with them while growing up. There was always this tension that I felt between us. My brothers, on the other hand, grew up knowing the whole family.

We were gathered at Mommy's studio apartment when she decided last minute to change plans. DJ was there, but Dino was not as usual. Dino would not have been himself if he appeared. I felt like the only one of her sons who refused to abandon her. She shouldn't have to bear the loss of all her children.

I could see DJ's mind churning a mile a minute in search of an excuse to bail. Since we weren't going to the reunion, why stick around? Mommy stayed one step ahead though and pushed a plate of hot soul food in his face—the little boy in him started licking and sucking on his fingers. Then he relaxed a bit longer to play big brother to me like he used to. We used to talk about everything back in the day. I could be totally honest with him because he was my big brother, my protector.

Still, up to that point, we never discussed my sexuality even though he must've figured it out after my housewarming. I don't know what he saw or heard that night. Mom kept looking at me out of the corner of her eye as if I was going to pick that moment to tell him I was gay and ruin the brother-to-brother vibe we were sharing. I was almost glad we didn't go to the reunion. The reunion would have been overflowing with some good food at the very least, but that day I got a chance to relive my childhood, back to a time when my big brother was present. But the moment was short-lived. DJ said his goodbyes before sundown. Mommy was happy the three of us were able to spend those few hours together.

"Can you clean up the kitchen, please?" she said as she walked out to go watch television. My response was insignificant.

After washing all the dishes and putting the food in the fridge, Mom and I fixed us two bowls of butter-pecan ice cream and put on a movie. It was some movie we came across on the Lifetime channel. The title never really mattered. They were all about a woman getting hurt, then overcoming her adversity by the end. Some were good to watch. Most were redundant. The one that we happened to catch halfway through was pretty good. We both stretched out on the couch and enjoyed the rest of the night. I couldn't believe that I used to sleep on that old worn-down couch, but it knocked me out, delaying my departure until morning.

●●●

Monday morning had again arrived and I treated it like a brand-new slate. Sean was officially out so I wanted to see how the day would flow without his influence. As soon as I walked in, the station owner, whom I had only met once, wanted to discuss my responsibilities. Mr. Martin Kolatch had bought WUGH about five years earlier and he had hired Sean himself.

It was a great opportunity for me to shine. I had to turn up the volume of my voice, relax and remember what my mother always taught me—treat people the way you would want to be treated.

After a condensed 60-minute conversation, Martin promoted me to assistant manager. He increased my responsibilities while he pursued a new programming director to replace Sean. Basically, he put me in charge of all talent booking in addition to my old, more administrative duties. I was so excited that I immediately sent out an email blast to all the promoters instructing them to begin calling me directly for all interview and promotional requests. Some of them hit back with congratulatory messages while others strictly wanted to know how long it would be before Sean's position would be refilled. Yes, I took it personally because it came from the promoters who never spoke to me when they visited the station. I simply replied, "TBD."

Other people in the industry were interested in the vacancy and how best they could apply. As time went on and digital technology evolved, jobs in the industry were shrinking. Physical sales of compact discs used to be the bread and butter for record labels. Thanks to the internet, kids no longer bought CDs. They could find it for free online. Still, oddly enough, the business model hadn't changed with the times. I just forwarded their resumes to Martin, hoping he would make the right choice.

The bulk of my day was spent filling one of Martin's requests. He wanted a list of the artists with new releases coming in the third and fourth quarters. A lot of research was required, but I pulled it together before the workday ended. On my way to the train, I got a call from Monty. He was one of the promoters I had emailed earlier.

"Congrats, sir," he said.

"Thanks, man. And where have you been? I haven't heard from you since my housewarming party last week."

"I'm cool, I'm cool," he responded.

"What does that mean?" I asked, refusing to ignore his shaky tone.

"It was just a lot to take in, Q. I'm not used to gay crowds like that where dudes are talking about dick and telling all their business."

"So you think my friends are super gay?" I asked while laughing.

It was interesting to hear what he must've been thinking that whole night.

"No, I didn't mean it like that," he said. "Come on, Q, you know me well enough by now."

"Do I? I didn't know you well enough to know about Bootnocka."

"What are you talking about?" he asked. "Did he say something to you?"

"No, your roommate said something to me. She asked me about you and him. She suspects more than you realize, Monty," I said as I could hear the steam blasting out of his ears into the phone.

"Yo, what the hell did you tell her?" he shouted.

"Calm down—I told Nicole to ask you herself. That's it. But, why can't you be honest with me about Bootnocka?"

"'Cause it has nothing to do with you. That's my boy," he emphasized.

By then, Monty was irate, screaming into the phone.

I said to him, "Monty, you and your boy have fun. I knew you weren't shit. You got issues, homie, and I'm tired of dealing with them."

He quickly responded, "And I'm tired of dealing with such a faggot who—"

Monty couldn't finish his verbal assault on me because I hung up the phone and hopped on the train. He seriously said that. Monty must've truly believed his bisexuality was equal to being straight. That was the way he talked to me, like a straight thug who got tricked into sex by a faggot. I had just started to get used to him being in my system. It took some practice and patience, but I compromised. Our friendship, I thought, was pure and only between us. Instead, I felt like a bad habit he wanted to break.

⬤⬤⬤

Later that night, my phone rang.

"So I heard about what happened," said Bootnocka.

"Did he tell you he called me a faggot?" I demanded.

"Wow, nah, he didn't say all that," Bootnocka said softly. "Yo, dude, I'm sorry you had to hear that. But you know Monty ain't ready for you."

"What are you talking about? We've been so-called dating for months. He knows me better than that. I can't wait to see him again so I can punch him dead in his face, then he can go play straight with the next faggot," I said as Bootnocka soon changed the subject. He went on to explain the real reason why he called.

"Let's hang out sometime, Q," he said.

I knew it was coming eventually. I was daydreaming that morning about the kiss we'd had at my housewarming. He put a spell on me. I hadn't felt that way since Kevin.

"So what would Monty have to say about that?" I asked.

"Are you serious? Monty dropped a dime and now I'm picking it up. And like I said, Monty ain't ready for you, Q."

Bootnocka was smooth with his words like songwriters should be. I agreed to hang out with him that weekend. We made no specific plans. We were going with the flow and underneath all the turmoil caused by Monty I could hear, in my head, violins play when Bootnocka came to mind. I was such a sucker for love.

I hopped into the shower for a quick rinse after another long day. Russ was watching television in his room before he barged into my room for the millionth time since I had been living there. I don't even know why I ever bothered to close my door. I was still butt-naked with the bottle of lotion in my hand. He gave me an odd look as if he'd caught me in the middle of a stroke.

When Russ realized what the lotion was really for, he jumped on top of me.

I cried out, "Dude, can I put some clothes on? You always do this shit."

"Hell no, punk," he said. "You ain't tough, I run shit up in here."

I struggled harder to push him off. By then, he had me in a chokehold from behind and his thighs were wrapped around my waist. He had on nothing but a pair of basketball shorts. They were his favorite pair and he wore them in the house every day. I rolled over again trying to break his hold. Russ had an erection. It was growing against my lower back, then he let me go.

"Dude, why are you hard?" I asked.

"Shut up, fool. If you were a man, you would know why," he replied sarcastically.

"Whatever—go handle that so I can finish getting ready for bed."

Russ stood there, spread his feet out a few inches and started feeling himself. I couldn't smell the alcohol, but I knew he must've had a few drinks. He wasn't running away like he normally would. He also wasn't moving at all in my direction. I was confused so I remained quiet. Russ, feeling himself even more, closed his eyes. I walked up to him with my hand extended out. I made contact with his body. He was mine in that moment. His eyes stayed closed. Gently, I massaged him. He took long, slow breaths. Taking position, I lowered my head to meet my hand. Just then, I think Karyn must have popped into both of our minds at the same time because we stopped.

"Hey, are you cool?" I questioned after pulling back, putting on a pair of my shorts and sitting on the bed.

"Yeah, dude, I'm cool," he said.

Russ had pulled up his shorts and started rubbing his hands against his face.

"Are you sure?" I asked. "I can't believe we were about to go there."

"Yeah, it's crazy," he said. "But I was just following your lead and you tried to take advantage of me, dude. That's not right."

Thank God Russ was joking. I didn't want to lose him as a friend.

I said, "But seriously…"

"I know, I know—it is your fault though kinda. I saw what you did to that singer dude at our housewarming. I had to pee and there you are Superhead in the bathroom."

"Well, that's what I get for not closing the damn door," I said. "But now you know Karyn can never ever…"

"Stop right there, don't even finish. Nothing happened. I don't want to lose either one of you," said Russ.

He went back to his room and closed his door, which he never did unless Karyn was visiting. I hoped that night wouldn't affect our friendship going forward, changing everything between us. I prayed Karyn would never find out I betrayed her briefly. She would never trust another man again, not even a gay man.

Control

My new responsibilities at work did not last long. After
only a few days, Martin had already hired Sean's replacement,
but not quite. It was the breaking-news alert that morning
as I walked into the station. Mercedes Newton was named
the new music director for WUGH and Martin had elected to
remain acting PD for the impending future. I couldn't blame
him for wanting to monitor his station more closely after what
happened with Sean. The Federal Communications Commission
is always watching, just like the streets.

Martin was a true businessman in every sense of the word
with an undergraduate degree in communications and a
doctorate in entertainment law, both from UCLA. However,
talent is not something one can study in a class. Some people
are born with it and Martin was not. Apparently, Mercedes
possessed many talents that impressed Martin so I had to do
my research. She had served as PD or MD for three different
stations in the three major markets of Chicago, Philadelphia and
Atlanta. She successfully made each one of those stations No. 1
in their respective markets. In short, she was a beast.

Martin took the two of us out to lunch to discuss his
rebranding strategy for the station. I always find it interesting
when you meet people who cannot seem to look you in the
eye for whatever reason. Mercedes must have been feeling
apprehensive about her new gig. Not once was I able to hold
her attention for any longer than 10 seconds. She, however,
kissed Martin's ass throughout the entire lunch. Every question

she had was directed toward him. My questions for her were glossed over and Martin didn't notice.

Finally, we made it back to the station and Mercedes wanted to meet with me one on one. She was beginning to remind me of the Toni Childs character from the television series Girlfriends. It was in her attitude, but she did not know as much about fashion. Once in her new office, she laid the law about her working style.

"I don't like to be caught off guard with pertinent information about day-to-day activities, especially involving my boss," she articulated. "I don't like nebulous information at all. Please keep it to yourself unless it involves me. Most importantly, never interrupt me when I'm talking."

She must have been referring to our earlier lunch. That must have been the reason why she barely paid me any attention. And where were her questions for me, regarding my working style? If that was how Mercedes was going to approach me on a brand-new slate, then I hoped she was prepared for a nasty fight. She stood to lose more than me.

Mercedes continued her dissertation for another 45 minutes. I interrupted her twice for clarification. I didn't care if it bothered her. I demanded the same amount of respect. We ran through the list of artist releases I'd submitted to Martin a few days before and she took issue with most of my recommendations. Everyone's opinion is not golden and no opinion really matters unless it becomes a proven fact.

Mercedes had a different perspective, but it didn't make my perspective wrong. She explained to me that she was going to rework the list based on her connections, never mind what the audience might respond to most or what the charts were saying. I refused to disagree since her title did read director. She went on to say that there was this new R&B singer newly signed to Def Jam she wanted to book. He supposedly had a great voice, was easy on the eyes and very charismatic. I had no idea she was describing Bootnocka.

"Please call Tina over at Def Jam and see when he's in our market for promo," she ordered. "I need to know before you leave today."

I left her office, returned to my desk, then called Bootnocka directly.

"'Sup, playboy?" he said after answering his phone. "You're not canceling on me, are you?"

"Nope, this is about business. My new boss wants to book you for an interview here at the station."

"I'm about to blow up," he shouted. "Were you telling 'em how dope I am and how my album will go diamond?"

"Okay, put your ego away," I said while smirking. "Give me your manager's info so I can get this thing booked, please."

Arrogance happens to be a bit of a virtue in entertainment. Bootnocka delivered the contact information. After that, I informed Mercedes that his management wanted to know our availability for the next week.

"Why did you call management?" she asked testily.

"Because I have a personal connection I wanted to utilize."

"Well, don't utilize it and call Tina like I said, please," she again demanded.

Her tone was very dismissive. I bit my tongue and made the call to Tina to handle the scheduling. Bootnocka was scheduled to come in for a brief 10- to 15-minute interview since his album was not yet complete. The label didn't want to blow their load too soon. Mercedes was satisfied.

The day ended and it was indeed a brand-new slate. While resting in bed that night watching the latest episode of America's Next Top Model, there was a knock at the door. Russ wasn't home and I was not expecting company. The knocks continued. By the time I made it to the door, there was no one in sight.

On the doormat, I found a magazine. It was an old issue of Essence from almost five years prior. I turned the cover page to find a small note that read:

Dear Quincy,

You may not remember this, but it is the magazine you were reading in the library the day we met and first exchanged numbers. I can't forget.

—Gabriel

It must have been a joke. Again, he could not be serious. I didn't even know what apartment his father stayed in otherwise I would have paid him a visit. It had been years and he was still holding on to the past. I know it was good, but not that good.

After taking another quick scan of the hallway, I took the magazine inside to join the rest of the periodicals on our cluttered coffee table. I knew I would eventually run into Gabriel again or he would find another way to run into me.

Do You Know (What You're Missing)

Bootnocka was scheduled to make an appearance at the station a couple of days later. Mercedes was waiting in her office for me to announce to her when they had arrived. I greeted them at the elevator. Bootnocka stepped off the elevator a bit shinier than I recalled. His dreadlocks were trimmed. His face was clean-shaven and the kicks on his feet had to be worth a few hundred dollars. That advance check from the label created a new man standing tall before my eyes. Tina, the label rep, looked surprised to see Bootnocka give me a full-on hug instead of a handshake.

"What's up, dude, it's good to see you," said Bootnocka cheerfully.

"Good to see you too," I said low enough so no one would hear. "You look sexy as hell."

I walked them to the green room and let Dove, our premier on-air personality, know that they had arrived. Dove and I had had a brief conversation earlier that morning about the new boss. Dove gave me some insight that she was well-known throughout the industry for being a difficult bitch. Overall, she was the type to tear down others just so she could get ahead. Dove advised me to always keep my eyes open and her advice was duly noted.

Right before Bootnocka was due on air, Mercedes came running into the green room saying that we both had to watch something in her office. Dove cued up a long commercial break to find out what the breaking news was about. Once we reached Mercedes's office, she told us to shut the door, then played a video on her desktop. The video featured none other than Bootnocka having oral sex with another man. It was major breaking news. I didn't know what to do or what to say. Mercedes and Dove were visibly mortified. I just stood there in shock as the two gay lovers went from oral to anal. Then, all at the same time, we recognized his sex partner. It was Monty.

Dove turned to me then said, "Oh my God, isn't that your boy Monty?"

I thought to myself—come on, Q, if there ever was a time to think quickly on your feet then the time is now.

"He's not my boy," I replied. "We don't talk like that anymore. But this is going to ruin his career. I can't believe it."

I could sense them looking at me out of the corner of their eyes, but I wasn't about to out myself based on someone else's bad situation. I needed to do it on my own terms. Besides, Monty had called me a faggot so he could kiss my ass as far as I was concerned. Bootnocka, however, needed at least a warning. I pulled out my cell to text him. Before I could finish the text, Mercedes and Dove ran into the green room to yank him into the interview before his team could become the wiser.

"Welcome back, y'all," said Dove, greeting the listeners. "As I mentioned before, we are joined today by one of Def Jam's latest signees. He goes by the name of Bootnocka. He's an amazing soulful singer and songwriter originally from Baltimore and has been endorsed by the likes of Brandy, Beyoncé and Diddy. Ah, but hold up, WUGH has obtained a groundbreaking new video featuring our new friend Bootnocka and it's not about the music."

"Oh, really?" Bootnocka said before snickering.

"Oh, yes," she laughed.

"So what is it, lady Dove?"

She replied, "We stumbled upon a sex tape with you in it and it's not with a woman. What's up with that, Bootnocka? Are you strictly knocking men's boots? Your audience deserves to know who you really are."

Suddenly, his manager stormed into the studio and dragged Bootnocka out by the arm before he could grab his water bottle to throw at Dove. Dove continued to berate him as he attempted to tear down the walls of the station. He was enraged. He kept asking his manager about the sex tape, but she had nothing to offer. I maintained my distance. There was no telling what he would say or do to me in that moment. In true form, Mercedes ordered me to follow them out of the building with a mini-cam so we could post the B-roll on the website. He happened to look back and noticed what I was trying to do.

"What the fuck, Q? Did you set me up?" he repeated again and again until he was out of sight, being carried away by his bodyguard.

I started to shake a little. I went straight to the restroom to pull myself together. It wasn't my fault, but it felt that way, like there was something more I could have done. I heard Mercedes paging me over the office intercom. I ignored it. Reluctantly, I called Monty to try to warn him. It went straight to voicemail. What else could I have done? I questioned whether I was somehow responsible for what happened. Those were two promising careers plummeting fast.

Another 10 minutes went by when my cell rang. Still seated on the closed toilet seat, I answered the unknown call.

"So I take it you saw the tape?" the semi-recognizable voice said from the other end.

"Who is this?" I asked.

"It's Nicole, Q—Montero's roommate."

"What tape are you talking about?" I said as I pretended to be stupid.

"The sex tape, Quincy," she confirmed. "With your boy and that gay-ass dread-head."

"Did you leak that tape, Nicole?"

"Sure did. He tried to play me," she explained. "A woman gotta do what a woman gotta do."

"Are you serious, Nicole? So destroy their lives 'cause you can't be happy?"

"Listen," she said. "I know he's your homeboy, but he has been lying to me for too long. He deserves everything he gets."

"And so do you, you miserable cunt. Why has it never occurred to you that Monty and I were fucking before Bootnocka came along?"

"What? When did…"

I ended the call.

My hiding spot was uncovered a few moments later. Mercedes had a field day telling me the reasons why she should fire me after I pulled my disappearing act. I just listened. She was right. It was my job and I made it too personal. Business and pleasure should never mix. Still, my heart went out to Bootnocka and even to Monty. My calls to them both through the night were still to no avail. I kept getting Monty's voicemail while Bootnocka's number had soon been disconnected. I assumed that meant our date that weekend was canceled.

Journal Entry #335

Thursday, July 3, 2003
11:00 a.m.

I had to skip work the day after that Bootnocka interview from hell. Mercedes is still mad I had the balls to do that since it was her first couple of weeks. But I was worried about Bootnocka. The start of his career was cut short just like that. I've been spending a lot of time watching his YouTube clips. One of my favorites has him getting dressed after a steaming hot shower, singing Jon B.'s "They Don't Know." The towel is beet-red and he sounds better than the original. He keeps trying not to show too much skin, but just enough to keep me and people like me glued to the screen. That boy is talented. But I still haven't heard from him. Def Jam's publicity machine is in full throttle. They had the video snatched down from every website. I heard the street teams are going around smashing all the copies being sold on the streets. The media is starting to forget not only the tape, but him also. It's all about the next story. Bootnocka's out of sight, out of mind basically. But I think the time will soon come for him to resurface with some hot new single that will have people bouncing in the clubs. Good music always prevails. So that's what the latest industry buzz is. Mercedes said in our last weekly meeting after having already heard some more of his album that she wanted to interview him again. However, the label won't be granting us another interview with him any time soon. I hope she's not surprised. I'm surprised they continue to book their other artists with us still. Someone must have some secrets. And I hear poor Monty moved out of that condo away from crazy-ass Nicole, staying with his family. I really hope everything is okay. No one knew about his alternative lifestyle. Monty hid it well. Monty hid me well since I never even saw a picture of his mom and dad. A few weeks have gone by so maybe we'll all soon forget. This has to blow over soon. I'm afraid for what my association with Monty will do to my career though. I don't want to be a casualty here. People don't understand how homophobic this male-dominated music industry can be despite the gays being all over the place. There's something ironic about it. Still, Monty doesn't deserve to be pulled out the closet like that. There's no happy ending in that. But me at home has been pretty normal. Russ hasn't been weird about me basically jerking him off that day. Actually, it's as if it never happened. I don't notice any change. Karyn was just here last night. Russ and I sandwiched her in his bed. There was no sex. We cuddled on her while watching the first season of The Sopranos on DVD. We had fun and thank God for that male code of silence. Russ scared me though when he told me and Karyn how he ran into Gabriel at the gym. Gabriel's got some guts nowadays. Russ said he noticed some dude staring at him from across the room, but chose to ignore the guy. Well, the dude eventually hopped every machine 'til he made his way closer to Russ. Gabriel introduces himself as my ex and tells Russ how we met. Russ swears that Gabriel looked as if he was high on something. I never understand how someone can pursue someone who keeps saying NO. You go that hard at work, not for love. I feel like I'm being stalked, but I can't be his victim. I will not be his helpless little victim.

 Stuck Pages, Vol. 1: Exposing the Heart of a Heartbreaker

Part Three (April 2004)

Tell Me If You Still Care

The Rude Boyz refused to quit. Roman and I walked into a hazy cloud of smoke while entering the Brooklyn headquarters to party with Prince that night. As usual, we were making another appearance at the Warehouse. We had marijuana, alcohol and some e-pills making their way through the apartment. Roman chose to tag along to witness all the fun instead of hearing me brag about it and, trust, no one minded Roman's beautiful presence. He was still one of the most attractive guys I'd ever come into contact with. I kept telling him to go model somewhere for some top agency, but he would just laugh it off. I guess he had very little imagination.

I also needed Roman's support in case I lost my cool. It was going to be my first time seeing Kevin in almost a year. Prince had been doing a great job of keeping us separated. He knew how hard it could be to get over the guy who was the first to rip open your heart. Still, I couldn't avoid him forever or avoid his steady boyfriend, Trey. It turned out that they were busy having regular sex in the same room Kevin and I first messed around in. The memories were taking a bit too long to fade.

Roman and I fixed ourselves a stiff drink, then joined Prince and the rest of the crew in his bedroom, the regular hangout. Of course, Roman and I both noticed a number of fresh faces. There were three to be exact. They all could have passed for the former R&B super-group B2K minus Raz B. Roman was probably trying to figure out which one of them was single and free. They were all his type. They were my type too so I hoped he picked wisely. I had my eye on the most vocal one. Prince then walked over to whisper in my ear that he was already taken.

"Who's taken?" I replied.

"The sexy shawty you keep staring at," he said. "Now, back up, boo—you're not even drunk yet."

I loved how direct most of my friends could be. We had no time for silly games. Prince briefed me on his latest relationship conquest. He called them conquests because he never knew how long he could stay faithful to just one person. Even though I had my challenges too, I was, at the end of the day, a monogamist. I believed in love, the true and unconditional kind of love. Prince, however, liked his variety and so did Roman. They were two of my only bad influences in terms of friends. Every Gemini needs to strike that balance between the good and the bad.

Getting back to the subject at hand, the Omarion lookalike, who apparently belonged to Prince, was killing me with his looks. He was literally the man I would have constructed if God gave me that ability.

His name was Anton. At 5'6" and about 135 pounds, I couldn't help but make him my main focus. He returned the favor pretty often. Prince wasn't worried though and seemed overly confident about the relationship. They had only known one another for two weeks, but Prince felt a serious connection. That's how some of the gays do. We fall in and out of love as if we never knew the meaning. I didn't want to test Anton's loyalty though. I respected my friendships way too much.

Anton's eyebrows provided the perfect amount of shade for his almond-shaped eyes. His nose and mouth were proportionate to the rest of his pretty face. I was truly exercising restraint and I needed Prince to recognize that. Roman had yet to get drunk so I hoped he also would show some restraint. I brought him to support my dilemma, not create a whole new one of his own. I'd much, much rather make love than have to get into another fight. I was sure we would have fun that night, or maybe I spoke too soon.

Kevin and Trey had walked into the room holding hands. I placed my drink on the windowsill. It could wait. My heart skipped a beat. In that moment, I realized that I really did still miss him, then, as quickly as it came, the moment passed. I picked back up my drink and smiled. The small talk ensued.

"Hey, Q, haven't seen you in a while. What's going on?" asked Trey while Kevin tried his damndest to ignore me.

"I'm good, man, just been busy with work and all. How are things with you and your relationship?" I asked.

We might as well put the cards on the table unless there was something I was not aware we should hide.

"No complaints. We love each other, isn't that right, baby?"

The question was directed toward his other half who still couldn't look me straight in the eye.

"Yeah, we're cool," replied Kevin in one of the most uninterested tones I had ever heard.

I simply nodded in the affirmative. Then, I joined Roman on the other side of the room. Out of concern, Roman gave me that are you okay look. I ignored it though because I wasn't sure how to respond. Nonetheless, the party had to go on. I just really hoped that night didn't become a disappointment. I wanted to have a good time.

After two hardcore drinks mixed and poured by Roman, I was definitely feeling better. My inhibitions were fleeting. In due time, the Rude Boyz had made our way to the Warehouse in typical fashion. It was like a rapper's entourage at an album-release party. But there were no rappers or, in fact, no one we recognized as rappers.

As soon as we hit the outdoor deck, I felt some random dude pull me by my arm to talk to him. I had no idea who he was, but, for some reason, a lot of Caribbean men think it's a turn-on for someone like me. They can be so extremely aggressive when there's alcohol in their systems. From the outside looking in, I'm slim pickings, which makes sense. My small frame somehow makes aggressive dudes like him feel as though I must be a bottom and a submissive one at that. My friends always enjoyed the entertainment of me giving a disgusted look then pulling away like he had a disease I didn't want to contract. In my eyes, it's not funny at all. Women don't even like to be treated that way so what makes one man think it's okay to do it to another man?

A bunch of us continued some of the illegal activities from the apartment on that deck. Soon, we were ready to hit the dance floor and scream over and over again above the music—Rude Boyz! It was nothing new.

Around us, there were those guys who loved and wanted to sleep with many of us, as well as the guys who despised our audacious nature that came to be simply because we were young, black and attractive. Someone would inevitably almost end up in a fight until the outsider would back down in fear of our sheer numbers. We fell into the Warehouse at least 20 people deep by the time we rebranded ourselves the Rude Boyz. You didn't have to like us, but you had better not disrespect us. That was our attitude.

The night came to an end and, once again, we made it back to Brooklyn without any altercations. I barely saw Kevin or Trey the whole night. I was proud that they kept their distance. However, the sight of them hugged up on the living room couch was making me want to vomit my 80-proof vodka all over them. Moving on is tough since there was no real closure.

Roman managed to behave himself that night. No drunk Roman's revenge occurred. Besides the three dudes he kissed at the club, he was by my side whenever I needed him to intervene, like in that moment. He grabbed me by the arm and we went to Prince's bedroom to sleep. It was only Prince and Anton in his king-size bed. My head hit the pillow and I was out cold. Next thing I knew there was someone at the foot of the bed shaking my leg in an attempt to wake me up. I sat upright and looked directly into Kevin's eyes.

"Can we talk?" he whispered.

"About what?" I replied.

"Someone might wake up so can we go out in the hallway?"

The clock read 6:33 a.m. The only noise in the apartment came from the radio left on in the living room. It was the WUGH weekend morning show actually. I followed Kevin into the building's stairwell. He didn't say a word until we both sat down on the steps side by side.

He said, "Look, I've just been thinking a lot lately and especially tonight. I knew I was going to see you, but—I mean…"

I could have driven a train through that gap between his words. Kevin was obviously nervous and wanted to collect the right thoughts.

"…I made a mistake," he continued. "Actually, I don't even know what I'm saying, but I know I miss you, Q, and I am sorry for what I did."

"What did you do? Do you really know what you did, Kevin?" I asked pushing him further. A simple apology wouldn't change what happened.

"I know exactly what I did and again, I miss you, and—I want you back."

"Dude, your boyfriend is right in there," I said.

"I don't care about him and he damn sure don't care anything about you if only you could hear some of the crazy shit that comes out his mouth about you. But I care about you. I always have. I was a stupid little boy when we met. I didn't know what I wanted back then."

"So, now you know what you want? What am I supposed to say to that? It's been almost two years, Kevin. Why now?"

He explained, "'Cause there's no one like you. The grass is not greener on the other side—all of that crap, Q. I didn't know back then, but now I do so I'm putting myself out there whether you feel me or not."

I thought for a moment. I always like to think before I speak. Regrets are what I try to avoid. No one had really had the kind of impact on me Kevin had. Secretly, I had always wanted him back, but never expected the opportunity to come. I told Kevin I needed to think about it. Chances were it wasn't going to happen though. I couldn't open up to him again when he was willing to break Trey's heart just to get what he thought he wanted. I was in Trey's position before and hated it when it happened to me. It really sucked not being able to trust someone you cared so much about. Kevin and I snuck back into our sleeping positions, hopefully without anyone noticing.

Later that morning, everyone went their separate ways. Trey was visibly confused by the fact that Kevin seemed to have warmed up to me in his sleep. He hugged me before they went out to grab breakfast. Prince and Roman also were confused. After explaining the bind I was in to two of my best friends, each of them said that it would be a huge mistake. Kevin could not be trusted. Prince also mentioned that he saw Kevin flirting at the club with one of Anton's friends. Supposedly, they lived in the same building complex, so my mind had been made up and, of course, I felt no need to even update Kevin. He was still the same person who dumped me on the eve of one of the best days of my life. Trey would learn his lesson soon enough, but it was really none of my concern.

On the walk home, I bumped into my father on Broad St. while he was driving. He pulled over for our usual predictable banter. He asked how I was doing, then how my mother was doing, then how my brother DJ was doing. He continued by asking when DJ was going to find a wife. I replied negatively. Then he followed up the rear by inquiring about my long-lost brother Dino. Again, I replied negatively. It was the same conversation every time, but I never knew exactly how it was going to end.

This time, he decided to end with an invitation to a church where he was going to be the guest preacher for the next couple of months. I hadn't been to church since my grandmother passed away. To me, it felt like I'd be walking into a set-up of the fire-and-brimstone kind. The doors would slam shut behind me. The ushers would rush toward me to restrain me from leaving while dragging me to the altar. All the parishioners would surround the pulpit chanting in Holy Ghost form. I would be unable to blink my eyes. My father would step forward continuously dousing me with holy water. The only salvation I would experience would occur by way of death.

In other words, I feared church. Actually, I feared a lot of religions. It had taken nearly my whole lifetime to accept that which I cannot change—my sexuality. However, I could not force others, including my father, to accept my newfound peace. He still believed I would change. He believed I would go to hell if I didn't change. So why would I want to willingly enter his church based on his beliefs? I just told him I'd made plans for that Sunday and I didn't feel bad for lying to him, considering the numerous times he had made promises and broke them without ever apologizing. The conversation finally ended and he drove off. I walked the rest of the way home.

Once inside, Russ got right down to business. We hadn't really spoken in depth to one another or been at home at the same time in months due to our hectic schedules. He immediately began his inquiries into the infamous sex tape and whether I knew about it in advance. I brought him up to speed on the incident at the station and how no one had seen Bootnocka or Monty in months. Russ just laughed. He laughed so hard, it broke me out of my laughter to think for a moment.

"What is so funny?" I exclaimed curiously.

"Dude, I respect you a lot for being who you are and being comfortable in your own skin, at least with me and Karyn. But those dudes were fooling themselves to think they could hide for too much longer. Karyn told me Monty really tried to play you too. They deserve what they got," he said.

I neglected to tell Russ about the f-word situation with Monty so I guess Karyn took that liberty. I wasn't mad. That's what partners do, they share. Russ also joked that he heard Bootnocka was teaming up with George Michael for his next single to be produced by Elton John and, to top it all off, Monty was going to be the love interest in the video. Russ couldn't help himself. I shook my head in light judgment. However, the jokes kept coming when he mentioned that the next party he was being paid to throw in the next few weeks was for Warner Music's latest hip-hop sensation, BFD.

"Salt Water Taffy" was their chart-topping debut single, which was comedy. Everyone mocked the song that soon became a No. 1 Billboard hit. Girls throughout every hood shook their salt water taffy with no shame, never mind the fact that salt water taffy doesn't actually jiggle. It's stiff and chewy, which is not sexy. The following night was the promo party and I was going to be in the building to witness the shucking and jiving firsthand with my flash camera in tow.

Never as Good as the First Time

The era of conscious and meaningful hip-hop had passed away after the new millennium. I saw it happening. It was a mistake for hip-hop to be called a lifestyle instead of a category of music. It is the way we live on many levels, but the circumstances are not fair. No one enjoys struggling in the ghetto and not knowing whether your loved one will make it home without being robbed or killed. It is not a healthy lifestyle to glorify or sing about.

On the other hand, hip-hop music's original intent was to be informative as well as poetic. The world was initially taken aback by some of the brutal language. All of it had a purpose to educate, uplift and shine light on the way we live in American ghettos. The fact that it evolved into a lifestyle just led the world to believe that we were proud of the unfair circumstances. Correction—we're black and we're proud as a people, not as a ghetto. Still, it was safe to assume that hip-hop would never be the same again.

A new generation was beginning to take over going into the 2000s. Their perspective was more watered-down and desensitized. Record labels then found a new cash cow by way of ringtones for cell phones. Teenagers have always been the biggest demographic buying popular music, and it became easier and flashier to download a song like "Salt Water Taffy" to your phone. Purchasing more than one ringtone became common and the cheesier the tune, the more ringtones it seemed to sell.

Developing new talent and real artists was no longer the strategy. It was cheaper to sign some desperate kids who could sell a million ringtones than to discover the next music icon. Thank God shows like American Idol came along. Whether you loved them or hated them, they brought some of the focus back to nurturing new talent. Still, acts like BFD thrived and I was looking forward to being entertained by the group the label classified as hip-hop.

●●●

As I was about to leave work to attend the BFD party, I received a call from Kevin. I sent it to voicemail. In it, he sounded a bit depressed or maybe it was his attempt to manipulate me into believing he was depressed and mournful over what used to be. I couldn't trust him. I didn't even want to talk to him because his words might strike the right chord in my heart. Kevin didn't deserve that. My plan was to continue avoiding him until I couldn't anymore.

I arrived at the party about an hour after it started. Industry folk usually liked to show up right before the artist appeared. I liked to arrive a bit earlier to avoid any madness outside at the door. It was my best friend's event, but I couldn't be sure if he would be at the door or if it would be some industry screener with a big ego. BFD had a current No. 1 hit so that brought out egos that would normally not be present otherwise. It was one of those events where people go to be seen as a mover-and-shaker, not because they support the artist's rise to fame.

The single "Salt Water Taffy" was blaring throughout the Cielo bar/nightclub, located in the Meatpacking District. The bar was fully stocked with Patron, the liquor sponsor. DJ Pound

Cake was spinning the latest hip-hop and R&B tracks. Nas, LL Cool J and Lil' Kim were all representatives of the past. By 2004, acts like BFD, Lil Jon and Chingy were top sellers. The hip-hop movement had indeed moved to the South. New York didn't have the clout it used to.

R&B music was suffering a separate fate. It was on a steady decline since the 1990s when hip-hop used R&B to get ahead. Bad Boy Records was a prime example of that. The platinum-selling trio Total was an R&B-singing group with strong hip-hop sensibilities. The Notorious B.I.G. murdered his verse on Total's "Can't You See," which became a classic over the years. It was a priceless collaboration. Fast forward to the 2000s and R&B had to use hip-hop to maintain its credibility and relevance (i.e., Usher using Lil Jon and Ludacris to help catapult his single "Yeah" to multi-platinum status).

As more guests began to arrive, I was blown away by how many people were still approaching me to ask questions about Monty and how he was doing. The sex-tape scandal was a diehard. The sweat began to build up on my forehead. I was unprepared for all the questioning so I just told everyone who asked that we didn't talk anymore. No one had the nerve to inquire further.

Then, fortunately, BFD made their way into the party. These guys were dressed like they were going to the prom with Shrek's baby sister. There were greens mixed with blues and oranges and other colors that should never be combined. Everyone wore their best poker faces and kept the shady comments to a minimum. In passing, Russ whispered, "Is the circus in town or what?" I couldn't stop smiling, which cleverly masked my judgment. Besides, after a few hours of a Patron open bar, no one was complaining.

●●●

The party was a hit. Russ accomplished the unthinkable and the label was more than pleased with how everything turned out. I was secretly wishing I would run into Monty at the event, but he was nowhere to be found. Again, my heart still went out to him. I was sure he needed a friend.

Russ and I rode the train back home to Newark, New Jersey. We were exhausted and both of us had to get up early the next morning. I had to work and he had an appointment at Atlantic Records to discuss the next event he was being contracted to coordinate. It was the usual routine as we walked into our apartment. We headed to our respective rooms to get undressed. Russ decided he would take a shower before going to bed and for the first time he paraded into the kitchen and through the living room with absolutely no clothes on. His private parts were on display and in full view. My flashbacks were thrilling. Still, I promised never to cross that line again. I know Russ felt the same way.

I hoped his nude strut was him being comfortable to do so considering we knew each other so well. If so, I had zero complaints. What gay man wouldn't want to see his beefy roommate walk around in the buff? It was the best of both worlds for me. We were great friends and I got to see all of him exposed. To stay out of trouble, we never again wrestled each other. Russ shouted out a simple goodnight to me before hopping into the shower. He did have me looking forward to some sweet dreams that night.

However, I woke up the next morning stressing about the nightmare I had overnight. I dreamed that Karyn walked in on what had occurred between Russ and me. Lo and behold, Gabriel was standing right behind her in the doorway. He was buckled over in laughter. Karyn's jaw was dropped. She started crying hysterically. I tried to jump up, but Russ kept pressing my face against his crotch. He wanted me to finish the job. Then Gabriel pulled out a knife and stabbed Karyn in the back right before I jolted myself up out of my sleep.

It was not a good start to what would be a stressful day. Mercedes had not eased up on me at work. She was so demanding and maniacal. She only cared if it was going to affect her job performance or lack thereof. She was quick to dismiss any concerns I might have, which was why I refused to use my relationship with Martin, the station owner, to my fullest advantage. I don't mind conflict. I never have as long as it leads to a middle ground of some kind. Arguing for the sake of arguing is pointless and I definitely hate wasting time on disagreements. Mercedes didn't seem to know the difference. She wanted it her way. In that case, Burger King is always hiring, but it was a radio station. Compromise was necessary. In time, I had faith that the conflict would work itself out.

I walked into the station a few minutes past 9 a.m. Mercedes had called a 9 a.m.-sharp meeting so, of course, I was late. I refused to take responsibility since she had called the meeting earlier that morning and called my phone to inform me in the middle of my morning commute. I couldn't make the trains move any faster. She rolled her eyes at me as I took my seat. She was going over the meeting's agenda. Somehow, Mercedes was able to convince the label to bring Bootnocka back to WUGH for an exclusive interview. Apparently, it was part of the label's strategy to revive his image and reputation, by bringing him back to the beginning of the madness.

We would premiere his official debut single and Bootnocka would explain on air that he is not gay. The person on the tape looked like him, but it was not. He would claim that the whole charade had been a ploy to destroy his career. Funny part was that they had a strong chance of pulling off the cover-up. The tape was rather hazy. Even though his face was visible, it could be argued that it was a lookalike. Mercedes said the single was, in fact, good enough to make the audience forgive him. However, none of us had heard it yet. The label was going to bring it with them to the interview and take it back once they left.

As soon as the meeting was over, my cell rang. It was an unknown number, but my intuition was telling me to answer it anyway. I was glad I did because it was Bootnocka calling.

"What's up, Quincy? What's new?" he asked.

"I've been trying to reach you for months and hoping you would call. Dude, it's good to hear your voice 'cause I never got the chance to explain what happened."

"There's no need. I understand now. You have a job to do and I don't believe you knew that would happen. I saw your text you sent me that day before I got the smack-down from your girl Dove over there," he said in jest. "My homegirl later had to explain to me that you were probably trying to warn me."

I assured him, "I was. I definitely was."

"But I think it's going to work out though. My label put together this whole story and we riding with it," said

Bootnocka. "I look forward to seeing you tomorrow. Make sure you save my new number. We still got a date to go on. I'll hit you up later."

I didn't get a chance to apologize and I guess he wasn't interested in an apology. It felt good though. I felt good. He seemed to be in a good place again. I hoped the cover-up-story crap would work. It was a long shot, but murderers have gotten off with worse defenses. Bootnocka was just a gay singer who didn't want to have to justify his sexuality at every turn of his career. If the cover-up made him feel better, then so be it. I was indeed looking forward to seeing him that next day as well as witnessing the interview.

Later, I spent most of the night talking to Prince on the phone. I told him about the numerous calls from Kevin wanting a final answer from me. We both convulsed over the situation. Trey thought he was still in heaven with Kevin. Sad thing was I think he was really trying to get payback for me dating his ex, Mitch. Poor, poor Trey—at least Mitch didn't do me dirty, or at least I never found out. Trey was going to lose his mind when Kevin eventually dumped him and he got hip to the fact that Kevin wanted me back the whole time. Karma can work for you or against you.

Prince and I also spoke about Bootnocka's interview the next day. Prince didn't believe the story would work, but he was not the average consumer. I maintained that if the song was really as good as they said it was people would be more than prepared to forgive and forget. Well, maybe not forget totally. In my opinion, that sex tape was equivalent to Kobe Bryant's rape case. Bootnocka didn't have that same type of celebrity, but if Kobe could get past that scandal based on his talents, then Bootnocka had a fighting chance. Bootnocka was poised to change the game of R&B. If Bootnocka could drop some seriously hot songs, he would be too valuable to lose and Def Jam was too used to winning.

Right before hanging up, I noticed that I had lost Prince's attention. It sounded as if he rolled over right on top of his official boyfriend, Anton. I said goodbye quickly. The last thing I needed was to be dreaming about Anton. I couldn't have him. My friendship with Prince was too important to me.

Full of Smoke

They were running 15 minutes late and Dove was doing a great job stalling the listeners who specifically tuned in to hear Bootnocka explain himself. The listeners were ringing the phones off the hook in an effort to ask Bootnocka personal questions. At first, we made the decision to keep the questions balanced. In other words, we wanted a question or two about his career, a question or two about his past and a question or two about the scandal. However, every caller wanted to ask a question about the scandal so we decided to increase the number of questions about the scandal to four so no listener would feel cheated. The callers always come first, rather that was what we wanted them to believe.

Another five minutes passed before Mercedes received the call that Bootnocka was on his way up to the studio. My pulse skyrocketed. I believe I was more anxious about seeing him than hearing the actual interview. Mercedes ran down to the elevator to handle the walk back personally. I waited outside the studio door. It was my job to cue Dove when he was coming around the corner. This was show-time.

"Sweethearts and gents, help me welcome back to WUGH one of the best up-and-coming voices of the next generation—Def Jam's own Bootnocka!"

"What's going on, people? Wow—I never thought I'd be back here. Good to see you, Dove."

"Is it really?" asked Dove. "'Cause you said some mean and strong stuff the last time we saw each other."

Bootnocka replied, "I said what I felt at the moment. And I don't want to do this dance again. I don't want us to start off on the wrong foot. I'm here to clear my name, not fight with you, beautiful."

Immediately, Dove's expression turned sour.

She said, "No need to flatter me, Bootnocka. I mean, are you saying now, as I've been told, that you're not attracted to the boys?"

"No, I am not. I never have and I never will be—"

Dove interrupted Bootnocka out of disbelief, then said, "So who is it on the sex tape giving oral and receiving anal sex from another man? You say that you're here to clear your name and I want you to have that opportunity. Our listeners have been calling all morning and afternoon dying to know the truth so please don't lie to all of the women who may still go out and support your debut album. But wait, don't respond just yet. We have to take a commercial break so it gives you a chance, Bootnocka, to think about how you're going to respond."

Dove closed that segment like a professional. This was like a dance. Bootnocka was one of the most promising R&B singers on the rise since Usher or R. Kelly. He had the full package, which was why Def Jam won the bidding war for his contract. Def Jam agreed to pay Bootnocka a million-dollar advance to sign with them. His sexy, rugged good looks and impeccable vocal tone and range made him a star by birthright. The scandal had derailed things somewhat, but so far he was not getting murdered in the interview. He just needed to remain confident and their plan might work.

Dove debuted Bootnocka's new song on the air after the commercial break. Our calls doubled in volume. It was a classic in the making that sounded like a remix of Mario's hit single "Let Me Love You."

"Without further ado, Bootnocka is here to plead his case to the listeners of WUGH. You have the mic, sir," said Dove.

Bootnocka took a deep breath and for the first time glanced in my direction. I don't think anyone noticed since they were busy hanging on his every word.

"I want all of my fans to know that I am not gay. It is not me on the tape. The other man on the tape is a con artist. Basically, this man wanted to manage me and I rejected him and then this tape appears after he learned that I signed my recording contract without him as my manager. It's an attempt to ruin me. And it's just that simple."

"Whoa, whoa, whoa, Bootnocka—I happen to actually know this other guy who's on the tape. He is well-known within the music industry. So you're telling us he set you up 'cause he couldn't be your manager?"

Bootnocka agreed, "That's exactly what I'm saying."

"And he recruited someone who looks just like you to put in this video too?" she asked.

"You know what I'm saying, Dove. I was so mad the last time I was here 'cause I know how much I love the ladies and it was crazy some of the stuff you were saying to me. I couldn't believe what was happening. I apologize to you since you were just doing your job. I mean that. But I swear on my grandmother it's not me in that tape and I can prove it."

"Okay, slick, what you got for us?" asked Dove.

"I'm not slick. I'm keeping it real. Dude in the video has this deep birthmark on his back that I don't have and I'll show you."

Sure enough, Bootnocka's back was smooth and free of any blemishes. Dove inspected thoroughly. She sat back in her chair and I watched this intelligent woman's defenses break down. The two of them started laughing and joking with each other. Dove mentioned that she felt the tape, as well as the acts on the tape, was vile and disturbing. She called out Monty on air, although not by name. She said if it was not true, then he had the right to challenge Bootnocka's claims. Until then, Bootnocka had received his pass from Dove. The callers had been supportive too. It's amazing how press works. One day you're a loser. The next day you're winning.

The interview was a success. Bootnocka and his camp were all smiles as they left the building. I was still a little dismayed at how it went down. I couldn't believe he was about to get off so easily. I wondered if Monty would resurface since his name had been stomped and spat upon. Bootnocka sent me a text soon after leaving the station. It was a proposal for dinner and a movie that weekend and I accepted.

●●●

Early Saturday morning, Karyn and I met for an overdue breakfast date. She was so busy with graduate school that we had to reschedule the breakfast twice. Russ, at least, was fortunate enough to catch her during her many class breaks. His entrepreneurial schedule allowed him to do that. Nevertheless, I was glad we made it happen. Karyn was the one friend who kept me grounded. I didn't have to pretend or hold back with her anymore. She got me.

The conversation was upbeat. She bragged about her 4.0 grade-point average and about how Russ was the best boyfriend in the world. I could have felt guilty at that moment if I hadn't buried the memory deep in my subconscious.

My breaking news to her about Bootnocka almost blew her out of her seat. She asked me if I could see myself with him considering everything that had happened. Honestly, I couldn't answer that until I spoke to him without all the lights, camera and action. He showed me a different side of himself during that last interview. Bootnocka stood up for his career and fought his way back into the hearts of his fans. I was really not the groupie type, but I had to admit that he turned me on.

Karyn, of course, warned me to be careful. He did slander Monty and he probably wouldn't hesitate to do it to me too if necessary. I also talked to Karyn about the situation with Kevin. Kevin was still calling daily trying to get the answer he wanted out of me. Karyn laughed at the whole thing. It was so ridiculous. Our next move was to do some shopping. We hit SoHo and spent a couple of hundred dollars because we could.

On our way out of Urban Outfitters, we bumped into Roman. Roman was on his way to Ford Models where he was going to meet with the creative director. They met at the club the night before. Roman was hoping the director would make good on his promise to feature him in a print campaign for Dolce & Gabbana. His big break had arrived. We wished him luck and I told him to call me immediately once he knew for sure. Karyn drooled her way through the next three stores. She kept talking about how good Roman looked and if she wasn't in a relationship—blah, blah, blah.

I walked her to her train so she could go study while I headed back home to get some rest and marvel over the outfit I had purchased to wear on my date with Bootnocka. Shopping is a habit for which I have no regrets. I'm not foolish with my money though. No piece of clothing is worth not being able to eat for a week. Now, for a day, I will make that sacrifice.

After I awoke from my nap, I noticed a missed call from Roman. He left a voicemail stating that he got the campaign and his life was about to change. As I was about to return his call, Bootnocka called in. The clock read 9:37 p.m. He was supposed to be picking me up at 10 p.m. I hopped up out of bed, then answered his call. He was in route to my place so I didn't have much time to shower and change clothes so I skipped the shower. I wore a canary-yellow, short-sleeved button-down shirt from Hugo Boss with a pair of dark True Religion blue jeans and my all-white high-top Adidas Originals. My haircut was still fresh too.

It was a brand-new record for me getting dressed in less than 20 minutes as Bootnocka was punctual. He pulled up in his new silver Cadillac CTS with the tinted windows for ultimate camouflage. It was a car fit for a celebrity and ripe for racial profiling so I advised him ahead of time to leave any illegal substances at home. His career could not bear another raid.

We rode off into the suburban hills of New Jersey to catch a movie. I wasted little time digging into his brain by asking, "So what happened to the birthmark on your back?"

He said, "I had to use part of my advance to get it surgically removed and it wasn't cheap, but it worked."

"Yeah, it worked. It took the hot spotlight off you but then you burnt Monty with it. How could you do that to him? Didn't he help you get your contract with Def Jam?"

"Is this an interrogation or a date?"

"It's a conversation about who you are as a person. Honestly, I don't know how I can trust you after what you did to Monty," I said.

"Monty will be okay. And I really can't talk too much about it, but Monty was taken care of."

"So you know where he is?" I asked. "And what does that mean, he was taken care of?"

The volume of the conversation increased a bit. He said, "Dude, please drop it. I signed an agreement that I wouldn't talk about it with nobody."

"Then you can take me back home since I don't know what else there is to talk about. It seems like you're willing to take down whomever to get ahead. I won't be your next victim."

Bootnocka pulled the car over onto the shoulder of the highway. He unbuckled his seatbelt so he could lean in toward me.

"Listen, dude, Monty is fine. I made sure of that before I agreed to say or do anything. Yes, he was a big help in getting me signed to Def Jam, but he wasn't an angel at all, Q. Have you forgiven him for calling you a faggot?"

"No, I haven't, but—"

Bootnocka cut my statement short, then finished, "Monty brought this on himself as far as I'm concerned. I didn't know his clueless roommate was his ex-girlfriend. We had a lot of sex in his room while she was home as if she wasn't ever going to figure it out. Monty didn't care about nobody but himself. You've known him longer than me. Have you ever met his children?"

"No," I answered.

"Exactly, it's because he barely visits them. You know that. He just sends the child support each month so he don't get locked up. And about my record contract, Monty wanted two-and-a-half times the percentage a manager normally gets. He's a selfish asshole so no I don't feel sorry for him. Like I said, he was taken care of. Now can we move on and enjoy our first date, please?"

The look in his eyes was warm. My antennas were static-free. He was right. I wanted Monty to be more than what he was. Still, at the end of the day, he was another grown-ass man who refused to take responsibility for his own decisions and here was this new man beside me with a bright future vying for my affection. But I had a couple more concerns to address.

"Can I ask just two more things? One, please tell me you don't have a grandmother to swear on, and two, do you really believe no one will ever find out for sure that you're gay?"

He said, "Well, one, my grandmother on my mother's side passed away before I was born. My father's mother was severely abusive so she can go to hell. Two, I will cross that bridge when I come to it. But unlike Monty, I don't expect you to live any differently. This is my choice so I do me and you do you. Cool?"

"Yeah, we're cool for now," I said.

"Brian," he said before reaching out to shake my hand.

"Pleasure to meet you, Brian," I said.

We forfeited the movie and decided to go straight to dinner. Over a plate of teriyaki chicken and sushi, Brian told me about his upbringing in his hometown of Baltimore. He grew up on the south side where he witnessed his older brother killed in a drug war. His parents, not able to carry the burden, split up a few months after the murder. Brian was only 15 years old at the time. Brian and his younger sister stayed with their mom while their father moved away to Los Angeles, California. They had been traveling to L.A. for summers ever since. That year was the first year Brian was not able to go based on his drama. It was much easier to stay low-key in Baltimore than L.A. He said his parents were worried that the sex tape would destroy his chances of reaching the superstardom he had worked so hard to achieve. Oddly enough though, Brian didn't seem to be worried much.

Dinner was gratifying. We substituted dessert for a lengthy French kiss in his car outside of my building. It felt just as good as the last one. I did manage to control my hands from wandering south. That wasn't the night for that. There would be others. We said our goodbyes then he skidded off down the block like it wasn't almost 3 a.m. in the morning. I looked up along the front of the building in search of any nosy neighbors and I found one—Gabriel. Our eyes locked, then I rolled mine, wishing I had never invited that boy into my life.

Journal Entry #394

Friday, July 21, 2004
8:38 p.m.

Oh my God, finally! Jordan, Roman and I were just on a three-way phone conversation and Jordan described my love life perfectly. He called me a serial monogamist. So I looked it up online. The website read—a societal mating practice in which individuals engage in sequential monogamous pairings. Basically, I romantically date one person at a time, but always looking out for that next date. The website also said that serial monogamy is closely linked to break-ups and divorce. When it seems so easy to jump from one relationship to another, the serial monogamist is very likely to escape. I don't know where this came from. My dream really is to find one man who can be as loyal and committed to me as I am to him. No secrets between us. No guessing games about how the other person feels. Of course, what someone looks like makes a big difference in this gay mating game, but that can go for everyone on the planet. We all want someone we are attracted to and want to have sex with and I don't think my standards are too high. Actually, I thought I had found that person in Kevin, then in Monty. It turned out I was wrong. But what am I doing wrong? I'm just following my heart, but Jordan thinks I'm following my dick instead. Roman had something to say, but I let it go in one ear and out the other. He can't talk. Still, I let him have his say. I love him for having his opinion. The more the conversation became about falling in love, the more quiet Jordan got. He kept dodging Roman's question about the last person he fell in love with. I knew Jordan wouldn't tell Roman that he's in love with him. I get it. Jordan realizes there's a strong chance he could scare Roman off so he'd rather keep him as a friend. Roman likes to run and hide from people he doesn't like sexually. On another note, I was lucky enough to have met the programming director for WUGH's rival station, WDDP. His name is Shelton Irwin. I met him at the Atlantic Records event put together by Russ. I'm thinking he might be able to help me out career-wise. Shelton spent most of that night hanging in VIP. He is also supposedly a friend of Mercedes's. I saw her hesitate introducing us. But I was excited 'cause I grew up listening to WDDP. WUGH only switched over to an urban format like five or six years ago. It used to be a rock station. WDDP is legendary though. It's how I first heard everyone from TLC to Jodeci to DMX. They were the first to play it all and Shelton has been with them as PD for over 15 years. It was truly an honor. He was so nice and humored me as I told him how much I loved his station. We exchanged numbers after he told me to contact him. His MD would be leaving soon so they decided to open up a couple of managerial positions as an alternative. Considering all I go through with Mercedes, a change of scenery isn't a bad idea. I reached out to him a few days ago, but he hasn't responded yet. And, of course, Brian and I have been seeing a lot of each other. To be safe, we haven't been going to any industry parties together because of the gossip that happens. Actually, we go so far as to barely speak to one another at different events. It works for us right now, keeping things private. He comes directly to my place to hang. It's easy to do since he's not a household name or face yet. It's only been a little over two months, but it feels so much

  Stuck Pages, Vol. 1: Exposing the Heart of a Heartbreaker

better this go 'round. I just love chilling with him. He keeps me laughing or thinking about something smart he just said. The music media have been calling him the Stevie Wonder of my generation. He sings like a raspy, caged bird, plays the keys with blurry fingers and wails on the drums. Billboard crowned him "Best New Artist," saying that he has the ability to bridge the generation gap. That's a ton of weight, but Brian is not backing down. It's one of the reasons why I like him so much. He's brave. He's also a little bit flamboyant behind closed doors, and he's bold enough to attempt dating me considering what it could do to both of our careers if folks found out. I see him at least two days a week now, mainly Sunday through Monday. The label and his management know not to bother him on those days unless it's an emergency or an appearance that's worth at least 50-grand. It's only a matter of time before people become suspicious though. This simply cannot last long. I just hope we don't get too caught up. I would hate to be blindsided like I was with Kevin.

Zoom

It was one of those days. For sure, it was a bright and sunny Saturday morning, but my mood was not aligning with the stars. I felt like I was floating outside of myself while my naked ego mocked me. My job was wearing me out. It didn't help to hear my industry peers continue to say sorry when they found out Mercedes was my boss. She had a hell of a reputation. Only her closest friends had nice things to say about her. Everyone else was just nice in their delivery. In short, she was stressing me so I needed to take a mental day off from work. I didn't want to be bothered by anyone. I turned my phone off.

Two hours later, I arrived on the sands of Point Pleasant Beach down along the Jersey shore. I went alone and planned to speak to no one unless they were a part of the ocean. The water scares me since I've forgotten how to swim. Apparently, some say it's a black thing.

I walked to the water's edge to inhale deeply. Ignoring the dingy shade of the ocean, I just listened to the waves crash against the shore. It was my alone time. No one else there on that beach mattered. Although, I did peek at the lifeguards to ensure they had a clear path to rescue me if necessary. I wanted to lose myself for a day, not a lifetime. Those suicidal thoughts have dissipated since my teenage years. My former psychologist would have been proud. Still, I wished I could figure out why I didn't feel proud.

There was not a cloud in the sky. It was sunbathing to the extreme. Then I suddenly lost it. While standing knee high in the ocean with my chin up, tears began to run down my face. They were not tears of joy. I was still in search for the real joy in my life. It was always there, just not always easy to see. It weighed on my mind that I was in a relationship where we couldn't express ourselves publicly. The mask and the disguise we wore felt unnatural. Brian seemed to be happy with it though.

I wished things were different. I literally woke up with the stress of work on my shoulders. How much longer could I take Mercedes's demands and disrespectfulness? And despite how hard I tried, I could not get DJ or Dino to understand our mother needed all three of her remaining boys.

Without warning, an ocean current managed to dislodge one of my feet from the wet sand underneath and I fell backwards into the water. My head was below water. I started freaking out. Then some strange lady in a long, white, chiffon dress dipped down, scooped her arm under my neck and brought me back on my feet. The nearest lifeguard stopped short of making the rescue. I wondered for a second how he would've executed it with his bulging body. Nonetheless, there was this flower child staring me directly in my eyes. She commented on the deep hue of red and cloudiness in mine. It was my best guess that the white lady was around 40 years old, a widow and listened to a lot of Janis Joplin. She spoke gently in a voice reminiscent of Cher's.

She asked, "Are you okay, my son?"

"I'm fine. Thanks for your help," I replied.

"No need to thank me, baby. It was all pre-destined just for you."

"Uh, what do you mean?"

She clarified, "Sweetheart, you have a lot on your mind and you need some grand answers, but you're not prepared for them."

"What are you, some kind of psychic?" I said lightheartedly, not expecting her to confirm.

"No, baby, I'm not. I'm a spiritual guide. Do you want to hear the truth about your situation? Or do I frighten you as much as your expression now indicates?"

I was scared. This lady was spooky as are most psychics. Then, before I knew it, she had moved inexplicably from my right side to my left. She whispered something in my ear I couldn't quite make out since my heart was pounding so loudly. She repeated it again in my ear.

She said, "Relax and know that you are capable of anything, but are you ready for the truth?"

Just like that, the woman faded into the background. Had she just delivered some sort of wild omen? What was that? How was I supposed to take that? It was ambiguous, yet typical. Leave it to a psycho to cause confusion then run off with your peace of mind. Still, I couldn't stop thinking about what she said. Was I ready for the truth?

On some level, I do believe in the supernatural. I believe the mind and spirit are capable of absolutely anything. The limitations are self-taught so I was not tripping over the fact that she was a psychic. I was tripping over what she said because I truly didn't know what the truth was. Her phrasing implied that I needed to have my guard up for something or someone. That was it. There wasn't much more to go off of.

On another level, I also think astrology (i.e., my Gemini nature) plays its part in the lives we choose to lead. Gemini is probably the most versatile sign of them all. According to Greek mythology, Gemini was the set of twin brothers, Castor and Pollux—sons of Zeus and brothers of Helen of Troy. Castor was mortal and Pollux was not. While on his deathbed, Castor was saved by his twin who convinced their father to allow him to share his own immortality. They were then converted into the Gemini constellation.

It was true. One side of me felt like an immortal combatant. On the other side, I was a flawed human being with the insecurities to match. Normally, I was on the good, strong and immortal side of my Gemini. It was the other side that made me question what I would do once I learned what the truth was.

The sun began to set on the horizon. It was time to head home. I didn't get a chance to listen to any music or really work on my tan since I was stuck in thought the whole time. There was always the next day if I felt up to it.

I walked by the lifeguard-post to thank him for being prepared to rescue me earlier in the day. A little flirtation never hurt anyone either. The lifeguard said he didn't recall that happening. I explained to him the entire ordeal, but he just stared at me like I was crazy. I was not crazy. I went on to tell him about the old white lady who pulled me up out of the water. He was saying that he saw me lay down in the water and it appeared as though I knew what I was doing. A few seconds later was when, as he said, I stood back on my feet.

Did I imagine it? No, it's not possible. The lady was real because I know what I saw. I know what she said. I know exactly what she was wearing, but I couldn't tell the lifeguard. He kept looking back at me as I walked away, I guess to see if I lost more of my mind in transit. I kept twisting my neck around to see his incredible body from behind. The exchange of looks came to an end as it was time to return to my life whether I was ready or not.

Anniversary

A little over a week later marked my three-month anniversary with Brian. I couldn't believe we'd made it that far. Unfortunately, Bootnocka was too recognizable by then so we celebrated the gay milestone indoors. Brian showed up again right on time. It was 9 a.m. and we had a full day ahead of us. I started cooking breakfast, preparing sandwiches for lunch and seasoning the night's dinner of grilled Cajun salmon and mixed veggies.

After breakfast, we watched the first of three movies for the day. Love, Actually is at the top of my list of romantic comedies largely because of the scene in which Mark confesses his love for Juliet using a stack of cue cards. It mixed that old Christmas cheer with good humor and a wide-open heart. There's not a woman or gay man in the world who wouldn't want to be in Juliet's shoes. Although, I believe most people would not have let him walk away that night without giving him a bit more than that cheesy kiss.

Then Brian followed up that flick with the 1999 gay film Trick. It's a movie about a lonely gay college student who meets the fling of his life on an NYC subway train. The fling also happens to be the stripper from the bar he visited earlier that evening. The attraction between two individuals from such completely different worlds is breathtaking. People are often more alike than we realize. Brian and I consummated the movie, then dug into our sandwiches for lunch. There was no way we could have kept our hands off each other for too much longer.

With a full stomach, I went into the bathroom to begin filling the tub with warm water and bubble-bath solution. I bathed Brian from head to toe. He couldn't stop smiling. I was glad Russ was not home to see it. I explained to Brian that there were only two rules: he could not touch himself and he could not touch me. It was part of my daylong appreciation gift to him. Silently, it was a gift to me also.

Since he had a debut album dropping in the next few weeks, Bootnocka had been working out even harder, maintaining his bubble butt I loved so gently. I hadn't felt that way for someone since I dated Kevin. Brian was a special kind of guy. He never let me see him sweat. It was like he matured tenfold since that blow-up at the station over a year prior. Besides the fact that we never really went out anymore, I had zero complaints. I actually thought I was falling in love with him.

Moments later, we were resting back on the living room couch when he said he had a surprise for me.

He started by saying, "Quincy, I want you to hear this song I've been working on this past week for the album. If you don't mind, I want to sing it to you. Cool?"

I gave him my blessing. Brian popped in the instrumental CD and began singing this soft ballad that had my name written all over it except no one else would have ever guessed. The lyrics spoke about our secret love that he hopes will blossom into a universal love. He understood us. He knew that double life would end if we didn't grow beyond it. The song, which had so much meaning, would be his signature ballad. That was just my assumption based on my expertise knowing good music when I hear it. I really thought I was falling in love.

We rounded out the movie selections with my all-time favorite movie, The Old Settler. Phylicia Rashad and Debbie Allen brought this film to light after having seen it performed on an off-Broadway stage. The screenplay tells the story of two sisters living in 1940s-era Harlem. The older sister, played by Phylicia, brings in a new roommate to help pay the bills. This new roommate is a much younger country man who eventually sweeps big sis' off her feet, but she soon comes crashing back down to earth after discovering some of his secrets. This movie delivers every time. I've seen it at least 50 times and this was Brian's first time watching it. Of course, he couldn't stop talking about that ending. It's definitely a gut-punch.

Dinner turned out great like that whole day in general. We kissed and kissed and kissed, then had more sex, which was on the borderline of us making love. Brian spent the night as usual. We headed out in the morning together as usual. I went off to work while he did the same at the studio. My baby had an album to drop.

●●●

Speaking of artists, pop icon Janet Jackson agreed to be the representative for our Aaliyah tribute that was going to go live on the WUGH website in two days, just in time for the anniversary the next month. There was no room for human error. It was the three-year anniversary of Aaliyah's tragic death. The tribute special featured the incomparable Janet Jackson, who also happened to be one of Aaliyah's idols, executing some of Aaliyah's signature dance moves. Janet had also surprisingly agreed to record an exclusive cover of "Are You That Somebody" for our WUGH listeners.

It was major. The label had already submitted the song to Mercedes and we all couldn't wait to hear the listeners' reactions. Janet slayed the song while adding her special touch to the arrangement. Time didn't permit a full-scale music video, which is why the song and performance video were separate offerings. The video was more amateur in its look and feel. It was simply Janet talking through some of her favorite Aaliyah dances. My responsibility was to make sure it all went according to plan. Mercedes had to stay behind for a meeting with the station owner to discuss next quarter's agenda. She was leaving the Aaliyah footage in my hands. I loved it. I was a very detailed person so that footage was supposed to be a breeze.

Before heading out into the field with our producer, director of photography and audio engineer, Mercedes ran down the list of everything we needed to capture. I inquired about the artist-release form that we required every artist to sign. It was a legal document giving us permission to use the footage anywhere and any way we pleased. The language was so loose that it amazed me how few artists, labels or managers actually took the time to read it. Once it was signed, there was no turning back. Mercedes told me not to concern myself with the form. She was working on it.

The shoot went off without a hitch. Janet arrived on time and gave 100% to the performance. I felt honored to be a part of something that I knew would surely be epic. Janet even kissed me on the cheek for being so nice to her during it all.

Once back at the station, Martin was beyond thrilled about the footage. We got a legendary entertainer at the top of her game paying homage to a fallen soldier gone way too soon. Not to mention, it was timely. Then Martin requested the release form so it wouldn't get misplaced or lost. I looked toward Mercedes for a response, but she just looked back at me like I had the answers. Martin was furious. He demanded to know whose responsibility it was to have the form signed. Our policy had always been that the artist had to sign before we began taping anything. We had been stuck with useless footage far too many times.

Again, Mercedes made me do all the talking until I explained that Mercedes said she would take care of it. I guess that was a mistake. Mercedes blasted back that I was the point person on that shoot and not to try to shift that responsibility onto her. I couldn't believe it. I know what I was told. Was she confused or scared for her job? Remembering how much she hated to be humiliated by her boss, I dropped my defense and gave in. Martin laid right into me like a honey badger on a beehive. I was also promptly written up for violating one of the business's most sacred rules. Mercedes never said another word.

After the ruckus, I paid Mercedes a visit in her office. She maintained that she never quite said what I said she said. Instead, she said her message was that she would help me get it if necessary, not to worry. It was literally a he said, she said moment. I felt trapped, not only in this situation, but in the job. Dove, and so many other industry friends, warned me about her. They were right. She was willing to do whatever it took to save her own ass. How was I supposed to work with a back-stabber? It was all I could think about throughout the week. Eventually, the label was kind enough to send over the release before the week ended. No harm was done, except to my career. One more false step and I knew I could be out of a job.

●●●

August 25th, for me, was not the great day that it was for everyone else at the station. It was a reminder of the lengths some people were willing to go to get ahead. I could barely even look at Mercedes at that point. I picked up my phone to call my idol Shelton Irwin from our rival station WDDP. He answered after the first ring.

"Hey, Mr. Irwin," I greeted him. "It's Quincy from WUGH checking to see how things are going in your world."

"Hey, Quincy, good to hear from you. Everything is straight over here. How about you?"

"Let's not discuss that now," I said jokingly. "I was wondering if you had some time this week to talk in depth regarding my future in this business. Hopefully, you can offer me some good insight."

My intention was to discuss my future at WDDP, but I couldn't tell him that over the phone.

He said, "Yeah, of course, are you free tonight?"

I was taken aback by how easy that was. Most people on his level like to lead you on for weeks, if not months, before actually making time to meet with a newbie to the industry like me.

"I sure am. Where did you want to meet?" I asked.

"Meet me at Bar 89 on Mercer in SoHo at 6 p.m. sharp. Please don't be late. I hate tardiness."

"I will be there at 6 p.m. sharp. See you soon. Thanks, Mr. Irwin."

"Please call me Shelton. See you at six, Quincy."

Bar 89 was a swanky bar/restaurant with great food and some infamous frosted-glass bathroom stalls. The glass door was transparent to the eye until someone locked it, which then activated the frost mechanism. Rumor had it that Bar 89 was frequented daily by kinky couples into exhibitionism.

Shelton kept his word by arriving precisely at 6 p.m. I just barely beat him as I took a position at the bar. He walked up to me all smiles to shake my hand.

"Good seeing you again, Quincy. I'm glad you called earlier. My apologies for not returning your previous calls."

"I know. You're a busy man. I get it," I assured him.

"So what are you drinking?" he asked.

In true executive fashion, he was getting right down to business. I ordered a Jack and Coke although a pina colada was at the forefront of my mind. The industry was big on appearances so I went for the manlier drink. Shelton shattered that notion by ordering himself a strawberry daiquiri. I really needed to work on being more confident in my decisions. The Jack and Coke burned.

"So what did you want to discuss?" asked Shelton, but before I could respond he followed up with, "Are you hungry? Let's get a booth. I definitely want to get some appetizers."

The lovely, blonde-haired, statuesque beauty doubling as hostess escorted us to a booth on the opposite wall. Shelton knew what he wanted without glancing at the menu. I wasn't hungry, but Shelton insisted that I eat some of the steamed shrimp and nachos. I then briefly explained my professional predicament to Shelton as we ate and he appeared to be engaged.

"Are you still close friends with Monty?" he inquired.

This green-with-envy question seemed out of place. I said, "No, I haven't spoken to him since the incident."

I prayed that he would change back the course of the conversation.

"Well, why not? You two were pretty close, right? I mean, I saw the two of you at every event," said Shelton.

"We were cool and used each other's connections to help further our careers. But he's gone now. I really want to talk about me if you don't mind."

Shelton pushed his plate of food to the side so he could lean in on his elbows.

He said, "Quincy, do me a favor and be honest with me. I knew Monty pretty well. I hooked him up with his very first promo gig. There's nothing you can say about him that would surprise me. Please don't play me for a fool. In fact, let me be straight with you. I can give you that dream job you've brought me here to ask for, but I need a little something in return."

"Such as, Mr. Irwin?" I responded. The formality was my attempt at keeping the conversation above the waist and professional.

"Okay, I said call me Shelton and since you want to play this game, let me just show you. Come with me," he directed.

Shelton rose up from the booth and began walking toward the restrooms. Like a shamed four-legged pet, I followed in his footsteps. It was clear that he was up to no good, but my curiosity was overwhelming me. The restroom was empty at that moment so he pulled me into one of the stalls and locked the door. The frost ensued as I gasped like my nana used to. He wrapped his fearless arms around my waist.

"Wait. Hold up. This is not what I'm looking for," I said forcefully.

"It is if you want the job. Stop frontin', Quincy. We're just two new friends getting to know one another, on the real."

His fishy breath and strong grip made it hard to consider anything except bailing from the situation. Besides, Shelton was not my type. He was nearly 20 years my senior and also dressed that way in a double-breasted, dull gray suit. After five seconds, I broke free, unlocked the door and returned to our table, leaving him in the stall stroking his ego. One restaurant patron gave me a disgusted look when I escaped from the stall with the dirty older man I just moments earlier had revered. It was shameful. Shelton was visibly disturbed when he made it back to the table.

He said, "Listen up, man—you have a lot to learn about this music biz if you think you're going to get ahead without doing a couple of favors. I'm going to be a nice guy and give you some time to think it over. I'm not asking for a lot here. I'm sure you gave Monty much more."

Those were Shelton's last words before exiting the bar. Fortunately, he dropped a one-hundred-dollar bill on the table to cover the tab. I felt like an idiot. I was then in a much worse position professionally. I called Brian for some consolation. He was disturbed to say the least. He brought me back to my senses. This was not the way to do business and it would not get me ahead. No man in his position would ever stop his advances and proposals after granting me the job. He was power-tripping because he knew he could. Brian also seemed to be somewhat concerned that I would even consider Shelton's demands for one second. I thought I was able to assure him that I wouldn't possibly have gone through with it, which was why I called him to talk it out. I hoped I was convincing. Losing some of Brian's trust over that douchebag would have driven me insane.

While taking the long walk of shame home, a familiar voice from my past startled me. I'm better with faces than I am with names, but her name was a hard one to forget. Dr. Cynthia Nutter taught my Voice and Speech Production class in my sophomore year at Rutgers University. She inspired me. It was as if she saw the real me I was born to be before life interrupted. I gleamed like a child star. She greeted me with open arms. Her energy had not changed one bit.

About five years earlier, I had shown up in Dr. Nutter's class while my peers did their best to select other instructors for the mandatory course. She had the reputation of being too intense. Some said she took her job way too seriously. For me, it was what I wanted. If I was paying for an education, then I wanted to get my money's worth. That's always been my attitude about anything I pay for.

Dr. Nutter took a liking to me from day one. Her goal for her students was to challenge, not just our hometown dialects and accents, but also to challenge our way of thinking. The purpose of her class was about acceptance of different people since discrimination was already too plentiful. She also happened to be the only African-American instructor of this course in the history of the university.

Coming from where I was coming from, Newark, N.J., I knew she could teach me much more than just enunciation. I learned that I was indeed different. She expressed to me privately after class one day that she could count on two hands how many black students had taken her class in her 10 years of teaching it. Standing apart from the crowd had always been one of my talents, but I was also raised in poverty. It was evident in the way I talked although I never noticed.

Ebonics was the term created in the 1990s by white elitists who wanted to segregate blacks who didn't sound like them. Fortunately, blacks by and large rejected and resented the term. In all actuality, what we possess is simply a dialect that I wasn't aware I had until I entered college and was exposed to people from around the world. In my ghetto, I was considered proper. In college, I was rudely awakened a number of times and I hated repeating myself again and again just to be understood. I took action to change it. Dr. Nutter was impressed with my commitment. She taught me code-switching. Being able to have a different yet personal voice fit for my current situation is priceless.

I can recall our very first presentation that I nailed even beyond my own expectations. Everyone had to write a poem and present it to the class. The poem had to touch upon the subject of self-esteem in some form. We would be graded on our creativity as well as our enunciation.

I wrote:

My Application

Authenticity Oftentimes
Doesn't express my insight.
Bending back and forth between classifications

Of what I choose to write.

Because you abandoned your verdict in my presence.
Then I somehow instinctively assumed that burden
With such reverence,

That I cried out
When I got stuck and fucked with the cock of fear
Encouraged by doubt.

Like the pansy I never wanted to be.

This application may be denied,
Like Prince, Ray Charles and Billie Holiday
Even after she died -
Initially deemed
By many decision-makers and career-breakers
To be unqualified.

Experience lacking.
No portrait of a barefoot dilapidated bohemian
backpacking.

I was brought here
Like a set of footprints in the sand.

Fresh carvings in my soul.

Paper bag removed from my head.
Striving
'Til my last breath soars
From the heavens of my deathbed.

You should know that I wasn't hiding.

Instead,
I dread the confines of popularity.
So my demons
Are sometimes more confident than me.

Or so they tell me.

I've been told that this position doesn't pay much.
And in this scheme,
This poetic scene
May seem to be a little nuts.
But passion has already been rewarded

So I sacrifice the bonuses.
The benefits.
The incentives,
I can't rely.

These are my own two feet.
In the pocket of a rhythm
Displaying my own drumbeat.

Now,

With my pleasure you bear witness
And I morph into gratitude.
My willingness to never quit this,
Now when can I be interviewed?

The class was dead silent when I finished. They sort of stared at me like I was butt-naked. Dr. Nutter began to applaud, which led to a standing ovation from everyone in class. I was humbled. Never did I think it was possible for me to move a crowd, but I did that day. Mine was the only A+ received and no one hated me for it.

Dr. Nutter brought it all back to me like it was yesterday. Seeing her again after all those years was not an accident. I needed to remember what I was capable of since I tended to get confused at times. She must've seen the uncertainty in my eyes because she simply said to me, before parting ways, "You're stronger and more talented than you realize, Quincy. Just believe or you'll lose everything."

Everything is Everything

I woke up the next morning feeling brand new, almost like a different person. Despite it being a gloomy and slightly chilly day in Manhattan, I had a spring in my step I hadn't felt in months, except when Brian was around. Maybe it was because I had finally made up my mind. My life wasn't going to change overnight, but my decisions could. It was the Quincy my mama raised me to be. I had been unsure about a lot of things up to that point when I knew deep down what was right. Shelton Irwin was not right. Working under Mercedes was not right. Dodging the persistent calls from Kevin was not right so that day I decided to answer. To my surprise, it wasn't Kevin's voice on the other end.

"Q, it's Trey. What's up with you?"

"Not much, on my way to work. What's on your mind at this hour of the morning?" I asked.

I really didn't need to ask, but I afforded him the courtesy.

"He's mine, Q," said Trey. "I don't know why he's been calling you so much for so long, but the fact is he's mine. I respected that thing you had with Mitch and now I'm asking you to respect what I have with Kevin."

"Well, the fact is you didn't respect what I had with Kevin. I came to you first before pursuing anything with Mitch. Next time I look up, you're with my ex, and not just my ex, but my first—my first boyfriend, my first love and now my first ex," I said angrily.

"Are you jealous, Q?" he said teasingly.

"This is petty. If you want to know the truth, please understand I am not jealous of anything you have. I have a man I love a whole lot right now."

That was the first time I said it out loud. I was in love with Brian.

"So please tell Kevin that I do not want him back and to please stop begging," I told Trey.

I actively disconnected the phone call. We were too old to fight over a boy who didn't realize he was a man with responsibilities.

Already onboard, the train seeped into the underground tunnel alleviating my angst about Trey's attempts to call back. I was sure he was overloading my voicemail at that very moment. Fortunately, Kevin was not on my mind. Brian was though. I had found myself falling in love again.

Later that night, Prince, of course, called for my side of the new battle of the exes. We laughed it up as Prince and I had become closer than Prince and Trey would have ever been. Trey's message for me delivered through Prince was that I had better stay away from Kevin or else. Since I had no intentions of being around Kevin, Trey's threat was not a factor.

What was becoming a huge factor was Prince's spike in drug use. He was the one who introduced me and a few of the other Rude Boyz to e-pills. During that period, Prince had added cocaine and sometimes heroin into his mix. He had been stone-high for our last five phone conversations over the previous couple of months. It was causing me to back away from one of my best friends in the whole world at a time when he probably needed me the most.

I just couldn't be there all the time like a number of his bad influences. They didn't have responsibilities. They coasted through their days and nights getting high and seeking the next high. It was anywhere between a half dozen and a dozen men staying in a three-bedroom apartment. Only a handful of them paid rent so there was nothing to do there but get high. Prince needed a new environment. However, I couldn't supply that for him and he would have never moved to Jersey. Instead, I prayed for him. I was thankful I had other things in my life keeping me busy.

Speaking of which, Brian had been super busy with his career. For the first time since we began dating, we hadn't seen each other in a couple of weeks. The label started flexing its muscle. They had him on a tight promo tour. His album dropped that very day and I couldn't feel more ambivalent about it. The buzz had been in his favor. He received a five-star album review from Rolling Stone magazine. VH1 had declared him an artist "You Oughta Know." Bootnocka's debut album was projected to sell over a half-million units in its first week. It was exciting news for his career, but not for our relationship. I wanted to see him more than ever before. I needed to share my secrets with him while I still had the nerve. I wondered if he was thinking the same about me.

Just then, Russ returned home from his daily jog through the park followed by an hour-long strength-building session at the local gym. It seemed like everyone around me was going hard in the gym while I stuck to my usual calisthenics routine. When he got in, I could see he was agitated for some reason. It turned out that he'd run into Gabriel again at the gym.

"So how's Quincy?" asked Gabriel according to Russ.

"Didn't you just run into him recently? And after speaking to him about you, we probably shouldn't be talking to one another," Russ had responded.

"Why is that? Do you have something to hide?"

Russ almost choked on his spit and it was clear to Gabriel that he had hit a nerve.

Russ told him, "Yo, what are you talking about, dude? Just leave me alone. You're nuts."

One thing insane people don't like to be called is crazy. Truly crazy people don't know they're crazy.

Gabriel, of course, fired back by saying, "Nuts? Ha—is that what this is about? Quincy has a way with nuts, doesn't he? The things that boy can do with his mouth is amazing. But I'm sure I don't have to tell you that."

Russ abruptly fled the scene and rushed home to confront me. He was steaming mad, not able to speak for a few moments, then the words gushed out. There we were, almost a year after, facing the mouth of the skeleton we both wished never existed in the first place. I had never seen Russ so upset. He kept pacing back and forth with very little eye contact. I assured myself that he wouldn't dare hit me. Before I lost faith in that affirmation, I assured him that Gabriel was and had always been crazy. He'd probably smelled blood then went on the attack with wild assumptions. Then I assumed the fact that Russ stormed out of the gym shirtless with only his sweaty basketball shorts and sneakers on probably confirmed Gabriel's suspicions.

Gabriel was going to become a bigger problem if I didn't stop him. He might go so far as to tell Karyn what he thought he had figured out. Karyn would be led to believe it was the truth just like Russ had. I could do little to ease Russ's trepidation. He retreated to his bedroom and shut his door.

Only a few seconds later, he shouted, "I trusted you."

That sent me exploding out the front door in search of Gabriel. His father said he wasn't home so I went to the gym to see if he was still stalking prey. He wasn't. My patience was getting thinner. The longer it took to track him down, the more conniving I figured he would become. I was sure of it.

The following morning, Russ apologized for overreacting to Gabriel's comments. He could see that he was being played and had probably planted more of a story than Gabriel could've imagined. I had a personal vendetta against Gabriel though. He seemed to be hell-bent on destroying the little happiness I had been able to acquire. I didn't know what to do, but I hoped I would have it figured out before Gabriel's main opportunity presented itself.

Russ also shared that Gabriel wasn't completely responsible for his foul mood the day before. Karyn had something to do with it. Two days prior, Karyn had bumped into her old flame Vincent on the street near school. Vincent served his minuscule one-year prison sentence and came off parole a couple of years later. Karyn had mentioned just the year before that she was dreading running into him again. Vincent never left the ghetto. He was still staying at home with his mother who lived just 10 blocks away from Karyn. It was surprising they hadn't seen each other much sooner. It was also surprising that Karyn didn't tell me first about it before she told Russ. I mean, he was her boyfriend so I couldn't be too bothered.

Russ said Vincent startled her by sneaking up from behind with his scare tactics as if the rape never occurred. Karyn was rendered speechless, of course. While frozen in fear, Vincent thought it would be a good idea to give Karyn a warm hug, again as if the rape never occurred. She said he still looked the same, yet stronger. Flashbacks of the night of the rape came and went. Karyn made an attempt at small talk before bluntly asking Vincent why he did it. It was the question that had haunted her all along. Russ took a long pause then proceeded to tell me that Vincent confessed that he didn't know he was doing something wrong.

In his own words, Vincent spoke about being the star basketball player with good grades and the perception and expectation that he had it all. That was until his friends discovered that he'd never had sex with his trophy girlfriend. It became the running joke. Vincent's manhood was called into question. They even began to accuse him of being gay since he couldn't get the girl. Vincent had the star power but was beginning to lose his teammates' respect.

After downing a couple bottles of champagne that night, he had been focused on getting what he wanted. Vincent admitted that he could think of nothing but his friends' reactions while in the moment of taking what he had always wanted from Karyn. It was never really even about Karyn. It was about his pride as a man. Like a ballplayer with less than five seconds left in the fourth quarter of a tied game, he scored. Karyn then asked why he couldn't just talk to her about it and Vincent responded by saying that it wouldn't have changed anything. No means no and he knows that now, he said. Vincent then apologized for what he did and how it may have affected her over the years.

Russ definitely needed some space. He had a lot on his mind. I knew how he felt. Karyn was the type of girl every man should want to protect, not harm. She was beautiful inside and out. Russ and I both couldn't protect her back then and we felt guilty about it. I hoped that was a chapter we could close and put behind us. Russ said that Karyn had finally been able to forgive Vincent after that conversation. Maybe one day, Karyn's father, Russ and I will forgive ourselves.

●●●

The shame was on me for having any doubts about my relationship. I was the very first person Brian called when he found out his debut album sold 676,233 units in its first week, snatching up the No. 1 position on SoundScan. It was the highest-selling debut for an R&B artist that year. That was a huge accomplishment when R&B sales had generally been on the decline. It was cause for a celebration, but Brian's promo-tour schedule was beyond packed. He called me from Los Angeles where he was performing at the Shrine Auditorium with T.I., Brandy and Kanye West. Kanye actually produced two tracks on Brian's album. The call didn't last long. He had to prepare for rehearsals. Brian was so excited though and it excited me that he was willing to include me in his happiness.

Before hanging up, he also told me that "I Can't Lie to You" was going to be the second single. They were going to begin shooting the music video the next day while in L.A. "I Can't Lie to You" was his signature ballad, dedicated to me, although no one knew it. The press had been pressuring him in interviews to reveal who it was written about since it seemed so personal and specific. It continued to be part of the label's strategy to milk the sex-tape scandal publicity for everything it was worth. In entertainment, any publicity can be good publicity. People were speculating whether it was indeed about a secret male lover or just a clever hoax. Brian, at the time, seemed unstoppable.

Journal Entry #492

Saturday, December 25, 2004
11:38 p.m.

The holiday season is here again. Stores are loaded with holiday cheer. Christmas decorations are on every light pole. It's a slow time of year especially in the music industry. During this period, you'd be hard-pressed to book an artist for an interview or even reach any execs by phone if you're not WNBC or something. Everybody is getting into refresh mode for the New Year. It's a time to clean out your email inbox, straighten up your work area and begin planning for any first-quarter releases and agendas. It's also a time of year when you are reminded of family and friends or lack thereof. Neither me, my brothers or my mother have ever been fond of the holidays. We never had that bond that I used to envy with other families. I was spared the drama my brothers had to endure and never really got inducted into my mother's side of the family. It made me yearn for what I didn't have. Now on my father's side, life was totally different. I had family around every corner in Jersey City. Reunions happened annually. Most of us went to the same church every Sunday, also in Jersey City on Communipaw Avenue. Afterwards, we all went to my grandmother's place to eat and the food was never a disappointment. My nana could really cook. I had no favorite dish because I loved them all—except the chit'lins. Whatever love I was missing from my father, I could get from his mother, his sisters, his brothers, or any one of my cousins. Sometimes I wonder what life would've been like if my mother wasn't so overbearing. Would I resent her now in the same way DJ and Dino do? But Larry never showed me any resentment in the short amount of time I was able to know him. The older I get, the more I realize that Larry had become the leader of this family. Now that he's gone, we've lost our way. And the holidays always remind us of this. The plan for Christmas this year was for the three of us to meet at Mommy's for a small dinner. We just could never count on Dino to show up. I came this morning to help her cut up the collard greens and season the chicken. DJ walked in just as we were about to count him out. The sun had already gone down. He was four hours late and said that he already ate with his girlfriend's family. Mommy was so mad. She cursed him out for being inconsiderate. She would've never bought so much food if she knew DJ wasn't going to be hungry. Mommy took a moment to grill him about why she hasn't met his new girlfriend yet when he revealed stupidly that he met her family almost six months ago. He said he meant to bring her to dinner tonight, but she had to work. What kind of work does she have to do on Christmas Day? I don't understand my brother. I know his new girlfriend has no idea what she's in for. The measure of a man is in his relationship with his mother. Once we got past the holiday tension, the three of us enjoyed each other's company. Mommy cooked baked chicken, collard greens, macaroni and cheese, white rice, green beans, cornbread, and banana pudding. We talked a bit about the old days when Larry was still alive and Dino had his innocence. DJ was close to tears. Larry was his rock he could always lean on. Dino looked up to Larry too. But I wonder if DJ realizes that I used to look up to him in the same way. With no gifts to exchange, the three of us parted ways. DJ went off to pick up his girlfriend from "work." I

went over to Jordan's to say Merry Christmas before coming back
home. Mommy turned in early as usual. Her curfew continues
to get shorter the older she gets. It's okay though. I got the chance
to speak to Brian briefly without my mother interrupting
because she wasn't getting all my attention. It's the ole guilt
trip of I don't get to see you that often as is. If there's one thing
I learned from being raised by my mother, it's that you do what
she says to do in her house or get out. This is a woman who is
used to loved ones walking out on her. Anyway, I haven't spoken
to Brian in over a week. He's now touring overseas in London
to help promote the album there. It's an amazing feeling to be
dating one of the most sought-after singers in music today.
The only thing that gets me down is thinking about how we've
only been able to spend five nights together since his album
came out three months ago. I'm suffering. I need to have sex with
my man. My sex drive is too high for me to be going through
a severe drought. I've been to the porno shop on 14th Street way
too much as a result. The workers now know my face. My
hormones are out of line right now so I need to see Brian as soon
as possible. And I missed him most while attending WUGH's
first annual holiday party a couple of weeks ago. The station
went big. Everyone, including Martin, brought their significant
others. There was karaoke, trivia, card games, and a performance
by Whitney Houston, who was extremely late, four-hours late
actually. She sang songs from her only Christmas album.
There was a moment during her performance when all the
couples were busy cuddling. Even Mercedes's evil ass managed
to scrounge up a date. How much longer can Brian and I keep
up this undercover thing? I keep thinking our love is too big
for all these small minds surrounding us. I'm falling hard for

him, basically, is what I'm trying to say. I can't wait to see him
again. Music-wise, he's still No. 1 on the Billboard 200 chart
with four Grammy nominations and the album last week went
double platinum. It's approaching seven-million units overseas.
He's flying into Chicago next week to tape a performance for
The Oprah Winfrey Show. But, he still won't have time for me.
And lastly, I have had enough of Prince and his drug habit.
I'm witnessing one of my best friends go from being a typical
pothead to a hardcore cokehead in just a few months and there's
nothing I can do to stop it. I'm outnumbered. He has too many
bad influences so I'm just hatin' if I say something. Prince
doesn't have much family so his friends are his family. Half of
the people in that apartment are on hardcore drugs, including
Trey. So I can only assume Kevin is using too. With work and
Brian on my mind, I haven't been able to see them as much as
I used to. Things do change though. Then there was that one
day last month I can't forget about. Prince and I got into that
elevator with a bunch of people all going to a friend's birthday
party. We were in this high-rise condominium in Dumbo,
Brooklyn. Passing the 30th floor, approaching the 51st floor
where the party was, I looked at Prince and he had streams of
blood dripping down from his nose. He couldn't feel a thing.
I used the reflection from the screen of my cell phone to show
him how serious it was. I pulled off my wife-beater to stop the
blood flow. Most of the guys in the elevator kept their distance
not knowing what Prince could have had in his system. Only
one nice dude helped me lie Prince down on his back once we got
to the 51st floor. The blood flow stopped and Prince said he felt
fine. But we didn't make it to the party. The party came to us
out in the hallway as news spread of Prince's nose bleed. Prince

 Stuck Pages, Vol. 1: Exposing the Heart of a Heartbreaker

was so embarrassed. He knew like so many of them knew. A nose bleed like that is usually associated with people who keep putting stuff in their noses that doesn't belong. I was hoping that incident would get him to slow down, but this is Prince. The boy lives on the edge of delusion.

Let It Flow

While en route to scout for new field-shoot locations in Yonkers for the second quarter, I spotted Monty sitting on a park bench talking with some boy. He was so deep in conversation that he didn't see me and the station's new intern, Iyesha, walk right past him at first. Iyesha, not having a clue who he was, gave me my distance to turn back and confront him alone. The guy he was with fell right under Monty's mode of operation. The dude was sexy. It was obvious that he owned a gym membership and appeared to be distracted by his charm. That was how Monty liked them.

"Monty," I plainly stated, standing in his periphery.

"Q? Wow, how have you been?" he said before giving me a man's hug.

"No—where have you been? Or is he the answer?" I asked amusingly referring to his male friend seated on the bench.

"Q—this is Tim. Tim—this is my ex Quincy."

It surprised me to hear him call me his ex. It was the first time Monty had ever classified me as anything personal to him. He just liked to always go with the flow.

Monty continued, "Tim has been a great help to me since, well, you know what happened."

"Yeah, seriously though, how are you? I've been worried about you in spite of what you said—" I said before Monty interrupted me.

"Dude, don't even do it. I won't go into detail here in front of everybody, but I was wrong, big time, for what I called you,

Q. It was me acting out. That's it. Being out of work all this time has me thinking about a lot of stuff I did wrong. But I'm good though. Def Jam took real good care of me, believe that," he said with a grin.

"What do you mean? Bri…uh—Bootnocka said they took care of you," I said with a slip of the tongue. "Was it a payout?"

"It was a payout, payoff, bribe, hush money—whatever you want to call it. It's taking care of my bills and supporting my kids. It's not taking care of my career though. I loved my job. I miss it. But that's my life. What's new with you though, Q?" he asked. "Who took my place?"

It was awkward. Monty drenched that last question in the lust of our past relationship right in front of his new playmate. I wish I could've warned the kid because I knew Monty couldn't have changed that much.

I replied, "Never mind that, I'm running late and still on the clock. Hit me up sometime if you still have my number."

"I do," he confirmed.

"Oh wait, quick question—what's the deal with Shelton Irwin? What does he know about you?" I asked.

"What? Why?" he inquired.

"Our paths keep crossing. I approached him some months back about working at WDDP. He mentioned he knew you."

"Stay away from that asshole, Q. He mentored me back in the day, then wanted to collect on his investment by fucking me. I'm not the first one he's approached and you won't be the last. But you don't need him. You got this, okay?"

He gave me some life and, in a look, assured me that he still cared. It was good to know our time together wasn't a complete waste. I nodded in his direction as if he was passing on great wisdom. I shook both of their hands, then linked back up with Iyesha to finish our day.

Three hours later, I got a text from Monty that read, It was good seeing you again. I replied the same. Soon after, Iyesha and I both received a text from Mercedes rushing us back to the station immediately. Getting off the elevator, we walked right into ground zero. Tables and chairs were almost unrecognizable. Spray paint scratched our throats and covered the walls throughout the station. The glass to the studio had been shattered into a million pieces. It seemed as though nothing was spared.

Mercedes informed us that the station had been vandalized by a handful of overzealous street rappers who wanted their music played on WUGH. I got the rest of Mercedes's sketchy story from Dove. Apparently, Mercedes promised these guys that she would add their song into rotation, but never intended to follow through on that promise. She said so to get rid of them. Therefore, Sammy McMurder and thugs took out their anger on the station. It was during work hours and there was nothing anyone had the guts to do about it. The goons held the lone security guard in the lobby at gunpoint. The police were called, but, of course, showed up a half hour too late to nab them. They were probably somewhere in far upstate New York laughing and joking about their thrill ride that day.

It's that street mentality in hip-hop that gets people killed. These rappers take their careers just as seriously as a Beethoven or a Mozart embraced classical music. Instead of batons, they sometimes wave guns. That's how it's done in the streets so why would the reflection of the streets known as hip-hop be any different? Sad thing was that the cops were aware of it too and tended not to treat incidents like this one with the proper amount of respect. Many cops think it's just part of the playing field that either needs to be dismantled or ignored. Seldom is there any middle ground.

That incident was documented by the authorities, but would never be resolved. They didn't care enough. To them, it was only hip-hop. We figured we would likely see those goons again at the next big industry party and we would all behave as if nothing ever happened.

Martin, however, was shaken up. He announced that he was shutting down the station for a couple of weeks so everyone had to work from home until all the equipment and supplies could be replaced. All on-air personalities would have a paid time off as the station would only broadcast continuous music, commercials and promos. He hired some small tech company to set up our wireless connections to work at home. It costs him a fortune, but it gave Martin some time to calm his nerves. He was literally shaking in his boots. I'm sure a rich Jewish man of his caliber had never before experienced something like that. I really hoped he wouldn't go off the deep end and sell the station, leaving all of us out of work. Only time would tell.

●●●

Running into Monty was the boost I needed. Since the previous summer, Shelton had continued to pursue something sexual. Now, armed with Monty's ammunition, I could feel comfortable telling him to go fuck off. I had been beginning to fall for his coercion due to my circumstances at WUGH. I felt trapped with little work experience to really pique the interest of some other radio-programming director. Mercedes didn't allow me to do much of anything but behave like a glorified assistant. Having Iyesha onboard, whom Mercedes hired personally, hadn't produced any different results. In fact, Iyesha spent more time with Mercedes than I did. They even went out to lunch together at least once a week. I had never been invited.

Out of the blue, I received an email from Prince's oh-so-fine boyfriend Anton, regarding his journey to finish college. He had mentioned to me a couple of weeks before that he had some college-related questions only I could answer since most of the Rude Boyz barely finished high school. He said he got my email address from Prince so I assumed our correspondence had already been pre-approved. Again, I didn't want any trouble. Anton asked some basic questions about credit transfers and course loads. I answered them to the best of my knowledge.

Before signing off, I did manage to sneak in a flirt or two. It's human nature and it was harmless. I could tell Anton was amused by the comment that read something along the lines of *I hope Prince is taking care of anything else you may need LOL.* He responded with a smiley face. There was no reason to go any further.

Full Moon

Every Sunday night you could catch the hysterically witty Harmonica Sunbeam at New York's Escuelita nightclub. Harmonica was a drag queen, essentially. Escuelita had been home-base for her comedic drag show, which attracted a young Latino and hip-hop crowd. Drag queens, in my opinion, have the strongest will to survive in a society where even gay men will shun them for being who they are. One cannot face that adversity unless they feel deeply that they have no other choice. It must be in the genes.

Still, drag queens can be a bit much. Most of them speak louder than my mother during her menstrual cycle. They always seem to fear nothing and no one. I guess it's where the best comedy originates from, that place inside the heart where you can laugh at all the pain that's eating you alive at times.

All across the country and in lands far away, there are drag queens causing multiple belly aches for audiences paying good money to hear some good jokes. Harmonica Sunbeam, a self-described comedian-in-drag and not actually a drag queen, hit funny with back-to-back combinations of humor. I had seen her out and about in New York City and she wasn't wearing drag. There was no shame she was harboring. It just appeared as though the drag was part of her act. He, or she, or however he or she liked to be called, separated himself or herself from the show. He looked like a regular guy sitting on the No. 2 train. I only recognized him because I never forget a face. I don't think anyone actually knew his real name, first or last. One thing for sure was that he was about his money as I heard again and again that he didn't play dress-up unless he was being paid to dress up.

That Sunday night, Jordan, Roman and I were going to check out the show. It started at 8 p.m. Jordan drove as usual. He picked up Roman first then scooped me soon after. The line at Escuelita was always wrapped around the corner, but it moved fast. Unfortunately, I didn't have the same pull there as I had at the Warehouse. The club was in Midtown Manhattan and sat in the basement two levels below ground. The steps were black, the walls were black and they had the nerve to have black lighting throughout the entrance area. Since no one wanted to be embarrassed by a bloody tumble downstairs, we held onto the stone-black walls on the way down. There were no handrails. We paid our fee before parting the large, black-leather curtain into two.

Once on the other side, Roman and I made our way through the crowd to reach the bar. Jordan simply followed. He was going to have one and not one more. Jordan was almost always the designated driver. He didn't always appreciate it. Fact was that Roman and I were younger than him. Jordan had his time of partying already. On top of that, I liked having a responsible friend in the group to keep a watch over us. It set my mind at ease.

Roman ordered the three of us Long Island iced teas. The drinks were pricey yet tough. I downed two of those drinks and I was feeling numb. That was when the party began. With only two minutes left before the start of the show, it was difficult to find a good viewpoint around the rectangular-shaped stage with the red-velvet curtain preventing us from seeing God knows what. The platform was about six inches higher than the standing-room floor. Harmonica's tongue would thrash catastrophically if someone decided to stay seated on the edge of the stage once the show started. Everyone got right up when those curtains were drawn.

The three of us found our spot stage-right behind a row of what Bobby Brown once called tender-ronis, so we took our positions. I got close enough to my favorite 'roni so that he would attempt to give me that back-up look, but realize last minute that he may want me to move in closer. Flirtation is an art form. Caught up in my moment, I looked over and saw Roman getting even closer to his chosen 'roni. That was the way we behaved sometimes. Jordan was not having as much luck though with his more mature and distant 'roni who was, Roman and I figured, too old to be even called a 'roni. We could tell he was older than either one of us, but still young enough for Jordan to be interested. Jordan's target kept glancing in his friends' direction as if to keep an eye on them. Roman was unaware of this. Jordan and I were, however, very much so paying attention while anticipating the start of the show.

The legendary Harmonica Sunbeam finally hit the stage when my 'roni was about to open his mouth to speak. Unlike Roman whose lip-lock with his 'roni was disrupted by the start of the show, I wanted to prolong the sexual tension between us. Besides, I did have a man. He hated these mind tricks I played on boys so he could never know how often I used them. I used them to get him.

Crossing that fine line of cheating was not an option though. I didn't know whether the grass was greener or just simply painted green. Brian made me happy, but flirting also stirred up feelings in me. It stirred up Jordan too. His target was beginning to open up to him, making sly remarks to Jordan during the show. He made me laugh a few times. My 'roni was still pretty and silent though and pretending to be mesmerized by Harmonica. Harmonica breezed through part one of her performance. Part two featured three male exotic strippers. There were new ones every week. The final act consisted of Harmonica's parting words as well as her lip-synch rendition of The Golden Girls theme song. She closed with it every single Sunday.

Following the show was the real time to party. The stage lowered, merging into the dance floor. Each of the three strippers gyrated their way to the three podiums strategically spaced out. All professional alcohol guzzlers headed to the bar for refreshers. That included our two 'ronis and the target. The three of them probably wanted to check out what the other side of the floor had to offer. Boys will be boys. As they were leaving us, my 'roni smiled and said "hello" as he brushed past my chest. I figured he was aiming to brush past a part of me much lower, but missed. I said "hello" in return. Roman's 'roni reluctantly pulled away from him to not break the bond he had with his friends. Jordan's target was the only one who gave up his phone number. Jordan nailed the bullseye.

Roman and I went to go get another drink, danced for the next two hours with random butch queens, then sought out Jordan. Party time was up. The crowd fizzled down to a skeleton of a dance floor. Many of them had to work in the a.m. except for me. I was enjoying my two weeks off.

Jordan was seated at the bar putting finishing touches on his bullseye. Roman and I were mistaken. He was not as old as he appeared to be in that other light by the stage. I actually told him so. He had a sense of humor so he just laughed at my bold statement. Jordan's target had a name. His name was Karl and he rode back to Jersey with us that night. He lived in Brooklyn not far from his other two friends who had hooked up and gone home with two other cuties from the club. Roman and I had scoped out the competition that appeared to be a homo-thug duo. Roman looked like a supermodel and I looked like a college-prep pretty boy. In our eyes, there was no real competition. It was a matter of taste.

It turned out that Karl was an assistant chef at the French eatery Daniel on East 65th Street. He studied at the Culinary Institute of America before getting that dream opportunity. His ultimate dream was to open his own critically acclaimed fine-dining restaurant. At 28 years of age, he was well on his way. I could see the sparkle in Jordan's eyes as Karl spoke. Jordan really lucked out. Chances were that Jordan would luck out again that night with Karl since they would be sharing the same bed. Jordan dropped both Roman and I off first. We said our goodbyes to Karl, but only momentarily. I was sure it was not the last we would see Chef Karl.

The Boy is Mine

After a long day of television watching and crotch grabbing, not only a straight man's hobby, a call came in from Prince around 11 p.m. I jumped at the opportunity to kick it on the phone with one of my best friends. Prince, however, broke my spirit by immediately saying, "Quincy can never be satisfied with just one man. You have to come for all of ours, huh?" I pulled the phone back from my ear to check the caller ID. I wanted to be clear that it was Prince on the other end. Then I heard Trey's sinister laugh in the background and realized I was on speakerphone.

"Why am I on speakerphone? You know how much I hate that," I said.

"Well, I hate that I trusted you, Quincy," Prince said angrily.

"What are you talking about? Can we get to the point, please?"

"First, it was Kevin. You couldn't let Trey just be happy in his relationship so they finally broke up thanks to you. And now I see you emailing my man making comments about taking care of his needs. Bitch, please. Who do you think you are?" yelled Prince.

"Prince, please take me off speaker because Trey has nothing to do with this. Kevin made his choice and you best to believe I had nothing to do with it. He's a whore, has always been a whore and Trey can't change that."

Prince turned off the speakerphone finally then responded, "Don't play with me, Quincy. Why were you emailing my man?"

"He emailed me about school stuff since he obviously couldn't come to you. I made one comment that was a joke hence the LOL at the end of the sentence. Do you even know what LOL means?" I laughed.

"I'm not dumb, Quincy."

"Then why are we having this conversation? It was a joke, Prince, and you know I wouldn't go after Anton because you're my friend."

"Whatever, bitch," said Prince. "I know you better than you think I do. You're just a slut and I don't trust sluts around me or my man."

"Is this really happening?" I asked.

I could hear more of Trey's inciting laughter in the background, which was making my blood boil. I told Prince, "Okay, get the hell off my phone and don't ever call me again. It's fucked up that you think I would try that after I spent so much energy avoiding Anton, and Kevin for that matter. You both can kiss my entire skinny ass."

I couldn't hit the end button hard enough on my cell. I was livid. In my mind, I could visualize myself blasting through my roof, fire blazing out of the soles of my feet, flying over to Brooklyn to handle the conflict face to face. It could have been the drugs forcing Prince to make those accusations based on an innocent email or it could have been Trey's bitterness over his break-up with Kevin, providing the ammunition Prince needed to confront me. Nonetheless, I called Jordan. He picked up immediately.

"I need your help," I said to him sincerely.

"What's wrong? What do you need, Q? You sound upset."

"I am. Prince just called accusing me of trying to take Anton from him and also for breaking up Kevin and Trey."

"Oh, Kevin finally dumped him too," Jordan chuckled.

"It's so not funny," I said. "I'm pissed off. I need a ride to Brooklyn. I won't be able to sit still long enough on that train."

"For what, Q?" asked Jordan.

"I want to beat his ass. I'll fight Trey too if he wants it. But I need you to also make sure I don't get jumped by those trifling addicts."

"Quincy, I will not. You are crazy. Calm down. Do you need me to come over there and lock you in tonight?"

"No," I said. "I need a ride. He knows me better than this. I respected his relationship from the start and told him so. How could he come at me like this now?"

"Isn't he still getting high on all kinds of dope?" asked Jordan.

"I guess."

"Then you don't need to be fooling with them anyway. They are self-destructing and you can't let them take you down with them. So calm down—take a cold shower or something, honey. You have too much to lose to go off the deep end like that."

I contemplated Jordan's wise words for a moment. He was right as usual, but I wasn't doing so well at calming down. Prince and I had been friends for almost five years. If anything, I know I deserved, at least, the benefit of the doubt. What are friends for otherwise? It was probably for the best. Prince and the Rude Boyz had become a bad influence in my life, from the drugs to the parties to the drama they loved to keep stirred up. I was certain Prince wouldn't be calling to apologize and I wasn't seeking an apology. Instead, I took Jordan's advice of taking a cold shower as I was burning up from the inside out.

Before turning in for the night, Russ barged into my room with some special news. Karyn was finally graduating later that week and he wanted to surprise her with a vacation to Aruba. where he was going to drop on one knee. It was no surprise. They had been serious about each other for over three years. I saw no signs of wear and tear like most relationships. He loved her more than ever before. Also, Karyn could not have been happier.

Russ had booked their flight for the next week so I was going to have the place to myself for the following two weeks. My instincts were screaming par-tay, but I was a bit partied out. It would have been great if Brian could have come to spend some time with me while Russ and Karyn were away. I didn't want to have to spend the entire time alone. Russ made me swear not to even communicate with Karyn until after they returned from Aruba. He said she was fishing for details about what he was planning since he'd told her to keep her schedule free. Russ couldn't trust that I would have been able to keep the surprise under wraps. It was fine. I was really good at keeping secrets, but also really bad at teasing people with them. Russ was right. I just needed not to communicate. Karyn knew me well enough to find clues where I wouldn't think they would be. I loved her for that.

Bad Habits

My two weeks away from work were almost up. Martin was reopening the station for business that Monday. It would all go back to normal. I was a bit anxious about it for obvious reasons. I had enjoyed the time away, yet I understood that nothing can last forever.

My brother DJ and I were meeting up for brunch that Saturday so I could get some things off my chest. Our relationship was becoming strained since I felt like I was being forced to choose sides between my brother and my mother. He told me things that he wanted to keep a secret from our mother when she already knew more than he gave her credit for. He never had anything pleasant to say about the woman who sacrificed everything to raise four boys. Not one of our fathers was man enough to really be a father.

My brother's father, George, whom he shared with Larry, was there on a financial basis, but couldn't deliver anything emotional to his two sons. If there was a physical altercation about to go down, George was there with his Muslim brethren in full force. However, when DJ needed to be schooled on his tough attitude, my mother had to do it alone. Whatever George gave, he gave out of his own guilt. Sometimes I wished my father felt that same guilt. Regardless, I needed to get deeper into DJ's head. I was going to behave like the big brother they always treated me as.

We met up at the local diner a few blocks from his new house where he resided with his girlfriend. He showed up right on time. My instincts were flaring, which was not a good sign. I didn't know where to begin.

"How's Marissa?" I asked inquiring about his girlfriend.

"She's good. How have you been?"

I said, "No complaints."

I mentioned to my big brother a few months back that I was seeing someone special, but he always failed to query as I was sure he would not have if I were straight. He must have known the truth since he kept ducking and dodging it like a bullet. I planned to spill the tea when Brian and I set our wedding date in the far future.

"Let me just get right to it, DJ. What happened between you and Mommy in the past?"

"What do you mean?" he responded by addressing my question with a question.

"Why do you shrink and behave like a stepchild around her?"

"You wouldn't understand, Quincy."

"Try me," I contested.

"The mother you know is different from the mother we grew up with."

"And?"

"And that's it. End of story. I don't know what you want me to say," he said.

I said, "I want you to tell me why a grown-ass man is still afraid of his aging mother."

"Quincy, that woman put us through hell when we were kids. She put the fear in us, then put us all out in the streets before we were 18, not even old enough to support ourselves. How am I supposed to act now?"

"Honestly, like a man—you're supposed to man up and show me, your little brother, what it's like to be a man. I've always wanted that, but you and Dino were too busy calling me big brother."

He said, "I love you, bro. I mean that, but this conversation cannot change the past. Now can we change the subject? I have some pretty major news."

I nodded in his direction. He broke the news that he and Marissa were expecting a child, the first for either of them. Then he followed up his great news with a plea not to tell Mommy. I was confused. How the hell was I supposed to keep something like that away from her? Was that even fair for him to ask? He was not even saying when he planned to tell her.

"Does Marissa know about all of this?" I asked. "Does she not ask why she hasn't met your mother yet?"

"She knows we don't get along. I told her I need some time before we bring my mother into all of this," he replied.

I had actually met Marissa for the first time a few months before. The two of us hit it off immediately. She was pretty, smart, educated, and had a great job that paid more in a week than DJ brought home in a month. It was obvious though that Marissa had been kept in the dark about her baby-father's family. At the time, I felt compelled to shed some light on the situation. I simply told her to be careful because DJ had done this before. He was always sweet, kind and endearing to his girlfriends in the beginning, then eventually his alternate personality surfaced with a vengeance.

Marissa wanted me to go further into detail, but I couldn't. He is my flesh and blood. I left her with a warning that she had chosen to ignore since there was a child on the way. The rest of our brunch was filled with talk about work and DJ contemplating asking Marissa to marry him. All I could do was shake my head. DJ ran off soon enough to join Marissa at her doctor's office for a prenatal visit.

No sooner than he could get up from the table and say goodbye, I got a call from Mommy. She called to brag, again, about hitting the Pick-4 lotto using Larry's birthdate. She hit at least twice a year ever since Larry passed on. She believed it was Larry's bittersweet gift to her from heaven. I let her know that I had just finished having brunch with DJ and my intended heart-to-heart conversation was a bust. She pressed for a reason why. Family secrets are supposed to be kept from people outside the immediate family, not from those within the family, especially not from the matriarch. Like only a mother could, she must have sensed the pregnancy.

She said, "Let me guess, his girlfriend is pregnant."

I couldn't lie to her about something like that. Mommy expressed her disappointment in DJ, but she refused to cry. She refused to show any sign of weakness. Actually, she took a moment to reflect.

"I've been through so much, Quincy, that I feel like I'm cursed," she said. "I feel like peace is not meant to be if I'm involved. I don't know peace. I was born to fight. I had to fight against my crazy grandmother who always made sure to let me know I wasn't worth the food she had to put on the table to feed me. Ruby was the only aunt to show love towards me, but then that gets tainted by these damn rumors that she was really my mother. I had an uncle who molested me very early on, then pointed a gun to my face as a teenager and said he would kill me if I ever told anyone. I'm a fighter. That's what

I do and that's the way I raised my boys. Unfortunately, DJ, Larry and Dino learned to fight too, but it was against me as their mother. I couldn't raise them by myself so I let my family help by babysitting and such. That was my mistake. It's my biggest regret in life. But I can't continue to fight this fight. I'm getting too old and so is he. If DJ doesn't want me to know his girlfriend or even his child, then so be it. I just wish he would have enough guts to tell me himself."

"Well, he did mention that he's afraid of you still," I said.

"That's bullshit. He's a grown-ass man about to be a father. Yeah, I was hard on them, but there's no need to be afraid of me. He just needs to respect me as his mother. I think it's something deeper that he doesn't want to talk about."

"Like what?" I asked.

"He probably blames me for Larry's death."

"How could you say that? I don't think so, Ma."

She explained, "His brother's death had a huge effect on him. He changed after that. He got meaner. I sent Larry off to Job Corps when he was 16 and completely out of control. It landed him in Denver, Colorado, where he stayed and that's where he died. Maybe it wouldn't have happened if I fought a little bit harder to keep him in line at home. Maybe one of us would've been at home with him when he had the aneurysm instead of him dying alone in his cramped house. And maybe my sons wouldn't hate me so much right now."

The conversation came to a close as my call dropped. I attempted to call her back a dozen times, but it just rang and rang, then went straight to voicemail. I was sure it was her way of saying I don't want to talk about it anymore. I understood our mother in ways I wished they did. Her heart was heavy and she had lost her will to fight in her old age. However, that conversation with DJ helped me put some things into perspective. I could no longer be in the middle. My mother needed me more than he did. Until he could man-up and deal with his mommy issues, I was unavailable. I deleted his contact information so I wouldn't be tempted. I wished DJ, Marissa and my new nephew well. As time went by, I prayed our deep wounds would heal.

Once home, my cell rang again with an unidentified number on the caller ID. Rarely did I ever answer anonymous calls, but I was feeling a little frisky at that moment. Surprisingly, it was Anton calling to check up on me. He had heard about Prince's accusations, through Prince, of course. Anton said he had broken it off with Prince. He added that it was primarily about Prince's jealousy. It was not their first argument of that nature. They had some physical battles trying to find a resolution for their reoccurring conflicts. Yet, every day exposed a new layer of conflict and the drugs weren't helping. Anton couldn't take it anymore. He explained it all to me in a span of 15 minutes.

We spent the next 15 minutes discussing his education. He had taken my advice. It was best to get the basic courses out of the way first so he wouldn't lose many credits if he decided to transfer to a different school. At the end of our 30-minute session, I suggested we hang out soon. There was nothing holding me back anymore. But it was sooner than I expected because he invited me to hang with him and two other friends at his house that night. His parents were away on vacation. I had less than three hours to get to Brooklyn before the start of their weekly movie night.

I walked down to the train, then hopped on the subway and arrived about two minutes late. The Lord of the Rings was blasting on the surround-sound. I had seen the movie twice already, but not in such an intimate setting. In the living room, there were the three of them snuggled underneath a large fleece blanket. The 60-inch flat-screen television hung on the opposite wall. Anton pulled up one end of the covers to let me in. I went ahead and got comfortable, removing my shirt, sneakers and jeans since they were in their underwear.

It was fun. Weed was being passed around. One of Anton's friends, Sam, made cocktails. Anton and I got a bit distracted halfway through the movie. Our hands began to wander across each other's bodies. He felt good. I imagined I must have felt good to him too. We tried to hide our movement so there would be no heckling from Anton's other friend at the opposite end of the couch.

Rashawn was not the most attractive guy in the room and he wore that fact on his sleeve. I had seen him out a few times in the clubs. He always seemed to be chasing some boy he couldn't have. It was always some boy out of his league. Rashawn wasn't ugly, but also wasn't average. Sam, on the other hand, was about six feet, two inches tall and slender. He was brown skinned with a pair of the fullest clean-cut eyebrows I'd ever want to see on a man.

Before long, Anton got up to go upstairs. Sam followed suit a minute later. Rashawn and I looked at each other, then decided to give chase. I wanted to know what was happening up there. Anton's bedroom was directly ahead of the staircase. The door was wide open as Sam and Anton sat on the edge of the bed talking. Rashawn asked why they came upstairs. Anton told him to shut his mouth and go back downstairs. It was rude, but apparently Rashawn was used to it. Then Anton got up, shoved Rashawn outside the room and locked the door behind me. There must've been a plan in action.

Anton ordered Sam to take his underwear off. I just stood and watched. Sam was shy at first. He acted like he didn't hear the command. Anton repeated himself while Rashawn banged on the door trying to get back in. For extra motivation, Anton leaned in and kissed Sam. I rubbed both of their backs. Sam's right hand reached in the front opening of my boxers, introducing me to Anton's mouth. They took turns performing. I lay down between them. We kissed, squirmed and grinded all over Anton's bed. Rashawn eventually gave up knocking. We were making the only audible sounds in the house at that point.

Anton surprised me when he pulled out a condom I didn't know he was reaching for. He put it on, but Sam and I both shook our heads in disapproval. I hadn't come prepared for that. I really wished I had known. We just finished each other off in a hurry. Anton seemed to be slightly disappointed. I bet he'd planned for a much more in-depth experience. Nevertheless, we swore to keep it amongst ourselves. No one needed to know what happened, especially not Prince.

The three of us made it back downstairs to join Rashawn who was mad at us for not letting him in. He pouted his way through the end of the movie as well as on our journey home to Jersey where the three of us lived. Sam dropped me and Rashawn off. That had to be the most exhausting movie night of my life. I couldn't wait for the next one.

●●●

A brand-new day had come complete with a ton of guilt about what happened the night before. It had slipped my mind that people in committed relationships are not allowed to do what I did. Most of my last day before returning to work was consumed by me moping around the house. The guilt was like a prison. I couldn't escape it. The only thing that made me feel somewhat better was thinking about all the desirable situations Brian must have been affected by while touring the world. He must have fooled around with at least one or two guys overseas and it was something I would never find out. Considering that, I couldn't beat myself up too much.

My moody funk soon ended when there was a knock at the front door. I was not expecting company so the first person I thought it could be was Gabriel. Was he leaving another unwanted gift on my doorstep? I rushed to the door barefoot and shirtless. Gabriel and I still needed to discuss his last run-in with my roommate. But on the other side stood one of the sexiest men I had ever seen in my life. It was my Brian. He was passing through town that night on his way to Philly to do an in-store signing. I had 90 minutes to say hello and lay my body on top of his. I didn't even want to think about how long it had been since we'd had sex.

Brian was just as excited as I was. He talked so fast. He stripped so fast. We lost ourselves in the moment until time ran out. His phone started blowing up immediately. The road crew was just blocks away, coming to take my man away from me once again. I did get a chance to mention that I had run into Monty recently. Brian was happy that I was able to finally close that chapter of my life. Going forward, it was about Brian. And he kept looking better and better every time I saw him. This was real love.

On Monday morning, I was speechless as Martin had really outdone himself. The renovations and repairs were top-notch. He'd updated the studio equipment as well as most of the DJs. Dove was the only one to survive the cut. She could thank that scathing Bootnocka interview. It transformed her career from being a radio personality to becoming a celebrity. Dove kind of made WUGH what it was. Without her, it was just a radio station to be bought by the highest bidder.

Mercedes was at work early, before I could arrive that morning, but she barely said good morning. She closed her door and kept it closed for the remainder of the day. I did notice that Iyesha had been in and out of there a number of times though. They seemed to be in the midst of a good laugh every time I passed by glaring through the glass. I made too many unnecessary trips to the printer. That day would've been a great day to talk about that quarter's goals. Instead, I was busy carrying out my assigned task of adding record-label fields to our entire database of over 30,000 on-air songs. My college education was failing me miserably.

On top of everything, I overheard Iyesha say something to Mercedes about the Alicia Keys concert at Madison Square Garden the previous night. What she said implied that they had gone together. If they went together, then it meant that they got complementary tickets from the label. Mercedes would never accept only two tickets. She would request a plus-one for her and Iyesha. In other words, she requested at least four tickets to see one of my favorite contemporary artists and I couldn't get one. The way she had each record label wrapped around her thumb, they felt obligated to always submit any tickets directly to Mercedes. They said they didn't want any trouble. I was told once by a label rep that it was Mercedes's responsibility to look out for her team. She didn't, but Iyesha appeared to be doing better than I expected the day she was hired.

After work, I raced down to Taj Lounge on 21st Street for a promo party. Jive Records was presenting their new teen pop/R&B sensation better known as Tamara. She was 17 years old. Her project sounded potentially promising even though the little girl referenced her crotch multiple times in those songs. She resembled a young Nia Long so every straight adult male in the venue couldn't keep their eyes off her. I was glad to see security by the door and it looked like they were packing in more ways than one.

As the night progressed, the label had to keep her upstairs on the balcony because the guys were getting to be too aggressive. Now what did they expect when she was wearing a skimpy mini-dress at an open-bar event? "Trouble," however, was the name of the title track to the album.

Superstar/Until You Come Back to Me

"Hello?" I said after answering my phone.

"'Sup?" said Brian in a melancholy tone.

"Wow, I didn't expect to hear from you again so soon. We just saw each other two days ago," I said while giggling internally like a child.

"Yeah, okay—who have you been with, Q?"

That question almost knocked me off my feet as I had just stood up. I asked, "What do you mean? I was with you just the other day."

"Q, please don't play with me right now. I got gonorrhea and you're the only person I've been with since we've been together. So who have you been with?" he repeated.

Brian was more demanding, but I was confused since I had no symptoms.

"Baby, I messed around on Saturday night, but there was no intercourse," I confessed.

"You know what…?"

"Brian, I fucked up."

"Yeah, you did. I'll get up with you later," he said.

"And when is that?" I pleaded.

"I don't know."

"Brian, let's talk this out. I'm sorry. Please don't leave me hanging like this."

"Dude—I can't talk to you right now otherwise I'm going to say some real mean shit. So to avoid any regrets, I'll get up with you later. Bye, Quincy."

Looking at the bright side of it all, thank God he didn't know it was a threesome. However, it was the dark side I kept finding myself on. What was wrong with me? Was I the true problem in all my relationships? Did I consciously or subconsciously sabotage what Brian and I had? Was I fooling myself into thinking I wanted a committed relationship when all I really wanted to do was avenge my broken heart? I didn't know how long it would be before I spoke to or saw Brian again, if ever.

Scream

It was his third hospital visit within the last two weeks. My father had been complaining of chronic chest and back pain. The doctors had no diagnosis. All the tests came back clean. Yet he still moaned and groaned on a daily basis. In the cab ride on the way home from the hospital, I distinctly watched him pick and choose his moments of weakness. First, he could hardly take a seat in the cab because it hurt him so much to bend his body. Then we reached his place and he exited the cab without any assistance or any complaining.

I always had my suspicions about his many medical conditions throughout history. He had bouts with migraines, sinusitis, asthma, acid reflux, muscle spasms, and a wide range of stomach issues. Still, no medical professional had ever been able to corroborate his claims. My mother remained the supreme cynic. Some of that cynicism had indeed rubbed off on me through the years. His conditions always seemed to be rather convenient.

During this period, his aches and pains were going to alleviate him from having to find a new job after being fired from his teaching gig for calling out sick too often. If he could have proved that he needed disability benefits, then he wouldn't need to work anymore. He had been out of work for over three months and hadn't even begun to look for work. He was too busy planning how he was going to spend his disability check when/if it arrived. For the time being, he still needed to eat and survive. I had given him almost $1,000 of my money since he'd first lost his job.

I was there that day to help him get situated back at home after his hospital visit. There was not much for me to do though. He was doing it himself. The trash needed to be taken out. Dirty clothes on the floor needed to be placed in the hamper. His comic-book collection needed to be organized as soon as possible so that was the main purpose he had for me being there.

My father began collecting comic books such as Superman and Batman when he was a preteen. Over 40 years later, he was still adding to his collection of 30,000-plus books. He had the very first Spider-Man comic to ever be issued. In other words, he was sitting on a gold mine. The plan was to sell the collection so he could live off that money until his disability benefits were processed. He was such a control freak that I wasn't allowed to handle the boxes. They were in special order despite the appearance that they were not.

We spent the next half-hour debating how to organize them because he knew exactly what he had in each box. I had to handle them in a particular way because as he said, "They are like my children". That phrase sent my head spinning. Before I knew it, I blurted out, "Lucky them." I attempted to move past my comment, but he shifted my gears in reverse. He wanted an explanation. Our moment of truth had been long overdue.

I kicked off the lid by describing our lack of a meaningful relationship and how I had always yearned for that father-son bond that we should have. I recounted the number of times we went out to play ball together when I was a kid—zero. I recalled the times we had heart-to-heart conversations—

none. I remembered the endless promises made to a little boy who valued his father's word—pointless. Having a child is one thing, but being a parent requires more than he was ever willing to give. Being selfish and self-centered is not the way to raise a child. It's a lesson I had to learn quickly otherwise the disappointment would have broken me into tiny pieces.

To this day, I hate to be let down after a promise is made. I don't know how to cope without internalizing it. Not once did I blame my father for this. I blamed myself like I wasn't worthy of not being lied to.

My father sat there staring at the floor for too long before he responded. He took the time to blame his past for what we needed to deal with that day. His own father abandoned him and his four siblings for a new wife and to help raise her kids. His mother raised them in the projects while on welfare. He longed for the day when he would have a child so he could be the man his father wasn't. He just never expected it to be so hard, but he said he did the best he could do. Refusing to engage or connect with your son is not doing the best you can do in my eyes. Much of what he said sounded to me like excuses. His crocodile tears went by the wayside since he was still actively moving boxes around like He-Man.

From left field, he suddenly brought my sexuality into question. I let him have a crack at trying to establish a connection between my resentment toward him and the shame I must feel for choosing a lifestyle that will lead me to the everlasting fire. I blacked out, but not totally. I remember the look of shock on his face when I told him how many times I attempted suicide because of how I felt about my sexuality.

Nonetheless, he followed it up with stories about his own brushes with voluntary death. It was irrelevant. My heart and soul were crying out for some understanding from the man I hadn't called Dad, Daddy or Father in almost 15 years. Where was the love and protection? Was the fact that I was born and him watching me grow up all the satisfaction he needed as a father?

While having a momentary loss for words, I blurted out an experience I never wanted him or my mother to know and had been suppressing since it happened. I didn't deal with the pain of it very well.

"You don't even know me. It's your fault, all of it. You never paid me attention and it's crazy what can happen to children when no one's watching. You never took that responsibility. You don't even know what responsibility means," I said.

"What are you talking about, Quincy?" he said nonchalantly.

The memory is still clear as day. My single father had dated more women than any man of the cloth should. Ms. Patterson, though, stood out from the pack. She was sweet. This nice lady could cook and dress. Basically, she was the prettiest, most put together woman of my father's past besides my mother, of course.

Ms. Patterson had two teenage daughters at the time. They were 17 and 18 years of age. I was only 11 when the three of us were left behind so the grown-ups could go out and do grown-up things. I was, however, petrified to be left alone with these two voluptuous, indiscriminate and horny teenage girls. Their eyes were always glued to me, making comments about how my eyes were too pretty for a boy. It was as if they had been waiting for their opportunity to get to know me better.

After the adults walked out of the house, I was led to the girls' bedroom for what they said would be lots of fun. I was stripped naked as they took turns performing fellatio on me. My body wouldn't respond to their advances and I could tell they were getting frustrated. Their last-ditch effort was to attempt stuffing me inside them. I didn't know what to think and whether what I was feeling was as wrong as it felt to me at the time.

In my mind, I escaped to that area of sub-consciousness where daydreams happen. It's where the imagination also resides. I know it well thanks to the many days and nights I spent in isolation at my father's house while I was growing up. There was nothing else to do but dream. Instead, this dream felt more real. Again, I was in the form of a tiger scratching away at its cage of flat, horizontal, wooden bars. Each swipe made me breathe more deeply. I didn't awaken from my reverie until I heard one of the girls scream, Oh my God, what are you doing? You're crazy!

I sat up in the bed and realized that it wasn't wooden bars I was scratching. It was the inside of my elbows instead. I bled onto the sheets. The girls panicked. It was almost time for our parents to return and we were then afraid to tell them what happened. Fortunately, I was wearing a black, long-sleeved sweater. To this day, when I wear a t-shirt, people compare the inside of my elbows to the stripes of a tiger. Still, no one could ever hear me roar.

Ms. Patterson spoke on the distance between me and the girls after they returned. My father simply shrugged it off that day. It was yet another secret I had always kept hidden inside my head and my father shrugged off my memory. He didn't want to believe me.

"Boys don't get molested by girls, Quincy—don't be stupid," he said.

Those were his exact words. I brushed off my heart even though it was carelessly bruised. He didn't understand nor did he have the capacity to. My final words to him in that moment were filled with rage and disgust.

"Don't ever again bring up my sexuality when you couldn't care less about any other part of me," I demanded. "I'm doing my grandmother, your mother, a favor by tolerating you and I don't know how much longer I can keep my promise to her. If she were still alive, you would be dead to me."

I walked out, head held high, and he didn't make one attempt to stop me. It did take a number of uncomfortable conversations throughout my life to classify what I had experienced as nothing less than molestation. For a long time, I believed what he thought it was since it was girl-on-guy, no matter the age difference; it was only sex. I had been exposed to sex with girls my own age prior to that day so there was no separation. What little boys are taught is boys crave sex with girls at any age unless the boy is gay. That's the way I had always thought about it. I abided by this law because I wasn't going to play the role of what would otherwise be known to the world as a faggot or a pansy or a sissy or any other variation. I never wanted to be considered helpless.

However, telling him I was in fact molested was definitely easier than the time I told him I was gay. Those two worlds are very different and they should never collide. I wished at times it was possible to suppress them both. A life minus that gross shame would be a mirror opposite. For Pop's sake, I had never intended for him to ever find out how badly he'd failed, just that he'd really failed to be the father I needed. It sucks somewhat that he still can't accept that. Anyway, it was my volcano moment and I would not have changed it for the world.

Journal Entry #597

Monday, June 20, 2005
6:39 p.m.

A lot can happen in a few months. The season will change. The position of the stars in the sky will change. Billboard chart positions will change. And people change. Two of my absolute best friends in the whole world are now newlyweds. Russ and Karyn eloped in Aruba after Russ popped the question. Their parents were mad as hell, but life goes on. Right now, they're in the process of finding their own apartment, which means it's time for me to move on and find my own too. I should be much better off living alone. I grew up that way and with no word from Brian since I burned him I will probably stay this way. It makes life a lot less complicated. My friends can keep me company if need be, but that pool is also shrinking. Of course, after getting married, I won't get to see Russ and Karyn much at all. I said good riddance to Prince months ago. That's a decision I will absolutely never regret, especially considering the new word on the street that he's now addicted to crystal meth. God bless him. Last week, drunk Roman had his revenge. Basically, Roman went to some fashion-industry party and had one too many drinks, which woke up his evil Gemini twin. Jordan said drunk Roman went ape-shit on other models he didn't think deserved better modeling campaigns. He actually spat on a few of them. The creative director of Ford Models fired him on the spot. Yes, it was the same guy who hired him to begin with. He was then escorted out of the party by security. But it

---

didn't stop there. Roman got into a fistfight with one of the security guards so they arrested him. Jordan wants me to help bail him out, but I'm not getting involved. I can't run to his rescue knowing he's on the edge of self-destruction. He needs help like only the judge can give him. But Jordan wasn't happy to hear me say that. He called me all kinds of evil bitches and such. He can't see that being in love with Roman is dragging him over the edge too. My love for Roman doesn't run that deep—sorry. But, on a happier note, Jordan is still involved with Karl, the chef. They spend a lot of time together and I see no signs of them slowing down. Karl is just man enough to keep Jordan's smart mouth in check and keep him happy in bed. Speaking of which, I've been busy in bed too. I stopped counting the number of partners I've had this year after I reached double digits. I'm having fun and living life with no strings attached. Why not? I'm too young to be taking these dudes so seriously. Men like to play the field. It's like a force of nature. Most relationships seem to be just about convenience. They conveniently make each person feel like they're worth more than they think they are alone. I overheard this one guy on the train complaining that his girl dumped him 'cause the weather got warmer. Some of these dudes get into relationships that will last the fall and winter, then they find excuses to break up around April. A female on the bus the other day said a friend of hers broke up with her boyfriend 'cause he was obsessed with online porn. I just want to find a good man like Russ, or even Karl. At the end of the day, I know I'm no angel. I broke Brian's heart, for God's sake. But is monogamy and commitment only real in fairy tales? Are my standards too high or am I lying to myself? Well, anyway, for the time being one thing is for sure, love don't live here anymore.

Lonely's the Only Company

The train-car lights were too bright for us to be underground. That train ride lasted about 30 minutes before it docked back home in Newark, N.J. Sometimes I listened to my iPod through the journey or I just decided to sit and people-watch. The number of characters present can equate to the capacity limit, yet the train crew insisted on packing us in like sardines. Typically, I huffed and puffed my way from one end of the tunnel to the next. However, the bald-headed professional dressed like a jock had captured my undivided attention. My best guess was that he was coming from the gym, which would make it his nightly routine at least five days a week. Or at least, I was hoping he had a job.

In this lifestyle, it usually spells trouble if a man as good looking as him doesn't have a line of work. The bills still have to be paid and women are not the only ones flocking to the pole. Men, especially gay men, make it look easy. Every gay NYC nightclub/bar has at least one stripper. Stripping, unsatisfactorily, doesn't pay enough so dancers are then commonly introduced to male escorting and prostitution or even pornography. It's all a slippery slope.

The escorts can be hard to distinguish from a tax-paying individual because all money is green. They look and act legit due to the influence of most of their wealthy clientele. They travel to and with clients continuously. After a brief conversation though, the transparency becomes obvious, but by then it's

too late for a sucker like me. All one has to do is stimulate me visually and somewhat mentally to get at me sexually.

Three train stops later, the sea of people parted to reveal a direct path to this gigolo type. We kept exchanging short glances. I had gathered that he was well-off. His Gucci duffle bag looked official. His vintage Nike dunks were worn, but still hot. I got caught up in the bulge of his chest and shorts. He stood about two to three inches taller than me. He reminded me so much of LL Cool J from the top of his head to the bottom of his feet. Still, I couldn't be sure if he was noticing me too or wondering why this skinny gay dude kept eyeballing him. Obviously, I was no threat to him physically so he had no worries if he was straight. If he was gay, then the final stop on the train would be the test.

Everyone hustled to be first up off the train, then up the escalator. I was close to the front and my jock was not far behind. I looked back a few times to confirm the mutual interest. We were off the train, yet still on track. He seemed to be following me as I walked up Raymond Boulevard to reach home. I doubted that he lived on my block. I slowed down my pace so he could catch up. When he got close, he asked me for directions to Broad Street. I told him I was going that way, which, of course, sparked a casual conversation.

"Are you from around here?" said my inquisitive jock.

"For the most part. Where are you from…?" I said purposefully pausing at the end of the question to leave an opening for him to introduce himself.

"I'm Dee and you are?"

I sighed a bit because Dee was such a nondescript name. I said, "If we must play that game, then I'm Q."

"What game? I'm just trying to talk to you," he said while giggling at me being forward.

"So what's up?" I asked.

"I saw you kept looking back at me so can I assume you're down?"

"Possibly, but down for what exactly?" I asked.

"Listen, there's no need to be afraid of me. You seem like a cool dude. We should go somewhere to hang out, get to know each other."

"And do what, Dee?"

I had to press the issue. By doing so, I got a minor cheap thrill out of it.

He replied, "I don't know. It depends, I guess. Do you live alone?"

"I have a roommate, but he's probably out working. I'm just a few blocks away since you're looking to hang out."

Dee had something special and I wanted to see it in private. We walked and talked until we entered my building. I started to make my way upstairs when he pulled me downstairs towards the basement.

"Wait—do you know where you're going?" I asked.

"This is the basement, right? I'm just trying to talk to you," he said for the second time.

Almost instantly, Dee got aroused and his white-mesh basketball shorts couldn't begin to mask it. He placed my hand around it.

"How does that feel?" he asked.

"Um, do we have to do this here? I mean, I live in this building so people know me. I would feel more comfortable in my apartment."

"How much?"

"What?" I replied.

"I'm working, dude. Nothing is totally free."

"Okay, I see we got our signals crossed. I'm not that guy. I can do and have done better," I said.

Dee, or whatever his name was, got offended by my statement. He pushed down on his erection as if that was going to make it disappear. Then he picked up his bag and told me that I should have known what it was about.

"You're playing games, dude. You had me walk all the way here thinking you knew the deal," he said while angrily poking me deep in the chest. "I should punch you in your face, punk."

That jock turned thug then breathed down on me like a dragon. My first thought was to swift-kick him in the nuts repeatedly into submission, but they could have been made of steel like the rest of his body. Luckily, someone came in the front-door entrance whistling and I could tell by the key of the tune that it was Russ so I called out his name. Dee caught wind of a bad situation so he ran upstairs and out the door. Russ recognized my voice from down below.

"Q, are you cool? What just happened? Did you know that guy?" asked Russ.

I explained to him the whole sordid ordeal. Russ was not happy that I would attempt to bring someone like that into our home. He went on about how he could've hurt me and/or robbed us. I agreed. There was no argument. I took a big risk. The tough thing, though, is being aware that it's a risk worth taking.

As gay men, we take these risks all the time otherwise it would be an even lonelier lifestyle. Since what we do is still considered blasphemous, we don't feel comfortable meeting at the museum, supermarket or the water cooler. Therefore, places like parks and subway stations become more viable for cruising. Honestly, it's a lot of the same guys you would meet at a bar or nightclub anyway. There are dozens of clubs full of lonely, slippery-when-wet men who are desperately seeking one night of fun over and over again. Loneliness, in my opinion, really should be the official eighth deadly sin. It devours like the others. Fortunately, this time, once again, I survived.

Work had been a similar game of survival. I was still on probation due to Mercedes's recommendation following the warning letter I had received the year before. It was the day of my annual performance review, which would determine whether I remained on probation or not. My relationship with Mercedes was still strained. It seemed the only time she wanted to talk was when she had some menial administrative task she wanted me to spend my entire week on. Then she assigned monthly goals that had absolutely nothing to do with the tons of never-ending admin work. And, of course, overtime was not an option and she told me that I must not be very efficient if I couldn't get it done during work hours.

It's the music industry. Work hours don't exist. One does what is required to get the job done. I was up against a wall. The glass ceiling was breaking my neck. I was essentially being sabotaged. Out of loyalty, I hadn't gone to Martin to discuss any of it. Once again, it's the code of the streets creeping into corporate America through the guise of hip-hop. Snitching had to be my last resort.

Then, out of nowhere, an interesting email appeared in my inbox with the subject, CONGRATS, IYESHA, in all-caps.

I gulped and sighed, then hit open to read the details. Iyesha had been promoted from intern to programming coordinator. I walked to Mercedes's office to get more information, but as usual she shooed me away because she was on the phone. She was in a congratulatory conversation with some record-label exec about Iyesha's promotion from the sounds of it. I didn't know whether to be mad or confused. Mercedes never mentioned to me that there was room in the budget for a new permanent hire. Once I got back to my desk, Mercedes called me back to her office to discuss Iyesha's promotion.

"Mercedes, what is going on? How come I didn't know about this since we're supposed to be a team?" I asked.

Mercedes rose from her chair to close the door before saying a word.

"Quincy, it's unfortunate you had to learn this way. It's my fault since I was supposed to discuss it with you first before you found out about her promotion. However, it doesn't change the matter at hand. We have to let you go. Martin and I both agree that this is not the place for you anymore. We haven't seen much of an improvement from you since you were put on probation and months have passed now. Iyesha has been a growing asset to this company so we believe her contribution will become even more paramount than it was as an intern," said Mercedes.

There was a moment of silence. Again, I didn't know whether to be pissed or feel completely bamboozled. The past year and a half flashed by in my mind like it was some horror film. How naïve could I have been? I couldn't help but stare relentlessly at Mercedes. It made her uncomfortable since she asked me to please say something.

"You know, I don't know what to say and my mama taught me that if you can't say something nice, then don't say anything at all. She raised me to have integrity, Mercedes. She never really taught me how else to deal, with people like you, when I should have just gone through you. It's all good though," I said as I continued to stare.

I then eased up out of my seat and walked over to Iyesha's desk to congratulate her personally since she seemed to be an innocent party. This was one of the few times I visited her desk. Ironically, it was the first time I recognized WDDP's Shelton Irwin in the group picture by her computer monitor. I asked her if she knew him well. Iyesha informed me that he was her uncle. The master plan went on right under my nose. I had no chance. I was helpless.

Mercedes was still in her office when I went back, then closed the door behind me.

"Off the record?" I asked.

"Okay—yes, off the record," she agreed.

"How well do you really know Shelton Irwin?"

"Shelton and I grew up in this business together. We've watched each other succeed and fail. He's like a brother to me."

"Off the record?" I asked yet again. I had to confirm so she would feel free enough to divulge.

"Quincy, you're an honorable man so I don't expect this conversation to leave this office. What more do you want to know?"

"Did Shelton have something to do with this?"

"Do with what?" she said cautiously.

My blood pressure shot up at that moment so I inhaled deeply when I really wanted to curse out loud, throw some chairs and break glass windows much like Sammy McMurder and his crew had.

She warned, "One thing you have to learn is always know who you're dealing with before you dismiss them. There are very few industry leaders with the rings in this game and it doesn't take much to get blacklisted. You're still young and smart so I'm certain you will land on your feet. Just keep your eyes wide open, please, with your next opportunity. God bless you, Quincy."

How dare such an evil woman bring God into it? If anything, it was my sign of divine intervention to leave WUGH and never look back. I couldn't bolt fast enough from the premises. I grabbed whatever tokens I could carry within my 10 fingers. Everything else was just fodder, although I couldn't control the commotion swirling in my head. My mind was racing to have it make sense.

Like a little boy with a fresh bruise, I instinctively found myself at my mother's apartment. She warmed up some leftover collard greens, yellow rice and fried whiting fish. It was all she had. Normally, I wouldn't eat the fish due to my fear of choking on the petite bones like I had done as a child. However, that day I just needed something to feed on. Both my stomach and my soul felt empty.

Still, I had no idea how I should react other than simply running away. Maybe South Beach was calling. Maybe the coast of Brazil or Jamaica was the cure. Or maybe I could escape to my wild imagination like I had been so used to. I wondered how long I could stay there before someone like my mother demanded I face reality.

I could hear her voice in the background of my thoughts, being as reassuring as it always had been. Nevertheless, I felt like a loser. My job and my man had done the absolute best disappearing act. They were here one day and the next they were gone. It was like all I had, again, was my mom and all she had was me. My duty was to save us both from just barely making it by.

"Money doesn't grow on trees, Quincy," my mother said while I was still in deep thought.

I took a few moments to lead her to believe that I had a plan. It just had yet to be formulated so I had to continue thinking. In spite of my contemplation, Mom finally sat down to break some news to me. She said it was neither good nor bad. It was what happens in dysfunctional families like ours. My tolerance was weakening. Mommy sensed it, then proceeded to tell me that my brother DJ and his father George had been keeping a dark secret from us for over 10 years.

My late brother Larry met his end some 1,600 miles away in Denver. He visited us at least two to three times a year, but we never got a chance to visit him. We assumed he died alone when, in fact, he'd had a new girlfriend who was three months pregnant at the time. George and DJ knew about it. They've always known about it. They also have been wiring money to the baby's mother every month since Larry died. It hurt like hell. I trusted George and considered him to be more of a father to me than my own.

Before I could get wrapped up in my selfish emotions, I looked into my mother's eyes for a reason why they would want to do something so cruel. What could she possibly have done to deserve it? That grandchild could've helped us with our grief, but they robbed us of that experience. They strolled in and out of our lives so freely like love was their motivation. My mother seemed more concerned with how I was going to react than how we were going to deal with those two cowards we called our family. I didn't know what I was going to do with George or DJ when they showed themselves.

Mommy ceremoniously was hiding behind her cloak of fortitude. Not even the recent news of a bastard grandchild was enough to tear through. That fortitude was probably part of the whole problem. Still, she was a woman who lost her son and the fact remained that her ex-husband and living son had denied my mother a lifeline to Larry's offspring. All the while, they laughed and smiled in our faces for years. Holidays and birthdays were part of the routine. Then George decided to drop a bomb like that on us.

"So why now? To what do we owe this honor of knowing the truth?" I inquired bitterly.

Apparently, the child's mother was beginning to wise up. She discovered Ellen Simmons was indeed alive in Newark, N.J., and had not died of a heart attack soon after her eldest son's death as she was told. I, on the other hand, just never existed to begin with. George had to come clean or the child's mother was going to. She had some stuff to get off her chest. Mom was apprehensive about that first conversation with her, but I was all ears. As far as what was in my sight, I needed George and DJ to stay out of it.

●●●

The day still burned even though the sun had fallen. It was a beautiful 75 degrees on that summer night of my termination.

I couldn't go straight home yet so I decided to head back into Manhattan to take in the sights. My phone had rung twice, but I refused to answer. I needed some space. In fact, that was where I needed to be—on top of the world. Prince once showed me a rooftop in Midtown that people in the know frequented to smoke weed or whatever else they were into. It was near the corner of 30th Street and 7th Avenue.

The building was 30 stories high with a minimum security presence. I took the elevator to the 30th floor, then climbed the stairwell to the roof. My fear of heights was diminished due to the amount of uncertainty I was feeling. I was uncertain about my career, my life, as well as the two male figures smoking weed and cigarettes off in the distance. It was too dark for me to make out their faces, but I had no intentions on backtracking to street level.

The panoramic view of New York City was beginning to open my eyes a bit and calm me down. Trouble seemed to come in droves, which had me falling deeper into myself. Instead of trying to find my place, I needed to let go and let life happen. God knows me. He knew my heart although my actions tended to come up short.

"Play on, player," shouted one of the male figures off in the distance.

I ignored it at first, figuring he was being loud thanks to the smoke inhalation until he repeated it again, this time standing in the light of the moon. He was talking to me. He assumed that I was waiting for someone to have rooftop sex with. Prince never mentioned that this rooftop had that sort of reputation.

I told the onlooker about my job loss, which led me to the rooftop haven. He felt sorry for me, then invited me into their hazy cipher. While going through the motions of introducing ourselves, I learned that Shahad and Carl both worked as engineers in the recording studio a few floors down. Carl soon bailed from the roof to take a leak, leaving me alone with Shahad. I could barely even give Shahad a good head-to-toe look considering the day I'd had. That was until a swift wind blew his joint about four feet away and he had to bend over to pick it up. The sun had arisen at midnight and made me want to burn my face with it.

Shahad's dark-blue Levi's jeans were sagging well below his waist. His red boxer-briefs hugged every curve, making me forget my troubles. I made eye contact with Shahad once he straightened back up. It was pretty intense. Something was telling me that we had something in common. Carl's trip to the bathroom was taking longer than it should have. The whole situation was a bit too convenient not to take full advantage of, plus I wasn't in the mood to waste any time.

"Yo, nice underwear," I said to Shahad while groping myself.

He almost choked on his last puff, but he soon smiled and thanked me for the compliment. Without trepidation, I unbuckled my pants to his visible delight. Shahad also wasn't wasting time because he dropped to his knees faster than a good little church girl. It felt as if I had just dipped my manhood into the neck of the Nile River. My own neck felt like a springboard.

My fear of heights should have been in full swing while I sat on the rooftop edge, but I was too focused on the tingling sensation flowing through the center of my body. I screamed out when it was over. Luckily, no one could hear me up that high. Shahad jumped to his feet still all smiles. He lightened the load of my troubles that day so I thanked him with a slight nod, zipped up my pants and made my way to ground level. I never said a word nor did I look back.

 Stuck Pages, Vol. 1: Exposing the Heart of a Heartbreaker

Can't Face the Music

Severance can be a beautiful thing. Instead of having to find a new job right away, I had been afforded a cushion in the form of some time to get over my shock. It was six months' worth of my regular salary to be exact. I woke up that morning due to me neglecting to disable my alarm clock. The clock was tuned to WUGH, playing none other than Bootnocka's second platinum hit, "I Can't Lie to You." I almost smashed it. The last thing I wanted to hear was the early-morning drive. Even the music in general was bothering me, not just Brian's. All of it reminded me of how twisted the entire industry can be. I grew up listening to the very stations I now loathed. Was anyone in it for the love of the music? Or was it all about the money?

It was not why I chose to go to college. Honestly, I would have gone a different route if it was about the money. I could've gone into engineering since math and science were my two favorite subjects in school. I chose music because it is my passion. I ignored the ugly cutthroat and back-stabbing rumors about the music industry. I elected to be on the side of the artists and make a creative difference from the business end of things. Just a few years in and I already felt like a has-been who had lost his first and second loves. People like Shelton Irwin I was sure wanted me to fail. I knew I couldn't give up on my passion, but my dream for success was fleeting. It was time for another drastic change in my life I could have never seen coming.

●●●

"It's time to have some fun. It's the weekend," hollered Jordan after I got him caught up to speed on my life. "Girl, you sacrificed a lot for that job. Fuck 'em. That Mercedes deserves everything she has coming to her. Now let's go find us some meat in the street and maybe in the process we'll also catch us a beat."

By that time, it was near midnight on a late Saturday. The seedy strip bar on 47th Street in Manhattan known as Stella's was about to swell the fiery ground from below. It was my first time going. Jordan had gone twice and said Roman and I had been missing out. Based on his description, the main bar sat on the ground floor to throw off passersby. This bar was also where the street hustlers and male escorts made their arrangements. They didn't get down and dirty right there. Instead, they acted social, then arranged a time and place to get down and dirty with their new or repeat clients.

Downstairs was where about 10 to 15 male exotic dancers performed solo acts on a stage barely large enough for any of them to do a split on. Jordan also claimed that he had seen guys giving strippers blow jobs in the back dark corners. I had to see it for my own eyes.

As soon as we walked in, Jordan's description became crystal clear. The spiral staircase to the far right led to the strippers' den. We paid our $5 cover charge, then descended deep into their lair of sin. A conspicuously voluptuous drag queen was working the microphone. Her name was not important.

However, the stripper on stage at that moment went by the name of Sex Appeal. He was sexy, dark chocolate with long black dreadlocks and a tight, corset-like six-pack. I noticed that his butt kept pulsating even when he was standing upright and still. When Sex Appeal turned around though, he could have literally beaten us in the head with that stick he was holding and he would never have to leave the stage. I mean he was not an average-sized man. He stayed stiff throughout his whole performance, flipping, bouncing and swinging about. I made myself a mental note to tip him well.

Who knew Stella's was the remedy I needed? Halfway into the night, three drinks and four lap dances later, I couldn't stop smiling. If there was nothing else Jordan knew how to do, he sure could put a great big smile on someone's face. He had that gift of the gab and used it cleverly. His sense of humor was jagged and rough, but hilarious. He could have been a politician if he had applied himself.

I took a look to my left and, of course, I saw one of the dingy strippers receiving oral from some large, round, pale-white male figure in the corner. Jordan called it. The sight gave me a funny feeling though. I was both disgusted and fascinated at the same time. That place was pretty awesome. It was like I had found a brand-new world. The most exclusive citizens were butt-naked under their thongs for the viewing pleasure of the regulars. The more cash we threw at them, the more body parts they caught it with.

Anyhow, all things, good or bad, came to an end so Jordan and I headed back to Jersey. We had spent over $250 between the two of us on alcohol and beef. Besides, I felt greasy. I didn't understand why dancers soaked themselves in so much baby oil like it was some kind of credible layer of defense.

While staggering from the bar, Sex Appeal had passed us going in the opposite direction. He then called out to me.

"Yo, slim with the slanted eyes," he said as I casually did an about-face.

Sex Appeal walked up to me, then said, "You forgot this." It was his business card.

"Ha. Nice. So this says you're a professional entertainer…"

"You were entertained tonight, right?" he asked, then I nodded affirmatively. "And you paid for it, right?"

I grinned. He was slick with his tongue in more ways than one. We had gone our separate ways, then Jordan said he had a confession to make as we rode back into Jersey.

"Okay. I'm drunk. I lost my job this week—had a good time looking at naked boys all night, and even got one of their numbers, and now you want to make confessions like we're in a taxicab or some shit. Like really?" I joked.

"Shut up, bitch. Act like you're not a failure and listen up for once," he said cutting me so deep I had to smile. "You know how me, you and Roman always joke about being a family? I'm the mother and you two are like my daughters, right?"

"Yeah, I guess," I said rottenly.

"And Karl is your new stepfather…" he continued.

"Get to the point, sweetie," I said.

He said, "Well, you also have a new sister."

"What are you talking about?" I whined.

"I met this kid who needs some help so I decided to bring him into the family. What? Are you jealous?"

"No, but don't you think it takes a vote at least? But I know you. He must be cute and quite vulnerable. I just hope you're not having the boy."

"Hold up—he's barely 19, and besides I have a man, unlike you, poor baby," he said as he amusingly rubbed the back of my head.

"Get off of me," I insisted. "So when do we meet this new sibling?"

"Roman already met him last week. We were saving your introduction for last with your ole evil ass. No shade."

I laughed. My friends knew me well. I could be very shady at times, especially to new people invading our inner circle for the wrong reasons. Too many people carry ulterior motives.

Once back at Jordan's apartment, I had the pleasure of meeting Latif. I emphasize pleasure because he indeed looked cute and vulnerable like a Butterfinger—appearing tender until one discovers that it's pretty hard, making the mouth water. Honestly, a lot of what I liked about Latif was what I liked about myself. He had great piercing eyes and large soft hands. We were both the same height and likely the same weight. He was kind of like a slightly younger version of me and I wanted to get to know me much better.

Jordan became boastful about the fact that we had hit it off so soon or so it seemed. Still, it was about 4 a.m., which meant that it was time to get some rest. Latif was sleeping in the spare bedroom while I slept on the sofa in Jordan's room. Before long, Jordan was knocked out. Latif left out of the spare room to use the bathroom. I could see down the hall that he wasn't wearing much, just a pair of boxer shorts that sagged off his thin frame. Something inside me took over. The next moment I was in his bed pretending to be asleep when he returned. He didn't say a word. He just cuddled up next to his new big brother/sister. It was a friendly cuddle so I don't think he expected me to be erect. I startled him a bit with a hug from behind.

He asked, "What is that?"

"Oh, that's the neighbors fighting downstairs. Jordan complains about them a lot," I said matter of factly.

"What is that in your pants?" he asked.

"Do I really need to tell you, Latif?"

"Are you drunk? We just met, Quincy."

"So? This is my welcome-to-the-family process. Besides, it's been a very, very long week and I could at least use a massage. Do you mind?" I said while turning over in preparation.

Latif hesitated, but soon climbed on my back. That space in between his legs felt like home. He hummed a little lullaby almost putting my intoxicated sexual urges to rest. Nonetheless, I stayed strong and diesel. After the massage, Latif made an attempt to roll over and call it a night. I then rolled over on top of him because my night had not yet come to an end. I kissed him. He got lost for a moment, then pulled away. I continued to taste his body more, nibbling gently on his neck. When I reached his nipples, he babbled, "That's my spot." Latif again pushed me away.

He was persistent just like me. I decided to go the distance. I stripped naked, then stood at attention by the side of the bed. Slowly, I rubbed my sweaty palm across my chest then down past my abs all the way to my spot. Latif shook his head in disbelief. If he couldn't satisfy me, then I had to do it myself. The night's many cocktails continued to drown out any shame I would have normally felt. Still, Latif refused to participate. He wouldn't even touch me, but he watched attentively. I finished what I started and threw the towel I found on the floor back into its pile. I hoped it was Jordan's pile of dirty laundry. Latif kept shaking his head at me as I got back into bed with him, passing out completely before I could even remember my head hitting the pillow.

Turn the Lights Down

Sticky fingers are like little magnets so I avoided touching anything unless it involved skin-to-skin contact. The bottle of lube sat nearby in arm's reach as I had been spending much of the past week trying to keep my troubles at bay. Russ no longer barged his way into my room since he got an eyeful of hardcore-gay porn on my television screen the other night. I bet he didn't even know that two men could perform in that position. He learned something new that day.

Still, Russ checked in on me each morning. He knew in his heart that I would get through this rough patch. Day by day, I was feeling better about the situation. Yes, I had no job, but I had some friends like Russ and Karyn who had offered to help me financially if necessary. Russ was going to stay in the apartment with me until I found a new job. I was thankful for the friends I had.

I was taking some time to be in my underwear, or less, and plan out my next move, to simply wallow in my own funk. Taking a shower might have been a good idea, but it wasn't a huge priority for me. I had been caught up in my flesh. Justin Slayer and Enrique Cruz had been keeping me beyond busy. I had found a new best friend in the internet. Sites such as KillEve.com and LewdDude.com connected users with over 100,000 lonely yet horny gay men around the world looking for a night of fun. I'd had about a dozen of those nights of fun crammed into a week since losing my job, but I didn't pay attention to the numbers.

It was my conscious decision not to remember the men I had slept with during those days unless it paid off. If it was mediocre at best, it was almost as if the sex act had never happened, in my mind. If he turned me inside out and had me climbing the bedpost, then I would never forget him and would probably want seconds, thirds, fourths, and so on. That week, not one of those guys were special or worthy of an encore. At any rate, the search for the next unicorn lover continued on.

After clicking on the umpteenth profile, there was a knock at the door. Russ was long gone, scouting new venues for his parties, and I was not expecting company. I hoped it was not some surprise visitor who would then be surprised by my refusal to be hospitable. The peephole was pitch black, which meant the fool was expecting me to open the door without actually seeing who it was. Of course, I made my way back to my bedroom without hesitation. The visitor then figured banging on the door would do the trick.

I screamed, "Who is it?"

The familiar voice shouted back, "Do I really need to shout out my name in this hallway?"

My heart dropped. That voice represented a new generation in music. I thought I had lost that voice for good, but the voice was back at my doorstep. Brian stood there in the doorway for a moment as I hesitated with fear that maybe I had done something else wrong to warrant his unexpected visit. He saw the trepidation written on my face.

"What's wrong?" he asked. "I hope I didn't make a mistake coming here, Q."

"It depends on what you came for," I said with my arms folded. As happy as I was to see him, I couldn't let him see me break down so easily.

"Can we talk—inside?" he asked.

"Yeah, sure—sorry—come on in."

Brian was headed for my bedroom when I stopped him cold.

"No, let's talk here in the living room," I said. "My room looks crazy right now."

"Um, okay, what's going on? I've never seen you let your facial hair grow out like that before. Is everything cool?"

"I lost my job last week, but I'm good, just taking some time to clear my head."

"Wow, that's crazy," he nearly shouted. "You actually cared a lot about that job. Do you need…?"

I interrupted him, then said, "I need to know why you're here. You can't expect small talk when we haven't talked in months."

"I know—that's my fault. You should have your guard up right now, but let's not act like I did you wrong. The fact is, I fell in love with you, Q, you played me and I still don't fully understand why. But I don't think you know why either. Do you?"

"I know it was stupid. I know it cost me the best I've ever had and I know I did not mean to hurt you, Brian. You're right. I don't know why I slipped up like that, but I think we could have at least discussed it. You have the ability to bail to another country where I can't reach you to convince you I'm still the same guy from before, that I just messed up this one big time. But for me, I'm stuck feeling like you had more important things to do anyway than be with me," I confessed.

"It sounds like you felt that way even before you fucked up," said Brian.

"Sure did," I confirmed.

"Quincy, are you serious? Do you know how many times I had to skip out on gigs or meetings just to spend time with you? I guess, in hindsight, I should've kept you in the loop about what was going on, but I didn't think you would see it that way. But, you know what, I get it."

Brian let out a deep breath, then patted the seat by his side. Immediately, I rose up to fall into my rightful position. It felt good.

"What do you get exactly though?" I asked needing more confirmation.

"I get you. I've missed you, Q, like hell. Have you been paying attention to or watching any of my recent performances on late-night?"

I said, "I've been avoiding them at all costs actually. I had to push my feelings for you aside once I got fired so I could deal with the most pressing issue basically."

"Understood, but you would have known how I still feel. My choreographer and I incorporated some cue cards into my performance of 'I Can't Lie to You.' Remember?"

"Yes. Like from my movie. That's hot. Wait—let's pull some up online," I said while pulling him toward my bedroom.

"But I thought your room was too crazy for me to go in there," he said teasingly.

"If you love me, you love everything that comes along with me, including this sticky, messy cocoon I've been chillin' in these days."

"Wow. Your keyboard feels like a sliding board. What have you been busy doing up in here?" said Brian as he doubled over in laughter.

"Just pull up the video while I hop in the shower real quick. Wait, how long are you here for?"

"I can stay the night if you want. I just need to tell my manager to cancel the hotel room. And we don't leave town again until tomorrow night, babe."

No words were spoken. I just smiled, then kissed his handsome face. I almost had forgotten how good my lips felt against his smooth cheek.

"Hold up though, why are you showering?" he asked.

"Because I stink and could use one maybe," I reasoned.

"No, you don't. Sit right down here on my lap. Watch this video with me now so we can take care of business immediately after. You smell good enough for me."

We watched the video for three whole minutes. That was about as long as we could keep our hands off each other. Brian was back in town and I needed to show him my appreciation. It was just like him to not get caught up in how disheveled my life had become. He was there with no regrets and yet so much to lose. Our bond seemed to strengthen the more our love was tested.

When all else failed, I wanted that feeling between the two of us to last forever. We braced ourselves on the bed of sour sheets and used-up packets of lube. Then we stripped and lost our clothes somewhere in the process of trying to outdo each other. Brian was my ultimate unicorn lover. Even his silhouette had a glow.

The sun had officially set. We were deep in the spotlight of the moon. With our eyes closed, we were giving the performance of our lives. No part of the stage was going to be unused. From the back of his neck to the crease below my ankle, we made contact. We couldn't nor did we want to shake that spotlight. His dreadlocks draped my left shoulder while I grinded up inside him. Minutes later, we switched places because we enjoyed taking turns at the microphone.

The temperature was rising. It felt like we were beginning to cook underneath the limelight. Brian whispered in my ear that it seemed a little bright in the room so I hopped up quickly to turn off the computer monitor. As soon as I came up for air, it was as if that spotlight simply shut off. We both froze like we had stage fright. I looked out the window and noticed someone on the fire escape with a video camera trying to hide in the cut. My first thought was that it must be the paparazzi and Brian must have been on the same wavelength because he ran straight to the window while I grabbed a pair of dirty basketball shorts to throw on to try to catch the guy at the bottom of the fire escape.

Out the door, then down the steps, I flew. I knew I could catch him in time. That video camera had to be destroyed. I broke out of the front entrance of the building. I looked to my right just in case there was an accomplice waiting to bash me in the head or something. I swung my head to the left to see the lifeless, limp body of the camera man. He was face down on the pavement in a pool of his blood, but I was still able to recognize him.

It was Gabriel. Everything around me shifted into slow motion. The hairs on my arms stood up. A couple of women walking by the building were screaming and pointing up at my bedroom window. Did Gabriel fatally fall in his attempt to escape or did Brian push him to his death? I ran back inside to discover Brian freaking out. He was holding Gabriel's video camera as the window curtains flailed in the wind.

"Quincy, we gotta go, Q. I don't know what just happened, but we gotta go," he said frantically.

"What happened, Brian? He's dead. What did you do?" I asked Brian who then dropped to his knees with the most frightening look of desperation.

He begged, "Quincy, please, don't do this to me right now. We don't have time for this. Please let's just get out of here until we can figure out a plan."

Was this what I prayed for when I said I wanted Brian back? And what was Gabriel thinking? Nevertheless, I started filling a duffle bag with clothes and toiletries, among other things. If it was within reason, it went into the bag. Meanwhile, Brian was on the phone with his manager, saying that we needed to leave town as soon as possible. No questions asked. I got dressed, then out of the backdoor of the building, we went into the darkness, before the approaching sirens could reach us.

Epilogue

I watched you watch me. It began with the occasional glance, something like a double-take. You wanted to be sure your lustful craving was valid. I, therefore, indulged you in light conversation full of glee, which filled the next couple of minutes until you realized there was more to me than just what meets the eye. Your glance had graduated to a fragile stare. There was no need for me to waver though. I greeted you halfway in the moment and then there was that nervous laughter that let me know you knew I knew what you wanted. You thought we could have something special like it was written in the stars. Without a doubt, I felt something, but my heart wasn't exactly in it. However, if I told you that, you might have been offended. If I just went with the flow and decided to have a little fun, maybe you'd move this mountain of discrepancy I owned.

Then, of course, in about two-weeks' worth of time, the sexual attraction between us would have settled. The sex would still be mind-blowing. We would have spent some time alone and figured out that we had very little in common. Still, stuck on the aesthetic, you would refuse to let me go. You wouldn't want to accept that great sex is not like the lottery. It's more akin to bodegas and Chinese restaurants in the 'hood. It's any and everywhere.

So you'd keep calling when there was nothing left to say. You like this and I like that. You go here and I go there. I know the difference between love and lust. You think they're one in the same. I would beg you to please stop calling. You're not the one for me, but unfortunately, it's hard to get rid of a dog that's learned its new favorite trick.

Then you'd change your story and want to be just friends when I have enough so-called friends. I would ignore every subsequent phone call until the dog in you tired from giving chase. You'd find a new lust-filled distraction eventually because you were not capable of tying me down. At that moment, Brian could barely do so.

I was done flirting with this particular concert promoter. His name was Pedro and, yes, he was a sexy Puerto Rican beast. Pedro bulged from his back to his arms to his chest and carried it on through his legs. He was not body-builder material. He reminded me more of a slightly beefier version of Mario Lopez, except he was devoid of personality. We were backstage at the Hammersmith Apollo in London, England. Bootnocka was performing there that night to a sold-out crowd. Pedro had spent the last 15 minutes trying to convince me that I should be choosing him as my mate for life. He had been going on about how every risk he'd taken had led to him reaping its rewards. He was boring me to tears.

Basically, he figured out real quick I must be gay since I played his game of hide-and-seek eye contact from across the room. Consequently, we found ourselves locked in a private conversation that I wasn't prepared to have considering what had just happened only 24 hours ago. A man died, or maybe he was killed. I wanted to believe it was an accident, but Brian had not broken his silence. That scared me. We had not had one moment alone together yet. He's been keeping his distance from me. No one else could tell though. Still, I was roaring on the inside.

Again, it had been 24 hours since the largest turning point in my lifetime. My mom was probably having a heart attack right at that moment or maybe she was stone-cold mad. The media was reporting that I was a person of interest, wanted for questioning in the bizarre death of an academically gifted young man with a seemingly bright future. Russ and Karyn must have been blown away by the possibilities of what happened. I'd have been a fool to try to reach out to anyone while being essentially on the run.

Brian and I had literally run from my apartment building in total silence. That silence maintained until we were picked up blocks later in a 007-style, all-black Suburban truck. After quickly and miraculously being issued a fake identity, I flew out of JFK airport on the next flight behind Brian's because placing us both on the same plane could have raised suspicion. Once again, he was able to distance himself from me when times got rough. Thank God it worked out, otherwise I would have been extradited back to Jersey alone by the authorities.

Brian's whole entourage had bought into this new fake identity of mine. They thought I was his cousin, DeAndre Forrester. I wondered how long I had until someone realized my true identity and what we did. Meanwhile, that dark fitted cap and oversized, black hooded sweatshirt were crucial to the disguise. They were like a second skin thick enough to repel any unwanted scrutiny. I looked like just another American street hoodlum, which was a departure from my usual pretty-boy swag.

This new identity though could be of service. It was a change for better or for worse. I could win or lose. Winning involved never ever looking back and allowing my last memories of loved ones to grow old and fade away. There would be no more use for online profiles, charge cards or even the truth. I would live a lie. Literally, start over and give life another try.

Stuck Pages, Vol. 1: Exposing the Heart of a Heartbreaker